Only a Secret

Kasper Ridge, Book 3

Delancey Stewart

Copyright © 2022 by Delancey Stewart

All rights reserved.

No part of this book may be reproduced in any form or by any electronic or mechanical means, including information storage and retrieval systems, without written permission from the author, except for the use of brief quotations in a book review.

Contents

Chapter One
Leaving Sasquatch in the Lurch

HARRISON

"Sasquatch, hit that thing again for me." I dropped the walkie-talkie to my side and watched with satisfaction as the chair lift in front of me hummed back to life, the four-man chairs gliding smoothly through the bottom station, pausing where riders would get on, and then swooping away up the hill toward the top, where Sasquatch stood at the other set of controls.

"Looking good, man." His voice came through the speaker at my side and I picked it up to respond.

"It better. Cost a fortune and the tramway inspector's

coming sometime this week." We'd ended up putting in a new ski lift with the help of a couple installation engineers. The old ski lift I'd been trying to bring back to life for the opening winter season at the Kasper Ridge Resort was an antique.

I'd finally convinced Ghost, the resort owner and my old Navy buddy, that springing for a modern system would pay off in the long run. A tough call, since the Resort was running completely in the red after a speedy renovation and ahead of its first real season, but it did give us two operational lifts—this one, and another at a halfway point that opened up another few runs from the top.

The construction crews had cleared and graded runs below the lift lines. All in all, it had not been cheap, but there'd be skiing when the place opened in November, and in Colorado, that meant people and money.

"I'm coming down." Sass's voice held a familiar note of joviality, one that typically meant trouble.

"Sass, no, do not jump on one of those—" I didn't have to finish the warning. Sasquatch had clearly hurled all two-hundred-plus pounds of himself onto a chair at the top of the lift, and I could hear his victory cry echoing down the mountainside.

He'd better not do that shit when the inspector was here.

As he came into view about ten minutes later, I watched him approach the station. The guy was always pulling pranks, making jokes. Even when we'd flown together back in the Navy, he often took things a bit too lightly for my liking. Flying a jet was life and death. Maybe a ski lift wasn't quite as high stakes as the F-18, but it still paid to follow the rules.

My oversized friend was still hooting and hollering as the chair brought him closer to the ground, and I decided I'd better give him a quick talking to. We'd be operating for real soon, with guests and impromptu inspections. There was no room for this bullshit. I switched off the motor and watched him swing to a stop, still a decent height in the air.

"Hey!" He called down. "Brainiac, your lift quit."

"Yeah, I stopped it," I yelled back up. Then I walked closer, so I didn't have to raise my voice. "Listen up, Sass."

"Oh shit, I'm in trouble with the professor." Sasquatch laughed to himself.

"Just listen," I suggested, looking up at his huge form, dangling overhead. "We're about to bring on staff up here, and you need to be setting the right example. No one rides without an operator at each end. Not us, not the college kids who are gonna be working here this winter, not anyone. It's dangerous, and pretty soon we'll be subject to pop inspections."

"Right, right." I didn't think Sasquatch was really taking this seriously, given the grin he still wore.

"Ghost is counting on this." It was a low blow, but I knew it would wipe that grin off Sasquatch's face.

He immediately looked regretful. "Yeah. Yeah, you're right. He needs this to work."

"He does. We all do. But especially Ghost." I didn't have to say more. Sasquatch knew the story. We'd all been looking out for our friend a little bit since he'd lost his flight status and been discharged after the investigation into the mishap that ended his military career. It had shaken him. Hell, it would have shaken anyone.

"I get the message, man," Sasquatch called as I turned and headed back to the lift station.

"Good." I called back, grabbing my walkie-talkie from the console and securing the station for the night. It was time for dinner, and I was starving. I headed toward the big patio at the back of the resort, the others were lighting the big fire pit.

"Hey!" Sass called from behind me.

The weather was good, and I figured he could jump from there if he got really desperate. He wasn't more than ten feet up.

"Hey!"

"You gonna leave him there?" Aubrey, Ghost's sister, asked, glancing past me at the hulking figure on the bottom of the chair lift.

"Till he learns his lesson." I gave her a grin and headed inside to get dinner.

When I returned to the fire pit, a plate full of smoked ribs in my hand and my stomach growling in anticipation, Sasquatch was ambling across the patio, grinning.

"Thanks a lot for that, man. Nothing like a little parkour before dinner." He poked me in the side, hard, but I held onto my plate and moved past him to one of the big Adirondack chairs around the fire pit.

"You made Sass mad?" Monroe asked from my side, where she sat with Mateo, her fiancé. Most people called her Annalee now, but we'd flown together, and the fierce blonde would always be "Monroe" to me.

"I taught him a lesson," I said, digging into my first rib.

"That was Sass mad?" Mateo asked, glancing after the hulking man who'd just ambled into the resort after cracking jokes and laughing loudly with Ghost and Fake Tom, who were both arriving to sit.

"Sass doesn't really do mad," Monroe explained. "But if he veers to sarcasm, you've struck a nerve."

"He needs to take things a bit more seriously," I suggested. I wasn't worried about Sass being mad.

"Or maybe you need to lighten up," she shot back.

I didn't have a response for that—it wasn't the first time it had been mentioned to me, but light wasn't really in my repertoire.

"We're all here, anyone got news?" Ghost asked from the other side of the space.

I glanced around, the faces of the crew that had been getting this place into shape all summer surrounding me. Ghost and his sister Aubrey had inherited the place—along with some kind of crazy treasure hunt that we hadn't solved yet—from their uncle Marvin. They'd recruited help as they needed it to get the resort back into operation, and in some ways, this group had become a family.

Some of us were former Navy fighter pilots, and some of us were locals. And then there was Sass's friend, Antonio, a former pro soccer player from San Diego. I hadn't quite figured out what he was doing up here yet, but then again, I didn't really know what I was doing here either.

I told myself I was just figuring things out. Helping a friend.

"Both lifts are working great, inspector coming this week," I reported. "Staff interviews beginning of October."

"That's two weeks," Aubrey said.

Ghost turned to his sister. "Those calendar-reading classes have really been paying off."

She threw a cob of corn at him.

"Marvin would have been proud of you folks," said Ernie, Lucy's grandfather and the oldest among us. He'd been up here his whole life, had known the first incarnation of the Kasper Ridge Resort, and been friends with Marvin. "This place is every bit as magical as it was back in the day."

Lucy leaned toward her grandfather and bumped his shoulder with a soft smile on her face.

"Thanks, sir. That means a lot," Ghost said.

"So the ski school and mountain staffing interviews are getting set up," Aubrey said. "We need to get some people up here for the rest of the operations too. Servers, housekeepers, front desk staff."

"Can you put out some feelers locally?" Ghost asked, focusing his attention on Lucy and Mateo, since they'd both spent most of their lives in Kasper Ridge.

"Yep," Mateo said. "Might want to extend the search if you're willing to offer housing, though. College kids will probably travel to stay here for the season."

I might have rolled my eyes. Because what we really needed was the mountain crawling with college kids. "Great."

Monroe leaned in close. "You did actually say that out loud."

I could feel the frown pulling the sides of my mouth down, but I decided not to let any more words out. Maintaining an upbeat attitude was not my strong suit, and I'd had more than enough of college kids.

"Aren't you a professor, Brainiac?" Fake Tom called across the dancing propane flames between us. "Figured you'd love college kids. All those young eager minds, desperate for you to impart your aged wisdom."

Fake Tom's real name was Will, but his callsign was based on his desire to be called "Maverick" back in the Navy. His last name was Cruz, so he'd thought it was a sure thing. But that isn't how callsigns generally worked, and his excitement at the name he wanted only led to everyone making sure he didn't get it. He'd recently proposed to Lucy Dale, who'd been brought in to help with construction at the resort.

There was a lot of coupling up going on up here. I was glad there were no more single women around. I was happy for my friends, but all this cheery romance was more than enough for me. It didn't really suit my current state of mind.

"Yeah. I was a professor," I confirmed, trying to keep any shade of emotion from my voice. I didn't enjoy conversation at the best of times. I did not want to talk about my recent departure from my non-tenured position as an engineering professor.

"I didn't know that," Antonio said, clearly in the mood to drive me over the brink with his good-natured questioning. "What did you teach?"

"Mechanical engineering," I said, shoving another rib in my mouth in hopes of signaling that we were done.

"And will you go back to teaching?" he asked.

Since no one else spoke, it seemed clear I was supposed to answer.

"I'm on sabbatical," I said. "And I need a drink." I rose, and turned, heading inside to the bar. I didn't want a drink—I'd spent plenty of time drinking before making the decision to come up here as I came to grips with my sudden freedom. But I definitely didn't want to talk about my current unemployment or the reason I had really been available to come up and play lift engineer at Kasper Ridge.

They'd find out soon enough if I didn't figure out my next career move pretty fast.

Chapter 2
Running Away to Colorado

PENNY

S hit. This could not be happening again.

"Maybe it's not that bad," Mom said, sounding annoyingly upbeat in the face of my world exploding. Again. "Maybe there's some way to capitalize on this, honey."

Her calling me 'honey' rubbed me the wrong way. We'd barely gotten back to speaking terms after everything, and that was only because of my father's death. I'd thought he was the one driving their actions all those years ago. But maybe I was wrong.

"There is no way to capitalize on my life imploding, Mom.

This is a bad thing. Most people would recognize that." My phone felt heavy and unwieldy in my sweaty palm.

"I do," she said quickly. "But when you're famous, you have to expect that people want to hear what you're up to. If you go quiet too long, they'll invent things."

Maybe. But I wasn't famous anymore. Not really. "Shit," I breathed, staring out the dark window of my Brentwood apartment. "I thought things were getting better."

"Want me to call Paul?" Her voice had turned sweet, cloying.

"Mom. I'm a grown woman. I can call my agent myself." Though I hated speaking with Paul almost as much as I hated talking to my mother.

"Okay." Now she sounded chastised. Like I'd swatted at her.

"Listen, I have to go," I said. Exhaustion was sweeping through me, a heavy layer of darkness matching the dark clouds suffusing the LA brightness outside my window.

"Talk tomorrow!" Mom chirped, her voice full of false glee.

I pictured her, ensconced in the cheap apartment she'd found in Englewood, the planes thundering overhead toward LAX at regular intervals. Her life was no better than mine, but I couldn't even fake happiness. She had a gift.

After I'd hung up, I pulled up the internet article again, unable to help myself. It was like having an aching tooth—you couldn't help prodding it with your tongue, over and over, testing to see if it still hurt just as much as it had before.

And this did.

It had been a second date, though why I bothered even trying was beyond me. The guy had sworn he didn't know anything about me beyond maybe having heard my name as a kid. He'd been charming. Handsome. Sweet.

And his bedroom had been plush and welcoming. And equipped with a camera, evidently. A camera hidden in the headboard, it looked like. A camera used to capture me being an idiot and trusting someone, yet again. Someone who was clearly going out with me under false pretenses.

I slammed shut the lid to my laptop, some sick part of me hoping I'd broken it. Then I'd have an excuse to stay off the internet for a while. To avoid the stupid headlines on those seedy gossip pages: *Child Star Caught in Another Sex Scandal! Our Girl Chrissy Isn't So Innocent! Playtime Never Ends for Penny Davis, aka Our Girl Chrissy.*

My little apartment, which had just begun to feel like home to me, now felt like a cage. Or a stage, which was far worse. There'd been a reporter waiting outside today, before I'd even seen the stupid video, and I realized now that it didn't matter where I went, what life I tried to have. Here in Los Angeles, hell —maybe anywhere in California—people would never let me forget that I was Chrissy Alexander, that she was all they'd ever want me to be.

I went to the bedroom, pulled a suitcase from the closet, and began stuffing it with clothes I didn't even see as they passed through my hands. I was going to have to leave. To run away. I might have been acting like a child, but if I stayed here, I'd always be one. I'd never escape Chrissy Alexander, my alter ego. I'd never figure out who I really was.

A plan formed slowly in my semi-numb mind as I gathered shoes and shoved them into the suitcase. It was less of a plan, really. More of a loosely structured Hail Mary pass of extreme desperation.

I sent a couple text messages. One to Paul, who promised to try to get the video taken down, and who—as ever—suggested a couple auditions I might like to go on. Delete. Delete.

The second text was the Hail Mary. But my old school friend Bennie responded almost immediately, every bit as sweet as she'd always been.

Bennie: Definitely! Come whenever you like! I have room!

That was all I needed.

I picked up my phone again and arranged the car service and texted Bennie back, then took a last look around my apartment. Whatever was here didn't feel like mine anyway. My mother could sell it. There was probably some sick asshole in this wretched town who'd buy Chrissy Alexander's bedsheets and pots and pans. Hell, they could auction it all off or something.

I sent another text from the car, letting my mom know I was leaving town for a while. And then I sank low into the leather of the seat, hoping that at this time of night there wouldn't be many people at the airport. I bought a last-minute ticket to Denver on the way to LAX. I could have chartered a plane, but that would have been a whole other thing, and I didn't want to drag some poor pilot out of bed at this hour. Flying commercial would hopefully give me a little bit of anonymity. A little pulse of panic fluttered in my bloodstream, but I tried to calm it as the car moved swiftly over the well-worn freeway.

Five hours later, the sun was just beginning to lift over the wide flat eastern horizon as the plane touched down in Colorado. Just another four-hour car ride, and I'd be there.

Hopefully Kasper Ridge was small and inaccessible enough a place to hide in for a while. Bennie had to teach today, but she'd set me up with a spare key, and her school day gave me time to actually get some sleep. I barely even registered the appearance of her house as I stumbled across the threshold, locked the door, and located the guest room. I climbed into bed and immediately passed out.

* * *

"Hey sleepyhead." I rolled toward the weight that had settled on the mattress, murky confusion muddling my thoughts. "Penny."

Where was I? I lived alone, so why was there . . . ah, yes. Memories of my harried flight from Los Angeles came sweeping back into my mind.

"Hi," I managed, turning to the voice and wrenching my eyes open.

"I can't believe you hopped a flight so fast," Bennie said, friendly and warm.

"I'm sorry," I moaned, my vision swimming and then clearing to find my old friend sitting at the side of the bed, smiling kindly down at me.

Bennie had a mass of naturally curly dark hair I'd always envied, and bright wide dark eyes that held every bit as much acceptance and kindness now as they did in my memories of her.

"Don't apologize," she said, smiling. "I'm so happy to have you here."

I struggled a bit with my limbs, which felt heavy and dull, finally managing to sit up against the headboard. "God, I needed to sleep. What time is it?"

"Almost five o'clock. I just got home from school a little while ago, but the girls are coming over, so I wanted to give you some time to wake up."

Alarm rang through me. "Girls?"

My face must have betrayed my fear, because Bennie reached a hand for my arm. "Just Lucy and CeeCee," she said, pronouncing these names as if I had any idea who these people were. "And Annalee."

I shook my head, both because I was not up to socializing, and because I didn't know who she was talking about.

"You'll love them all."

"I'm not in a peopling place, Ben. Maybe I'll just hide in here?"

"Definitely not," she said, laughing at the suggestion. "I haven't seen you in years. I'm dying to catch up."

"A quick internet search will tell you everything you need to know," I whispered, dropping my eyes shut and rubbing a hand over my face.

"Oh no," Bennie said, a gentle hand taking my own from my face. "Are you okay?" Her tone was soft and concerned—so different from my mother's barely concealed excitement over my drama.

"Well, I pretty much just abandoned my entire life to come here. It was the only place I could think to go where maybe no one would read those trashy sites."

One side of Bennie's mouth lifted. "Small towns are awful for gossip, Penny."

My heart sank.

"But this one is full of good people. No one will bother you here, no matter what's on the internet. You can stay as long as you like."

Her reassurance helped, and I settled back against the headboard, feeling a little lighter.

"So get up and do whatever you need to do. The girls will be here in a half hour for dinner and *Bachelor Bay*."

"You do not watch that trashy show."

"Oh yes, we do!"

"But you're a first-grade teacher. Isn't that kind of seedy for you?" I knew about *Bachelor Bay*. My agent had even suggested I go on the show as a bachelorette. That was the fourth time I fired him, but Paul just wouldn't take a hint. He told me we were ride or die. Sometimes I thought about how old he was, and hoped maybe die was coming soon.

"First grade teachers need to have fun too," she said, her posture stiffening a bit.

"Of course, I didn't mean—"

"Get up!" she laughed, standing. "You've got your own bathroom there and you can come out when you're ready." She pointed to a door I'd assumed was a closet, and then disappeared back out of the room.

Bennie was a good friend. She'd lived in Los Angeles a long time ago, and we'd been friends in middle school, during the years when I'd insisted that I wanted to go to public school, when I'd thought that would be the path to a normal life. And for a couple years, it was. The kids in Los Angeles were used to fame, and for a while, they let me be Penny Davis. But in high school, everything had exploded. And by then, Bennie's parents had moved here, to Kasper Ridge.

* * *

I emerged from the bedroom full of something that felt like fear. I could hear the voices of Bennie's friends echoing down the little hallway. They sounded light and friendly, and I stood there for a minute, listening.

What would it be like, I wondered, to live up here, to have Bennie's life? To go out and have friends, and teach school—though that was not something I was equipped to do. But the rest of it. What would it be like to be allowed such a normal, happy life?

"He didn't say that exactly," a voice was saying. "It was more like he suggested that sex was better at high altitude because the air was thinner."

"How would that make it better?" another voice asked.

"I have no idea. Fewer molecules between you or something . . . Will is not a scientist."

The voices all laughed at this, and I felt a little bit of weight slide off my shoulders. They weren't talking about me. That was good.

I took a deep breath and stepped into the living room.

"Hey," I said to the ladies standing in Bennie's kitchen.

There were three of them. One was petite, with long dark hair waved around her shoulders. She wore a pair of tight jeans and a shirt that was cut low and revealed an athletically curvy frame that made me a little self-conscious of my own less-than-fit physique. The woman next to her might as well have been Marilyn Monroe—she was blond, buxom, and gorgeous. I fought an immediate urge to dislike her that must have come from going to too many auditions too early in life where I was constantly pitted against other girls and taught to see them as competition. And the third was tall and slim, strawberry blond hair pulled back into a ponytail and bright blue eyes assessing, but friendly.

"Hey Penny," Bennie said, coming around the little counter to take my arm and pull me closer. "I'd like to introduce you to my friends. This is Lucy, Annalee, and CeeCee."

"Hi," I said, feeling awkward and disoriented. "It's nice to meet you."

"You too," Lucy said, pouring a glass of white wine and sliding it toward me. "It's so great that you were able to visit for a bit."

I nodded, accepting the glass and smiling at the smaller woman. "Thanks."

"How long are you staying?" The blonde—Annalee—asked.

I glanced at Bennie, who smiled encouragingly. "I really don't know," I said. I hoped this wouldn't lead to more questions, but I didn't need to worry.

Annalee grinned. "That's my story too," she said. "Though now I might stay forever. This place does that to you."

"Or maybe Mateo did that to you," Lucy said, raising an eyebrow.

"Have you been here before?" CeeCee asked me.

I shook my head, letting the cool crisp wine flood my mouth. I felt it work down my throat and could almost sense myself relaxing as it made its way through me. "Never."

"You'll love it. River rafting, rock climbing, hiking," she listed.

"Skiing," Bennie added. "Right, Lucy? You said they got the lifts going."

"They did," Lucy confirmed. "At the Kasper Ridge Resort," she told me. "So there will be skiing this winter for sure."

"I don't know how to ski," I said, beginning to feel more comfortable as I realized these women weren't expecting anything from me beyond a bit of regular conversation.

"Perfect time to learn," CeeCee said.

"CeeCee thinks everyone is equipped for outdoor adventure," Bennie told me. "She runs the adventure shop up here."

"All you need is a willingness to try," CeeCee said.

I smiled, looking between the friendly faces of Bennie's friends. Not one of them had given me a sideways glance, not one had mentioned *Our Girl Chrissy*. I didn't know if Bennie had briefed them ahead of time, or if it was possible I really could just be Penny up here.

Either way, even if it was for only one night, I was going to enjoy it.

Chapter 3
Peopling is Scary

HARRISON

"How's the interview schedule looking?" I asked, coming in the front doors of the resort from my run a week before we were slated to begin seeing candidates.

Aubrey had been in charge of following up with those who'd responded to the call we'd put out on various sites, and scheduling. She stood behind the grand front reception desk, looking tiny next to its imposing form.

"We're just about full, actually," she said, her voice giving away her excitement. "Hopefully most of these will work out and we won't have to do multiple rounds.

"What did Ghost decide about housing?" I asked her. We'd gone back and forth. We had the full un-renovated east wing, but having half the resort filled with college kids working part time for the season probably wouldn't scream "luxury" to those guests paying top dollar to stay in the west wing and ski.

"Not part of the deal except in special circumstances. We put together a list of rentals out in town."

Town was not huge, but there were apartment buildings and condos here and there, and lots of people went to warmer climes for the winter. This would give them the option to rent their homes for additional income.

"Good." I didn't want to be sharing living spaces with guys who were probably more at home in a frat house than a luxury resort.

"Didn't want to spend your winter surrounded by youngsters, old man?"

"I'm not that old," I bit out. I wasn't. I was a couple years older than the other guys, but hell, I was barely thirty-five.

"I know, but it's so much fun to give you shit." Aubrey winked at me and then turned back to the screen in front of her.

I headed back up to my room, pleased to have some down time before things got crazy here on the mountain. Maybe I'd be able to figure a few things out before then. I couldn't hide in the Colorado mountains forever, but I just didn't know what was next.

Upstairs I took a shower, dressed, and then sank into the leather chair in front of the desk facing the window that overlooked the front of the resort. There was nothing in the view beyond dark green trees and the sense of something bigger looming out there beyond the thick screen of branches. Maybe it was the mountains themselves I sensed, maybe it was nothing quite that concrete, just my own sense that I was shrinking somehow. Smaller than I had been when I'd been teaching, when I'd had the respect of staff and students at Archer University. When I'd known what I was supposed to be doing.

I pulled up my email, a surprising tension wrapping my shoulders and clenching my jaw. I'd passed my CV to several friends in academia, hoping there might be an engineering opening at another school. There was nothing waiting in my inbox though, and a surprising sense of relief washed through me.

It wasn't that I didn't want to go back to work, I told myself. Everyone enjoyed some time off now and then, and that's all this really was. My own misfortune had coincided nicely with Ghost's need for some help, and so here I was. But if a university reached out, I'd jump at the chance to get back into the classroom.

Wouldn't I?

* * *

We'd been screening movies regularly once a week since the movie theater's renovations had been completed. There was a pile of ancient films in the projector room, and though we'd updated the equipment, Ghost had thought it would be cool to keep the old reel projector working so we could watch the old movies. There was something nice about the way we were holding onto some of the old pieces of the resort.

"What is it tonight?" I asked him, taking my seat in the back row as usual.

Monroe and Mateo slid in on my other side and she bumped me with her shoulder. "You're looking especially grim today, friend," she said. "Someone fart in your waffles this morning?"

"Mature," I told her.

Monroe and I had been close since she joined the squadron years ago. I'd watched her evolve into a ridiculously adept fighter pilot, and she was even more skilled at fending off sexist barbs and unwanted advances in that male-dominated world.

I respected the hell out of her, and sometimes wondered what it would have been like if we had dated as everyone had always suspected. Maybe life would be better now somehow. But I couldn't resent the happiness she'd found with Mateo, even if the contractor wasn't my favorite person. She deserved to be happy. And truth be told, I didn't really like most people, so Mateo was probably quite likable to anyone else.

"This is another Annie Lowe feature," Ghost announced from the back of the theater. "*Riding the Range*," he said, beginning to read from a piece of paper he pulled from his pocket. "A sweeping western about—"

The back door of the theater opened again and Lucy Dale hurried in, three other women at her back. "Sorry we're late," she said, guiding them up front to where Fake Tom, her fiancé, was holding a seat for her. Before she sat, she turned to address us. "You guys remember Bennie and CeeCee. And this is Penny." She waved at the women following behind her. I watched as the women waved to the assembled group, and then turned to settle themselves. I'd met Lucy's friends before, but not Penny. I'd definitely have remembered her.

Penny was striking, and I was finding it hard to take my eyes from the defined angles of her face as she looked out at us all uncertainly—the full lips, the dark lashes sweeping up over dark eyes. She turned to sit, and I stared at the back of her dark head as she gracefully settled into a seat next to Lucy's friend Bennie.

"What's wrong, Brainiac, a little starstruck?" Monroe asked me. When I didn't respond, she went on. "She's sweet. I met her at Bennie's the other night when we watched *Bachelor Bay*."

"What the hell is *Bachelor Bay?*"

Monroe blew out a breath, rolling her eyes. "Of course you wouldn't know. I forgot that you grew up in a hole and you take pride in staying there."

"I didn't grow up in a hole. I grew up overseas."

"Didn't they have televisions and movies overseas?" she asked. It wasn't the first time she'd teased me about being clueless when it came to pop culture.

"I spent my time doing other things." Mostly because my father insisted on it. It would have been nice to have had a vague idea what kids were talking about back when I was one, but at this point, I was glad for the childhood I'd spent in books and cultural immersion.

Ghost had begun reading aloud again. "A sweeping western about settlers in Colorado and their homestead wives. Lowe portrays a tough-as-nails settler's wife traveling out to meet her husband after he's established a home for them in Colorado's rugged mountains, and in an unusual twist for movies made before the 1970s, she is the hero of this film."

Monroe let out a whoop at that news.

"Girls rule!" Lucy called from the front.

"Well, I'm not gonna read the rest of this," Ghost said, tucking the paper back in his pocket. "Let's watch. We can analyze the feminist themes over whiskey when it's over. Don't forget to—"

"Look for clues!" Sasquatch boomed, his voice filling the small space.

"Right." Ghost disappeared into the back to start the film. I could hear Lucy whispering to her guests about Ghost's treasure hunt—the series of clues that his uncle had left him along with this resort, a hunt we'd all been dragged into in one way or another, though none of us knew where it was supposed to lead. So far, the biggest revelation had been that the actress Annie

Lowe was actually Ghost and Aubrey's Aunt Lola, Marvin's wife. I wasn't sure there was any actual treasure, but the idea of it was kind of exciting.

The movie wasn't long, and soon we were gathering in the bar at the front of the resort, another routine that would be coming to an end as soon as we began hosting actual guests. I'd miss the routine, but maybe it was just another signal that I needed to move on, figure my stuff out.

"I thought she was a badass," CeeCee was saying, describing Annie Lowe in the movie we'd just seen. "Giving her husband that ultimatum and telling him what was what. And shooting the bear!"

"That's my aunt!" Aubrey laughed, holding up her whiskey glass.

"To Aunt Lola," Ghost called. And after we'd all shared the toast, he spoke up again. "Anyone get anything out of that?"

"Other than the fact that western mail order brides are terrifying?" Sasquatch asked.

"Like clues," Antonio said at his side. The soccer player was quiet most of the time, and now he sat at the far end of the bar, sipping whiskey and keeping himself slightly apart from the rowdier group of former fighter pilots. Bennie's friend Penny sat a little apart too, and I watched with an uncomfortable feeling in my stomach as he turned to her and asked some question, low enough that I couldn't hear.

The rest of the group went on analyzing the movie, dissecting it for potential hints about where the treasure hunt should take us next. We'd hit a bit of a stopping point and I could feel the frustration that Ghost and Aubrey shared at having felt like we were close, only to hit a wall.

"So Aunt Lola was engaged to that Rudy guy," Aubrey said. "But what difference does that make? She married Uncle Marvin. End of story."

"Maybe that's not even part of the story we're supposed to figure out," Fake Tom said from Lucy's side. "Why does it matter who he married? What does that have to do with money?"

Aubrey shrugged and Wiley did the same at her side, shaking his head.

As usual, I was less comfortable in the middle of the group than I would have been off to one end, but the newcomers were ensconced in my usual spot at the end of the bar, still talking in quiet tones.

Normally, I would have excused myself to the quiet of my room, but something pulled me to the little twosome taking at the end instead. I didn't want to look too closely at exactly what drove me to wedge myself into the conversation between Antonio and Penny. It had something to do with her, though. Everything to do with her, actually.

She was gorgeous. And intriguing.

"Hi," I said, taking the stool next to her.

She turned to me, an uncertain look in her eyes. "Hi."

"Harrison." Antonio nodded to me, his easy smile lighting his face.

"Did you enjoy the movie?" I asked Penny.

That uncertainty remained, and she seemed to think about her answer for a moment. "I did," she said softly. "I love old movies. I'm kind of a movie and television junkie, I guess. Hazard of the life."

I had no real idea what she meant by that, so I just nodded.

"In town just for a visit?" I asked, feeling every bit as awkward as usual making small talk, and yet driven to keep Penny talking. I liked the look of her, but something else about her drew me in. Something less specific, less identifiable.

"Not sure, really. I might stay for a while if Bennie can

tolerate me. My life, uh . . ." she trailed off and sipped her drink. "I'm just kind of in between things."

I nodded. That, I definitely understood. "Same," I told her.

Antonio had risen as we spoke, and now he leaned down. "Nice to meet you," he said. "I'm going to head up to bed." I felt a little guilty at potentially having driven him out of the conversation, but it was hard not to be a little pleased at having Penny to myself.

He left, and I was gratified to see that Penny's eyes didn't follow the well-built ex-soccer star from the bar, but remained on my face instead.

"So, Harrison, is it? Like Harrison Ford?" she asked.

I smiled. "More like Benjamin Harrison. Twenty-third president."

"Of course," she laughed.

"What?" I feigned surprise. "You aren't familiar with the many storied acts of the Harrison administration?"

She ducked her head and a piece of dark red hair fell in front of her face as she laughed. "Sorry, no." She looked back up at me, and the contrast of the dark lock of hair over the pale skin of her cheek sent a forceful jolt of desire through me. Penny was beautiful.

"Well," I began, trying to tamp down the sudden realization that my body was reacting to this woman in a way I hadn't reacted to anyone in a very long time. "Harrison enacted some key legislation relating to the military and to trade practices in the US."

"So your parents named a newborn baby after him. Naturally," she laughed.

I sipped my whiskey, loving the sound of her laughter. It was rough and dusky without being harsh. Like she had some kind of rugged landscape hidden inside her, and her voice resonated with the echoes of it.

"Right. My parents were odd that way. My dad was a diplo-mat, so government and law were the only things he really ever thought about."

"And your mom?"

"I don't really know. She died when I was little, so I grew up with my dad, trailing him all over the world for his job."

"I'm so sorry about your mom," she said softly. "But it sounds like a fascinating childhood."

I thought about that for a moment, her sincerity as she offered condolences making me miss my mother suddenly, in a way I hadn't felt in a long time. "It made me a little different, I guess. Less good at . . . regular people." I didn't want to delve too deeply into that topic—it was my greatest failing, as far as I was concerned. "What about you?"

She narrowed her dark eyes at me for a moment, those full lips pursing like she was trying to figure something out. "You're asking me about my childhood?" she said, and something in her voice made me think it had been a stupid question. Or that maybe she'd already told me about it.

But she hadn't.

"I didn't mean to pry," I said. "Sorry."

She laughed again, the sound pulling at the desire growing inside me. "No, you're not prying. Just caught me off guard, I guess. Most people act like they already know me."

What a strange thing to say. I thought about it, intrigued further by this unusual woman. Why did people assume to know anything about her?

"I'm not super good at people either, that's all," she said, smiling broadly and lifting her glass.

We touched the rims of our glasses together, a little toast to mutual social awkwardness, and then we sipped our drinks. And I couldn't help feeling like life at Kasper Ridge had just gotten much more interesting.

Chapter 4
Chrissy Gets a Job

PENNY

I was getting a glass of water in Bennie's kitchen before heading to bed when I felt her step into the space behind me. She didn't say anything, and when I turned around, she was standing, arms crossed, a funny little smile on her face.

"What?"

"Saw you in intimate conversation with a certain former fighter pilot over at the resort," she said, her voice cheerful and almost singsong.

"You'll have to be more specific, sounds like they're all former fighter pilots." My defenses went up immediately, even though it was Bennie. My instincts had taught me to keep my private life private, though that had never done me much good.

"The surly one who never talks to anybody."

"He didn't seem surly," I said, thinking of the serious slate blue eyes, the grim, somewhat stoic expression Harrison had worn before we started talking. "Just . . ."

"Just hot," Bennie supplied.

"He's attractive," I agreed, keeping my tone noncommittal. He was more than attractive, but there was little point to me goading my friend. I was here short term, and it sounded like he wasn't staying around long either. Plus, given what had happened the last time I'd attempted to date, I was pretty sure any hopes of romance were off the table.

"And?" she asked.

"There's no 'and.' We were just talking." I finished my water and put the glass into the sink. Part of me wished there could be an 'and.'

She nodded, wrapping a piece of hair around her finger. "So while you were flirting with Brainiac," she started.

"I wasn't flirting, Benn. The thing is . . . he didn't know who I was. That was all. I haven't gotten to talk to someone who didn't know *Our Girl Chrissy* in years. Maybe ever."

"He didn't?" Her head jerked up slightly. "Did he grow up under a rock?"

"He's a little older than us, and I guess he grew up overseas. His dad was a diplomat." I leaned my hip against the counter, remembering how intriguing Harrison's past had made him seem as we talked, how refreshing it was to be just a person to him. Not a former child star with multiple scandals in her past.

"Well, that's gotta be different," she said, smiling. "I'm glad you got to talk to him then."

"Me too. It was nice to not be me for a bit." It occurred to me that Harrison would inevitably figure out what I hadn't told him, and then he'd probably ignore me altogether. But in the meantime, it was refreshing.

"Hey," she said, stepping closer. "You're always you. Some people just make assumptions that you are a whole lot different than you actually are because of that silly show."

"Right." But sometimes even I had trouble feeling like an actual person, not just a vestige of some sitcom character.

"Anyway, Aubrey was telling me that they're hiring for a lot of seasonal positions over at the resort."

I tilted my head. Where was she going with this? "Like ski instructors," I said. We'd talked about that too.

"And back-office people," Bennie said. "Reservations and finance. Payroll, admin, that kind of thing." My friend watched my face, looking like she was waiting for a reaction. "You know, if you wanted to stay a little longer. You could maybe work at the resort?"

Just the words 'back office' lit a little flame of interest in me. The last thing I'd want would be to work in front of a never-ending parade of people, most of whom would certainly recognize me. I'd be Chrissy forever, every day. But getting to do some kind of real-world job out of sight of the public was intriguing. "That's actually kind of interesting," I said aloud.

"Right?" Bennie asked, her face lighting up. "You could work for the winter, help with the opening, stay with me." She emphasized this last word, but wiggled her eyebrows with the next, "and get to know your fighter pilot a bit better."

"Even if I stay, he's not planning to," I told her. Then added quickly, "and I'm definitely not thinking about it like that."

"Definitely not." She grinned. "Should I call Aubrey in the morning and get an interview set up for you?"

"Interview?" I hadn't considered that. I had never actually been interviewed.

"Yes, that's usually the first step."

I nodded. Of course it was. "Right. I just. I've never gone on an interview. I've been on auditions . . ."

"Do you have a resume?"

I shook my head. My high hopes flagged. There was no way I was qualified for any real jobs.

"Okay, we can work on that tomorrow. I'll text Aubrey and share your info, and you guys can set up an interview."

Though I was suddenly nervous and worried, the idea stoked something to life in me, some hope or excitement I hadn't felt in a while. A real job. Like an actual regular person. I only hoped I was qualified.

* * *

I had thought I might have a week or so to prepare, but Bennie met me in the kitchen the next morning holding three bags and balancing a mug of coffee as she was heading off to school.

"Texted Aubrey before I went to bed last night."

My stomach clenched the same way it always had when I'd gone to an audition, waited to hear if I'd been chosen.

"She said she'd text you about coming in today."

"Today?" I dashed to the bedroom where I'd left my phone charging. Sure enough, there was a text from Aubrey, asking me to come by the resort at ten.

"Oh my god," I said, suddenly terrified. "We didn't even have time to do the resume."

"I told Aubrey you don't have one officially. She knows your background."

And that was the problem, wasn't it? Everyone thought they knew me. Aubrey knew what she'd seen on television and read in tabloids. I wondered why she was even going to bother with the interview.

"Okay."

"Why do you sound less than excited?" Bennie asked, frowning at me.

"I don't know," I told her honestly. I wanted to be excited, but it was all happening really fast. "I basically ran away from home and now I'm considering getting a job?" I hadn't really planned to stay here. I hadn't planned anything.

"Did I move too fast?"

"No, it isn't that. I guess I'm just trying to get used to the idea." I stared at my hands in front of me, wringing one another like they were interrogating each other for answers.

"Hey," Bennie set down her coffee and a bag, and took one of my hands, stopping it from strangling the other. "You don't have to take the job if she offers it. Right? You're just exploring options, seeing what's possible. If you want, you can tell her no thanks and head back to Hollywood tomorrow."

That made me feel a little better. She was right. I was in control. The idea of heading back to California, however, definitely didn't make me feel better.

"Okay," I breathed. "Yes. Okay. Thanks, Benn."

"Call Jepsen. He'll give you a ride."

"Your brother?"

"He's the only Uber up here."

"Oh, okay." I pulled out my phone to make sure I had the app installed.

"Just text him," she said, typing something into her own phone. "Here."

A contact popped onto my screen, and the name Jepsen Summers appeared, with a phone number.

"Thanks."

"I can't wait to hear how it goes when I get home," Bennie squealed, giving me a quick hug and then heading for the door with her bags slung over her arms again. "First graders await!"

"Bye," I called after her turning back to the empty kitchen

feeling a little nauseous. Did I want a job? Really? Did I want to stay here?

* * *

Three hours later, Bennie's brother was dropping me off at Kasper Ridge Resort, his little Toyota pulling around the grand driveway and coming to a stop beneath the massive overhang.

"There you are, m'lady," he said. He'd offered me gum, water, and dental floss over the course of the short ride, and told me he was striving to disrupt the on-demand ride service with full-service offerings.

I wasn't sure how that would go for him. The ride itself, on half-bald tires around potholed mountain roads, was disruptive. I could give him that, at least, as my stomach identified the fact that we'd come to a stop.

"Thank you," I said, fishing some bills out of my purse.

"I can't take your money. You're family," he said.

"Oh. Um, okay, thank you." In Los Angeles, everyone was only too happy to take my money. Especially family.

"Give me a call when you're ready to head back."

I watched Jepsen pull away and then turned to the big resort, the wood and dark iron structure looking even more grand in the day than it had when I'd come to the movie the other night. The resort had a rustic air about it but was imposing enough to suggest luxury. I took a deep breath and headed inside, where Aubrey was waiting at the massive reception desk.

The lobby was brightly lit, making the space feel opulent and welcoming at once, and soft music played somewhere. I half expected to see guests milling around, and had to remind myself the place wasn't open yet.

"Hi again," I said. "I'm Bennie's friend, Penny."

She made a face, her eyes widening and her mouth pulling

open. "I know who you are, Penny, we met the other night." The face quickly morphed into a grin, and she bounced out from around the desk. "Let's go. I'll show you the back office and we can talk back there."

I followed Aubrey through a set of doors at the back of the lobby, near the grand staircase, where we went down a short hallway to an open area. One side of it had windows that faced the back patio, each set up with a workspace in front of it—a monitor and a chair, and a stack of drawers down one side of the desk. Ticket windows, I realized.

There were desks centered in the room as well, and a door at the far side, which Aubrey led me through. This opened to a small office, which had a window looking out over the back patio and a well-equipped desk with a chair in front of it. Aubrey sat behind the desk, and I took the other chair. I had no idea what to do next. This wasn't like any audition I'd been on.

"This is a nice office," I said, glancing at the view out the back window. It overlooked a big patio with a firepit in the center, Adirondack chairs spread around it, and the ski mountain rising away from us in the distance.

"It was my uncle's at one point," Aubrey told me. "He liked keeping an eye on everything, I guess. We had to tint that window—it was super bright in here."

"Can people see in?" I asked. The glass was darkened a bit, but it would feel a bit like sitting in a fishbowl, I thought.

"No, not at all," she said. At night, you can see if the light is on in here, but you can't actually see through the window.

That was a nice touch. I liked the idea of being able to see outside without anyone seeing in.

"I'm glad Bennie texted," Aubrey said, facing me over the desk with an easy smile.

I settled onto the edge of the chair, trying to look interview ready.

"We're hiring a lot of positions over the next few weeks as we prepare for opening, but we really need to get a few back-office positions filled right away. There are a couple things that might work, depending on your skill set."

She was barreling ahead as if I'd already been hired. "She told you I don't have a resume? Or any actual job experience?"

"She did," Aubrey confirmed, the smile never faltering. "But I'm kind of into lived experiences as much as resumes, and you're a friend of a friend, so you get a bit of leeway there."

"What kinds of office jobs are you hiring for?"

"We need a bookkeeper like yesterday," she said, rolling her eyes. "Archie is awful at keeping things organized, and we're not exactly flush with cash at the moment."

I nodded, listening, excitement growing slowly inside me. Finance was the one thing I might be qualified to do.

"We need someone to oversee the ski school. Not a ski instructor, but someone to manage the scheduling of instructors, the online reservation system, which is separate from the hotel's main system. All that stuff."

"Would that person be interacting with the public then?" That would not be a good fit.

Aubrey shook her head. "With the ski school staff, yes, but not outside this window." She pointed to the window, and I imagined legions of skiers and boarders wandering around.

"Okay," I said slowly, not sure if I should mention my degree or tell her anything else yet.

"We're also going to need someone to handle HR. Staff management, benefits coordination, that kind of stuff."

That was definitely not me.

I cleared my throat, hoping my voice was not going to betray my peculiar nervousness. I needed to project confidence, and tried to tap into my acting skills. "I actually have an accounting degree," I told her. "So the bookkeeping job sounds kind of like a fit. I'm good with numbers."

She straightened in the chair, grinning. "Really?"

I wasn't sure what the right answer was to that, so I waited for her to accept that I wasn't joking about the degree.

"So . . . do you have any kind of experience managing accounts? Like keeping track of expenditures, future planning budgets and stuff?"

"Kind of."

She waited, so I decided to expand.

"My parents managed my career when I was a kid. But by the time I was old enough to wonder, it was pretty clear they were not the best at it. They'd spend wildly and we'd end up getting behind on the mortgage payment or having to wait for my next check to get groceries and stuff."

"You're kidding," Aubrey breathed. "I assumed you would have been paid well for that show."

This was the first time Aubrey had mentioned the show—I'd almost begun to wonder if she knew about it or if Kasper Ridge was a magic black hole where no one had ever heard of *Our Girl Chrissy*. I lifted a shoulder. "I was. I mean, for years, I had no idea about any of it. I thought it was fun. I didn't even realize I had a job. But by the time I was ten or so, I understood that I was the cash cow for my parents, and they depended on my income for everything." I'd never blatantly told anyone about all of this, but Aubrey's kind eyes and soft smile made her easy to talk to.

"That's a lot for a ten-year old."

I nodded. "And they weren't putting anything away for later."

Aubrey frowned.

"So I started reviewing the accounts when I was about

twelve. They were sloppy about everything, and didn't do any kind of planning. Even as a kid, I knew that wasn't right.

"I got my GED when I was fifteen and took online college classes while I worked. I got my accounting degree when I was nineteen. By then, the show had ended, and my parents had spent pretty much everything, minus what I'd managed to sneak into my own savings."

Aubrey's face reddened. "That's such bullshit," she whispered. "Sorry, I mean, I know they're your parents . . ."

I shook my head. I'd long since accepted that my parents weren't the peanut butter and jelly making, hug-giving types. They were more like the sell-a-scandalous-tape-of-your-own-kid types.

"No loyalty there," I told her, swallowing hard. The next part was not something I'd planned to talk about, but I already knew I was going to tell Aubrey everything. "Either way. They sold the video of me when I was twenty. Cut the guy in for a third."

"What?"

By now, I failed to get irate about this, but it was nice to see how awful Aubrey thought it was.

"You probably heard about it. Or saw it. It was everywhere for a while."

Aubrey was shaking her head slowly back and forth.

"Anyway," I practically sighed this word. "Sorry, I didn't actually plan to get totally into all this. Just wanted to explain how I gained experience managing finances. I moved out right after that and terminated contracts with my parents as my managers. I took half of what they made on the sex video and tried to start over."

"That sucks. Did you keep in touch with them?"

I shook my head. "Not until recently. My dad died, and my mother reached out. I probably should have stayed away, but I felt sorry for her. They were so codependent. She was waitressing by then." Probably the first real job she'd had since having me.

Aubrey's eyes were huge, and I wondered if I'd revealed too much.

"You grew up so fast," she said, sounding impressed and sad all at once. "And did you have to find a job too?"

"I went on a lot of auditions. Did some commercials that paid okay. A couple magazine ads. But every place I showed up, I was *Our Girl Chrissy*. No one wanted a has-been child star to grow up. Especially after the scandal."

"That's so shitty."

It was, but I'd accepted it a long time ago.

"You're hired," Aubrey declared, springing up from the desk. "When can you start?"

"Um . . . now?" Relief washed through me, along with a healthy amount of confusion. Was this what I wanted? Bennie and I had agreed that I didn't even have to decide right away, that I could say no.

But what would I be going back to in Los Angeles? Mom, who was probably only going to become more and more dependent now that Dad was gone. An empty apartment. More auditions? And the newest scandal. Nausea turned my stomach as I considered going back.

"Great," Aubrey said. "Paperwork first." She tapped a few keys on the computer and brought up a form for me to fill out. "You'll be the first official employee on the Kasper Ridge Resort payroll. Archie will be so relieved."

"He's the guy they call Ghost, right?"

She nodded. "My brother, yeah."

I was just beginning to get all the names and callsigns figured out. Bennie had given me a little review.

"It's confusing," Aubrey said, waving me toward the chair behind the desk. "You get used to it."

As I took the seat she'd vacated, I turned back to her, uncertain.

She flashed me the grin I was coming to see was her natural expression. "This is your office, Penny."

I sat up straight and looked around, worried for a second I might actually cry. It felt so monumental, and so important. "This is amazing," I said. "Thank you."

I would be happy here. Away from the eyes of people who thought they knew everything about me. Doing a job I would be good at, in a place where I could be a real person for a change. "Thank you," I said again, taking the mouse and beginning to fill out the forms.

"Come find me out front when you're done, and we can get started."

I smiled my agreement, and when Aubrey had gone, I took a moment to lean back in the chair and gaze out the big window. This. Was. Perfect.

Chapter 5
Give Ghost a Kiss

HARRISON

I'd thought about Penny a lot since I'd basically inserted myself between her and Antonio down at the bar. There was no point lying to myself about it—I was drawn to her. And now her throaty laughter and flashing eyes filled my head unexpectedly. Inconveniently.

I spent the day after seeing her walking the ski runs out back with the resort designer Ghost had brought in when he'd begun researching getting the place permitted in time for winter.

"It's surprising how set up you are here," Frank, the guy

we'd been working with, said. "I guess the old owner must've put a lot into it the first time around."

I was relieved to hear it. The one thing that would definitely throw a wrench into the plans would have been not passing final inspections, but with these guys to help open up the new runs and a bit of clean up on the old ones, we were in good shape.

"A lot of times, we'll do the topographical map," he was saying as we returned to the resort proper, "and then when we get up here we'll find a rock the size of a house that we didn't see from the satellite survey. You guys got lucky. The only thing here is that depression on the side of the peak, but it's in the trees at this point, so as long as you keep the barriers up over there, it doesn't really matter what it is."

"What do you think it is?" I asked him, wondering if it was anything we would need to worry about in the future.

He shrugged. "Just a cave or crevice in the underlying rock, most likely. We'll keep an eye on it, make sure it doesn't get any bigger. Shouldn't be a problem. You guys are all set up here, good to go for the season."

"Good to hear," I said, a noticeable load lifting off my shoulders. The designers had weighed in on the actual grading and slope of the runs, and even made suggestions about traffic flow at the foot of the resort, giving us some things to think about for future expansion plans. Of course, I wouldn't be here by then, but it was a help to Ghost, no doubt.

I stood on the back patio, thanking Frank for his time—and for the permits I finally held in my hands—as the sun neared the tree line, casting tall shadows across the patio around us. I had an odd sense of someone watching me, watching us, but I couldn't identify what had set off that internal alarm. It was an old instinct, maybe born in the Navy, but I was used to trusting my gut. The ticket windows and the one on the office next to them reflected the sun's rays back at me, and I squinted toward them. Maybe Aubrey was in there. She'd spent a lot of time setting up for the influx of staff we'd be seeing before long.

Frank left, promising to come ski this season to see the place in action, and I was about to head inside when my phone vibrated in my pocket.

I was not a fan of live synchronous communication in an age when there were so many alternatives that did not involve having to actually speak to another human being. And I'd been with Frank all day. I was tired of people. But the screen showed a name I hadn't thought about in a while, and I had an idea—or a hope—why he might be calling. I settled into one of the Adirondack chairs, leaning my head back against the wide planks, and answered.

"Gator. What's good?"

"Brainiac. How's Ghost's Folly coming along?" His wry grin was apparent in the tone of his familiar voice and I could practically see him shaking his head as his eyes glinted—waiting for his jab to land. Gator had been our squadron commanding officer when I'd first joined, and though we hadn't served directly together long, we'd kept in touch. He was a few years older, and had retired at twenty years and gone on to found some tech company in California.

"Ghost's Folly," I said, a chuckle escaping me. "That's pretty on the nose. Though I think this thing is going to pay off for him."

"The hotel or the treasure hunt?"

"Which one is his folly, according to the gossips?"

"Both," Gator said. "But everyone's really pulling for him," he added, his voice more serious.

"The resort is looking good. The hunt is stalled at the moment. No one can figure out what his uncle had in mind or if there even is any kind of treasure to find."

"It's a good distraction for him, though."

"Yeah, it is." Ghost's career had ended tragically, and I didn't like thinking about what he might be doing if he wasn't completely immersed in the details of getting Kasper Ridge up and running again.

"Hey, you got a job lined up? Heading back to school soon?"

Ouch. I hated having to admit that my sabbatical was actually more of a joblessness situation than anything else. So I didn't. "Uh, no. Still just figuring out what's next."

"Good. Yeah, you should take the time you need. But I've got another idea to throw at you, something you can factor into what I'm guessing is a pretty complicated decision-making matrix. Probably a huge whiteboard next to your bed or something, knowing you."

"How'd you know? But it's actually on the ceiling."

"Grease markers on the mirror?"

"Exactly."

"Well, add a new column up there."

"What should it say?" My curiosity was piqued. This was what I'd hoped Gator might be calling about after catching wind that he'd been contacting a few guys from the fleet about jobs.

"I'm hiring. I need a guy with your skills to interface with the client."

That was exactly what I wanted to hear. Not so much the 'interface with the client' part, but I wasn't sure it mattered. I needed a job. I tried to keep a professional tone. "Gonna need a little more. The client is . . ."

"The Navy, man. We won a huge contract, and I'm staffing up. You'd be basically running the program. With me, of course."

"That sounds like a lot of people management." I couldn't picture myself running staff, dealing with client engagement. There was a reason I liked teaching. . . although maybe "liked" was a strong word. I liked being in the front of the room, controlling the environment, knowing it was all on a timer.

"Nah. I've got a guy for that. I need his technical counterpart. Someone who actually understands the product."

Much better. Now I was really interested. "And that's me?"

"It could be. The sensor we're building is a lot like what we had in the fleet," he explained. "A few minor differences that make it a pretty big upgrade. Navy's putting it on the F-35."

"Huh."

"Well there's an interested candidate if I've ever heard one."

"Sorry. Just thinking." And I was. Hadn't I been waiting for an opportunity? Digging through my network to make something pop? I'd assumed it would be another job in academia, but then I'd heard about what Gator was up to and pinged him on LinkedIn in hopes he might consider me. I'd proven I wasn't cut out for teaching. My last university had definitely decided that one for me. This was going to be a good fit.

"Look, the pay's good, and we can definitely negotiate on that front. You'd need to be out here though, as soon as we can get you."

Wheels turned in my head. I'd promised Ghost I'd handle the first ski season. That was non-negotiable. "When do you need to know? Ski season's just about to start up here. I kind of owe it to Ghost to stick around for a while."

Gator let out a noisy sigh. "Fucking loyalty. This is what you get for hiring goddamn sailors."

"Sorry, man." But I wasn't. And I knew he didn't resent the loyalty that our time in the Navy had bred in us all. It was one of the reasons he was calling me in the first place.

"Nah, it's good. Ideally, I'd have you here tomorrow. Realistically, I can wait until spring."

"Yeah?" Spring would be perfect.

"But I do need a decision, Brainiac. Just need to know I've

got the right guy coming. And if you don't get here until the snow clears, I might need you to consult a bit between here and there."

"I'll think about it for sure." I had already decided, but figured it was prudent to hold off dancing with excitement and accepting before I'd even seen the pay. More weight lifted from my shoulders. This was turning into a banner day.

"Let me know soon."

"I will."

"Give Ghost a big kiss for me."

"I won't."

We hung up on that note and I stayed in the chair on the quiet patio, my mind spinning around the idea of moving to the coast, working a real job, pulling in a good paycheck. There was something satisfying about the thought, and putting my skills to use would be rewarding too. I'd certainly never get rich running a ski school for Ghost. Hell, as far as I knew, I wasn't even getting paid to do it, at least not beyond living expenses and the monthly check he referred to as a "stipend."

I didn't have expenses, so it didn't really matter. But one day, I thought, maybe it'd be nice to have someone to take care, someone I'd need a little job security for. Maybe even a kid . . .

I pushed that thought away. Kids were the ultimate investment, and once you pulled that trigger, there was no walking away. I wasn't sure I was cut out for being a dad anyway, especially not after my clear failure at being the kind of touchy-feely teacher the university wanted me to be.

Maybe it'd be a good fit. Working in the lab for Gator, advising the program guy. Testing, documenting . . . that was what I was good at. Keeping my head down and my mouth shut.

I was about to stand and head inside when the back doors slid open and Aubrey came out, trailed by the face that had been popping into my head off and on for the last day. Penny. It had already been a pretty good day. Seeing her again was the cherry on top.

"Hi again," she said.

"You remember Penny," Aubrey said, bouncing on her toes as she was prone to do. Aubrey wasn't tall, and sometimes I thought she bounced as a way to make herself bigger, but it was probably just an effort to contain the incredible energy that seemed to zip around under her skin at all times. "She's Kasper Ridge Resort's first official hire! She's our new bookkeeper!"

I turned to Penny, a little surprised. "So you're staying." The idea of seeing her every day was exciting, but I tried not to let my face give me away.

She smiled, her shoulders giving a little shrug as her eyes met mine. "I guess so."

That news gave me a little lift. I was happy she'd be around, and I wondered if she might be up for spending a little more time together. Of course, getting involved with a co-worker had completely different implications than dating someone who was temporarily visiting a friend up here. So was Penny suddenly off limits? And why was I even thinking about this? Yeah, she was gorgeous and sexy, but we'd just met. And now I was most likely leaving.

"That's great," I said, taking a step back, and turning to head inside. "Welcome to the team," I called over my shoulder, basically trying on a phrase I thought sounded right in the circumstances. Instead, it sounded forced and awkward.

"Thanks," she called back.

I went up to my room, telling myself I'd settle on a path forward now that one had presented itself. I checked my email, just to make sure I hadn't been offered a teaching position in the six hours since I'd last checked, and wasted some time looking at employment pages at universities who probably didn't want me any more than my last employer did.

Gator's offer sounded good, and though I didn't have any job offers from academia, his email was waiting for me. And the numbers were impressive, benefits were tight. It was like the perfect answer had just fallen into my lap.

There was no point dancing around it. I emailed him back, accepting the offer. I'd start in the spring, when the snow began to melt and the ski operations up here shut down.

And until then, Penny and I would be co-workers.

Chapter 6
Cookies Can Be Dangerous Too

PENNY

Aubrey, who was so talkative and full of energy it was somewhat draining, walked me through the entire resort, showing me all the recreation spaces, the yurts out back, the ski shop that was slowly acquiring gear for the season, and the restaurant, from which a heavenly garlic smell was coming.

"Is the restaurant open?" I asked, my stomach rumbling as I realized I hadn't eaten lunch.

"Not for anyone except staff," she said. "Smells good, doesn't it? Want to stay for dinner?"

I didn't, not really. Being "on" all afternoon for Aubrey had exhausted me, but there was something pushing me to accept the offer. Or maybe someone.

I'd be lying to myself if I pretended that knowing Harrison would be around hadn't factored into my decision-making process, both in coming to talk to Aubrey and in accepting this job. The other parts were clearly things like: needed the cash, needed some direction, needed an escape from my mother and my current scandal back in LA. But Harrison was in there somewhere.

"Does the resort have any kind of 'no fraternization' policy in place?" I asked Aubrey quietly as we headed toward the kitchen. I wondered if Aubrey could see right through the question.

She laughed loudly. "If it did, we'd all be screwed."

I chuckled along with her, relieved, but didn't really feel in on the joke.

"I mean, I met Wiley again because he came to set up the bar. Lucy and Will met on the job, and Annalee and Mateo, too. Actually," she grinned at me, her eyes bright with fun. "There might be something in the water up here. Better look out!"

I laughed, wondering just how transparent that question might have been. I wasn't looking for anything serious, but I could admit that I was interested in the guy they all called Brainiac. He was so different from other men I'd known, and the fact he didn't seem to know who I was helped a lot, though I doubted that would last long. Had I ever met anyone who didn't already have a preconceived notion of who I was? I couldn't remember anyone except Bennie and now, her friends.

Eventually, Aubrey and I had plates of steaming lasagna and crisp salad in our hands and we headed outside to the patio, where a few other familiar faces from the movie night I'd attended were already seated, eating.

"Hey guys," Aubrey called, pulling everyone's attention to us. I felt my face heat. "First official Kasper Ridge Resort hire here. You all met Penny at movie night. And now, she's our new bookkeeper."

There was a low chorus of greetings, and I did my best to acknowledge everyone with a plate in my hand. "Welcome!" Aubrey's brother called out. "That'll be a huge relief. Aubrey is notoriously bad with numbers."

"I am not," Aubrey said at my side, her voice rising.

"Well, you're not good with numbers," he went on.

Audrey huffed as she led me to a table where there were a couple vacant chairs.

"Remember that time you—"

"No need to stroll down memory lane," Aubrey interrupted loudly.

Her brother just laughed, and a few other chuckles rose from those around us.

"Jerk," Aubrey said as we sat. But her dark mood slid away just as quickly as it had arrived, and she put a hand on my shoulder, introducing me to the others at the table, Annalee, who I had met already, and Mateo, who I'd met briefly at the movie.

"Good to have you on board," Annalee said.

"It's all starting to feel real, huh?" Mateo asked Aubrey.

"It is," she said. "We passed inspections today for the runs and lifts, and now we have our first official hire."

"How are bookings looking?" Annalee asked her. I tried not to stare at the beautiful blonde as she spoke, but there was something about her that I envied. Sure, she was curvy and had glowing, gorgeous skin, but she also possessed an air of self-assurance I wasn't sure I'd ever have.

"Getting there," Aubrey said. "Opening week is booked up."

"Seriously?" Annalee said. "That's great."

The back doors of the patio opened, and I tried not to look

too interested as Harrison approached, carrying a plate. He wore a dark grey soft-looking long-sleeved T-shirt and dark jeans that wrapped his clearly muscular thighs. I wished my mind wasn't leading me to wonder what he might look like with that shirt off, but I couldn't seem to help it. His eyes were blue, almost grey, and the salt and pepper in his sideburns gave him a distinguished look. He glanced my way with a quick smile. "Mind if I join you?" he asked, glancing around the table.

"Wouldn't matter if we did," Annalee said, and I suppressed a laugh as Harrison purposely dragged a chair over, inserting it too close to Annalee and bumping her several times as he settled himself. If I hadn't known that she and Mateo were together, I might have assumed she and Harrison were a thing.

"Asshat," Annalee said as Harrison took a huge bite of lasagna and grinned at her.

"Ignore them," Aubrey suggested. "They're like siblings. You know how all these pilots are."

I shook my head. "Not really."

"They're like children when they get together. All their silly nicknames and inside jokes." She frowned, but she didn't actually look bothered.

"I think they're call signs," Mateo offered. "Not nicknames."

"Like in *Top Gun*," I blurted, feeling immediately moronic. These were real actual fighter pilots, and all I could do was name Hollywood caricatures of their lives.

"Exactly," Annalee agreed. "Except no one gets called cool stuff like Maverick in real life. Maybe in the Air Force." Harrison snickered at that, and I felt like I'd missed a joke somewhere, but was enjoying being part of the conversation, nonetheless.

"So you were Brainiac, right?" I asked Harrison, who nodded. "And what was your call sign?"

"That's Monroe," Harrison told me. "For obvious reasons."

"But sometimes," Annalee said, "if you show up thinking you'll get a cool call sign, your peers will quickly divest you of the notion. That's what happened to Fake Tom." She looked across the patio to where Lucy sat with Will.

I laughed. "I heard that story."

"He thought it was such a sure thing. I mean, he's got that hair."

"He does have nice hair," I agreed. Thick, unruly in a very sexy way.

"But you don't show up letting people know you'd like to be Killer or Torpedo. That's a sure way to get called Plunger or Pop Rock." Harrison chuckled.

"Remember P-WOC?" Annalee asked Harrison, grinning. She said it like "pee-wok."

"What does that mean?" Aubrey asked.

"I can't remember what it was originally," Harrison said, smiling in a way that made his steely blue eyes dance. My stomach flipped a little as he focused his attention on me. "But there was a point when we were in Atsugi, Japan, and the guy got ridiculously drunk a little earlier in the day than was strictly acceptable. Anyway, one of his enlisted maintenance guys had gotten a box that had been sitting in their workspace, and P-WOC started insisting he'd seen it move."

"A box? With holes in it or something? Like a pet?" Aubrey asked.

Harrison shook his head, and Annalee laughed. "No," she said. "Like the kind of box someone sends from home with cookies and magazines inside. But he was hammered, and he decided there was something dangerous in the box, so he ordered another guy to take it outside and shoot it."

"Shoot the box?" I asked.

She nodded, grinning.

"Um. Why, exactly?" I laughed.

"Not sure what the logic was there, but it turned out to be a box of cookies from the guy's girlfriend. So we called him 'Pointless Waste of Cookies' from then on. P-WOC."

We all laughed, and for the rest of the meal, I couldn't stop my gaze from straying to Harrison. There was something about him that I found compelling—beyond the muscled arms apparent beneath the sleeves of his T-shirt, or the clear confidence he conveyed. He was reserved, almost like he was holding himself back. And every time those slate-blue eyes flickered over my face, I felt like I'd gotten a little too close to a flame.

It felt like there was something there. Something mutual. But I knew if he didn't already know who I was, he would soon. And whatever seemed interesting about me now would be overshadowed in a heartbeat by tabloid headlines or photos he could find with a quick Internet search. It probably wasn't worth thinking about.

When we were cleaning up our plates, he appeared at my side, taking my plate from my hands and disposing of it for me.

"Thanks," I said.

"Sure," he replied. "Congratulations on the job."

I nodded as we headed back out to the patio, side by side, as if there was some unspoken agreement between us to go sit together. My stomach flipped as Harrison led me to a double Adirondack chair positioned at the edge of the patio, away from the fire pit where the others were gathering, drinks in their hands.

"Can I get you a drink?" He asked.

I didn't normally drink much, but there was something about the environment that made it feel right. And if I was going to sit here with this handsome fighter pilot, maybe a bit of courage was in order. "Sure."

"Do you drink whiskey?"

"Not on the regular," I told him. I rarely drank outside in public where someone might catch a photo, but figured this was probably safe.

"Wiley's family makes this stuff out in Maryland. It's good. Half-Cat."

"I'll try it," I told him. "Ice though, please."

"Be right back."

Soon, Harrison and I sat side by side as the mountain behind the resort fell into shadow, the environment taking on a silence that felt loaded, as if it was gearing up for the sounds and movements of the evening to officially begin.

"Aubrey told me you got all the permits today to get things operational," I said, glancing at the handsome profile next to me and feeling a rush of interest slide through me. "She said you did a lot of that yourself."

He shrugged. "I just did the research and made the contacts to get things going," he said. "Tried to rebuild the old lift, but the thing was an artifact. We'll put it on a back run, but we needed something more modern up front."

"That's pretty impressive."

He blew out a noisy breath, as if blowing away the compliment. "I do okay with building things. Not a lot of conversation required."

"You seem okay with conversation."

He glanced at me, the corner of his lips lifting. "You're easy to talk to, I guess."

Warmth flooded my chest and I smiled back at him, sipping the whiskey and settling into the gathering darkness. "So have you changed your mind? Are you staying here for life?" I asked him. "Becoming a ski bum?"

"Nah. Just till I'm sure Ghost is set up. Archie, I mean."

"And then what? Back to the professor gig?"

"Truth?" He said quietly in a way that got my attention. I faced him again. His eyes were dark in the dim light, serious.

"Yeah."

"I was let go. They don't want me." The words were matter of fact, but there was a deep thread of emotion behind them. I sensed that he had wanted to stay, that being let go wasn't something he'd expected.

"Why not?"

He glanced around, as if he didn't want to be overheard. "More truth," he said, taking a sip of his own drink as if he needed to be braced for this next part. "I was up for tenure. Thought I had it made. But there were two of us in contention. The other guy was a lot less experienced. Younger."

"And he got it?"

"He did."

"Why?"

"They said he had a more empathetic teaching style." Harrison shrugged. "He peoples better than me. I sucked at massaging those little egos and lifting up those developing minds."

"I doubt that."

He settled back into the chair. "Maybe you could make a call on my behalf."

I laughed, though I felt my defenses rise a bit. If he had any idea who I was, or who I used to be, that might have been an actual suggestion. "I'm sure that wouldn't do any good. Credibility isn't my strong suit."

He glanced at me, but I didn't feel like getting into any details about the scandals that had plagued me since I'd reached adulthood. I still couldn't tell for sure if he knew what I was referring to, but he didn't ask.

"So I need to find another path," he said. "A buddy called

today, actually. My old C-O. Offered me an engineering gig, which I accepted."

A little flicker of dismay wound through me. "So you *are* leaving?"

"Not right away. I'll work here through the season. But at some point, I need a real job, right? Actual pay. Some kind of security."

I nodded, feeling more disappointed than I would have expected to at the thought of him leaving. "Yeah. Me too."

"What about you? Planning to stay here now that you've got the gig?"

I didn't have a good answer. "For now, yeah." I didn't have much to return to, but I couldn't hide forever.

"Will you miss Los Angeles?"

I shook my head. "Definitely not."

There, at the far corner of the darkening patio, it felt like Harrison and I sat alone inside a comfortable bubble together. The voices and occasional laughter of the others floated our direction, as did the flickering light of the fire pit, but no one disturbed us, and we faced away from the group, staring out into the darkness at the edges of the resort grounds.

We didn't speak for a while, each of us sipping our whiskey. But there was something actively happening between us that I could feel. A drawing in, a leaning almost, toward one another. And when my glass was empty and I set it down on the ground beside me, I straightened up to find Harrison's eyes on me. A jolt of desire shot through my body.

"Penny," he said, his voice like smoke.

"Yeah?" His gaze was focused and clear, and I felt like something big was coming.

"I'm glad you'll be here this season," he said. "I'd like to take you out."

Surprise sent a bark of laughter out of my mouth before I could catch it, and Harrison's eyes widened slightly.

"Or . . . not?" He said, clearly unsure what to make of my reaction.

I covered my mouth with a hand, mortified that I'd laughed and now he was discouraged. "Sorry, I didn't mean to laugh. Nerves," I explained.

He waited, and I felt the air between us grow thicker with tension. Then he tried again. "Would you want to go get dinner this week? In town?"

My stomach was twisting around under his serious gaze, every nerve in my body shuddering in frenzy at the laser-focused attention he was giving me. Going out in town would likely mean being recognized. But I didn't want to say no. And he'd find out who I was eventually. Maybe sooner was better.

"Truth?" I heard myself whisper. His head inclined slightly, encouraging me. "I'd like that a lot."

We exchanged numbers, said a somewhat awkward good night, and as Jepson drove me back to Bennie's house after a long afternoon at Kasper Ridge, my phone pinged with a text.

Harrison: Truth?

Me: Okay.

Harrison: I'm really glad you're going to be here a while.

I liked Harrison's truths.

Me: Truth?

Harrison: Always.

Me: I'm looking forward to dinner.

Harrison: How's tomorrow?

Me: Sure.

Harrison: Text me your address. I'll pick you up at six.

I smiled, feeling strangely young and naive, when really, I was the opposite of those things. But if Harrison really didn't know about anything from my past, then I could be someone else entirely with him. I could be myself. The girl I was meant to be. At least for a little while.

Truth? I couldn't wait.

Chapter 7
A Surly Pilot at the Surly Fox

PENNY

"You've been here a whole week, and you've already scored a date with one of the few eligible bachelors on the mountain. I've been here since high school, and . . ." Bennie gestured around her little house as if to highlight that it was, in fact, devoid of eligible bachelors.

"It kind of just happened," I told her, dropping my gaze to the coffee mug I held in my hand. I'd gone straight to my room the night before and Bennie had gotten home late. We hadn't had a chance to catch up, so I had to wait until morning to tell her about work and Harrison.

"And he seriously has no idea who you are?" Bennie was curled on one end of the sofa, her own coffee steaming in her hand.

I shook my head slowly, widening my eyes. It shocked the hell out of me too. Not because I expected to be recognized out of some egotistical belief that I was just that famous, but because experience had taught me that whenever I managed to get comfortable in some new environment, someone would make a big deal about my past and essentially ruin it. "I don't think he does."

"And no one over there told him?"

"I guess he's really good at compartmentalizing if they did. But no one over there has even asked me about the show." I wondered how much things would change if it got out.

"I'm surprised."

"I am too," I admitted. "But it's such a nice change."

"You made the right call, getting out of LA."

"Thank you so much for letting me crash here. I will be paying you rent, too."

"No you won't." Bennie straightened up, looking horrified at this announcement.

"Of course I will." I didn't have the money I should have had after years of being paid well to be Our Girl Chrissy, but I had enough, despite my parents' best efforts to ruin me as well as themselves from a financial perspective. I didn't want Bennie to feel like I was using her.

"I honestly don't want your money," Bennie said. "It doesn't feel good to me."

I made a face at my friend, but wouldn't push the issue. Instead, I decided, I'd find other ways to pay her back.

"I'd better get ready for work," she said, popping up from the couch and setting her mug on the coffee table. "Do you have to work today?"

I shook my head. "I officially start Monday. Yesterday was like orientation. Lots of paperwork and learning where everything is."

"So exciting," Bennie said, reaching out to squeeze my shoulder.

As my friend got ready to go to school, I pulled my laptop out onto the kitchen table and braced myself to go through the email I'd allowed to pile up since fleeing Los Angeles.

By the time Bennie had left, I'd been through most of it, but there was one from Paul, my agent, that I popped open just as the door clicked shut behind her.

Hey Penny: Wanted to get in touch about an opportunity, and I get the sense you're screening my calls - ha!

Don't worry about the articles. That stuff will blow over. You know this—you've been through enough of it by now.

New opportunity, and I really want you to consider this one.

They're doing a reboot of Our Girl Chrissy.

I nearly slammed the laptop shut, but morbid curiosity kept me reading.

Keep reading please before you say no…

It's a reunion show. A kind of "Where are they now?" thing, plus ten episodes with a new setup, showing Chrissy as an adult, living on her own.

Give me a call. I've got all the contract details. The money is good.

For obvious reasons, they'd really like your participation, but they've let me know they will work around you if you say no.

It sounds like they'll point to the current scandal as the reason though, which will just rehash something we'd rather bury. Kind of an offer you can't refuse, huh?

Call me — Paul

My heart felt like a kettlebell inside my chest, pulling everything in me down. Why couldn't I just walk away? Why did my past life have to color every single thing I did?

I stood up and walked to the window, thinking about his words. Basically, if I said no, they'd use the current scandal as the reason. I could see the articles splashing across the television screen now, one after another, as some smug narrator talked about how troubled child actress Penny Davis hadn't been able to join them because of her current personal issues. They'd probably even drag out the previous scandal, painting me—not for the first time—as a troubled woman prone to poor decisions and living some kind of damaged life. And if they saw that up here... would it change the way Harrison looked at me?

I already knew the answer.

But if I said yes . . .

I shook my head. Paul hadn't given me any idea of time frame. And I'd just made a commitment to Kasper Ridge. I had a real job. A normal life.

If you didn't count hiding rent free at a friend's house in the mountains.

I squeezed my eyes shut, willing my brain to figure this one out. Why was nothing ever simple?

I turned and went back to the kitchen, pushing shut my laptop as I passed it. I would answer Paul later. When I'd had time to think. For right now, I was going to make an egg, and think about what I was going to wear tonight when I went to dinner with Harrison.

A little flicker of excitement flashed through me, making me feel lighter, almost giddy.

* * *

Bennie came home around five, and found me sitting on the couch, reading a book. I'd recently stumbled into a series of romantic comedies about a winemaking family with a bunch of brothers. It was silly and fun, and a complete escape from everything I worried about in my real life.

"Isn't that where I left you?" Bennie joked.

I dropped my tablet to the side. "I've been relaxing today."

"Good!" She gave me an evaluative look after dropping her bag into a chair. "But shouldn't you be getting ready for your big date?"

My stomach flipped as she said *date*. "I probably should," I agreed. "I've been putting it off because I don't know what to wear. I didn't really put a ton of thought into packing, I did it so fast. And I wasn't packing for dating."

Bennie grinned. "I have a few things that rarely see the light of day," she motioned for me to follow her down the hall to her bedroom. "But it's not like there's a lot of call for dressing up in Kasper Ridge. Even for a date."

"So no chiffon. Got it."

Bennie laughed. "I don't have a ton of chiffon or tulle, luckily. Only one garish bridesmaid dress a girl from college made me wear a few years ago."

"No thanks. Unless it's lime green."

"It's burgundy, so I guess you're out of luck."

"Damn."

Bennie pulled a few things from her closet, among them a flowy floral top that caught my eye.

"Maybe this?" I asked, holding it up. "I have a pair of white jeans and some high sandals."

"You and Lucy and the high heels. Just be careful." Bennie shook her head.

"Lucy was wearing high shoes this week, wasn't she? Is she trying to look taller?" I remembered the petite dark-haired woman's shoes because I'd coveted them a bit when we'd met. They were gorgeous. And very high, considering we were in the mountains.

"Lucy Dale is the only woman I know who can hold her own bossing around men all day and look like a complete bombshell by night. She's always been girlier than anyone else I know up here."

"I like that," I said, thinking about a tougher version of Lucy working around the resort, directing teams of men twice her size.

"She's pretty awesome." Bennie nodded at the shirt in my hands. "Go put it on. Let's see how it looks."

I did as directed, finding her in the living room digging through her bag. She heard me come in and turned to face me. "Oh yeah," she said, eyeing me up and down. "That's perfect."

I felt pretty in the silky shirt, and the shoes weren't so high that I was worried about stumbling. That was one thing Hollywood had done for me—I'd learned to be comfortable in heels at a very young age.

"Thanks, Ben." I spent the rest of my time curling my dark auburn hair and putting on a little more makeup than I wore during the day, pushing down the jittery worry inside me that was a mixture of nerves and the lingering effects of Paul's email.

I considered telling Bennie about the offer, but decided not to let it ruin the evening.

When the doorbell rang, I was ready to go, and I beat Bennie to the door to answer it.

Harrison stood there, looking perfectly calm and collected in a button-down shirt rolled up his forearms and a pair of dark-wash jeans that fit him to perfection. The light green shirt made his grey-blue eyes pop, and the touch of silver at his temples gave him a worldly look I found ridiculously sexy.

"Hi," I said.

His lips curved up on one side and he didn't say anything for a beat. Then, in a low voice, he said, "Sorry . . . I was speechless there for a minute. You look incredible."

The praise warmed my skin, and I felt my own smile widen. "Thank you."

Bennie stepped to my side, grinning at Harrison. "Don't keep her out too late, young man," she said.

Harrison's smile dropped a bit, and he looked between us. "Uh, sure."

"You remember Bennie," I said poking her shoulder playfully. "She's just kidding."

"Right," he said, still looking uncertain.

"Have fun," she said. "You going to the Moose or the Fox?" Her tone suggested these were the only two options.

"Are all the restaurants up here named for animals?" I asked.

Harrison nodded. "Yeah, and it gets better. It's the Toothy Moose or the Surly Fox."

"Descriptive," I noted.

"No making fun of our town," Bennie said, frowning between us.

"No worries there," I told her. "So far, I love it here." I was telling the truth. From the moment I'd arrived in the tiny town of Kasper Ridge, I'd been made to feel welcome, right at home, and blessedly normal.

"We will be heading to dinner at the Surly Fox," Harrison informed us both. "If that sounds okay to you, Penny."

"That sounds perfect," I told him, stepping back to grab my purse. "See you later," I told Bennie, who winked at me in a way I was pretty sure she thought was sly.

As soon as the door closed behind us, I felt like I'd entered some alternate universe. Harrison put a hand gently on the small of my back as we descended Bennie's front porch steps, almost like he was guiding me, or making sure I didn't fall. A thrill shot through me at his touch. He opened the passenger side door on a huge black SUV, and then smoothly moved around to the driver's side and slid in. He moved as if every step was practiced or choreographed, and I wondered if that self-assuredness and grace had come from flying jets or if it was something he'd been born with.

For a few moments, neither of us said anything, and the twisting two-lane highway that seemed to connect all parts of Kasper Ridge flew beneath the wheels of the car. After a moment, Harrison spoke, so low I almost didn't hear it.

"Truth?" he asked.

My stomach jumped a little—I liked having what felt like an inside joke with this man.

"Please," I said.

"I'm nervous."

I looked over at him, unable to detect the slightest bit of nervousness in the relaxed position of his body in the seat, one hand slung casually on the steering wheel as the other sat in his lap, steering from the bottom of the wheel when we moved through turns. Everything about Harrison screamed competence and self-control, from the stoic expression he seemed to wear all the time to the solidity of his well-muscled body. He definitely didn't seem nervous, but as I considered the man taking me to dinner, I felt my own nerves spike up.

"You don't look nervous," I told him.

"I hide it well."

I felt a little smile lift my mouth at the idea that I could make a guy like this feel nervous. "Well, if it helps, I'm nervous too."

He glanced at me, his lips lifting a tick in one corner as those flinty eyes flashed.

"I'm nervous because I haven't been on a date in a really long time," he said, turning his gaze back to the road. "And never with a woman I found as innately attractive as I find you."

Wow. We weren't holding back, I guessed. I felt my cheeks flush. I was definitely not used to this straightforward kind of assertion.

I did not know how to answer that, but it struck me as odd that a man as handsome and self-assured as Harrison didn't have women falling down at his feet. I was about to ask a question when the sign for the Surly Fox appeared ahead, and we pulled into the parking lot. Harrison switched off the car and got out, coming around to my side to open the door. He didn't appear to be affected in the least by the truth bomb he'd just dropped.

And as I took his strong, firm hand and slid down from the seat, I realized I was in serious trouble. I liked this man. I was intrigued and more than a little attracted. He saw me as a woman he wanted to get to know, not as a conquest like so many of the guys I'd dated, who'd only wanted to say that they'd slept with someone who used to be famous. For once, this wasn't about Chrissy. It was about me.

Harrison's hand found my low back again as we climbed the two steps up to the front door of the restaurant, and as he opened it for me, our eyes met. And held.

My blood heated and the pull I felt to him was a physical force like nothing I'd experienced before. I didn't know what this was, but if it was mutual, there was no way the night was going to end without this fire between us combusting.

I couldn't wait.

Chapter 8
Here, Have Some Cake

HARRISON

Penny was wearing white jeans and heeled sandals that made her legs appear longer and shapelier than they had before, combined with a low-cut feminine top that hung in a way that made me want to slide it from her shoulders and explore. She looked beautiful.

As we walked into the Surly Fox, I was not the only person who noticed her.

"Reservation?" The young hostess asked me as we moved to stand in front of her podium. Her eyes were frosted with a shade of startling blue, and her eyelashes seemed to match. It was not an especially good look. And I had plenty of time to consider it, because as I told her my name and reservation time, she swung her exotic gaze to Penny and kept it there. The girl's eye widened slightly, and her mouth formed itself into a little "o" shape as she gawked at my date.

"Harrison Ketcher," I said a second time, leaning into the podium and blocking Penny a little with my body. "Seven."

The girl recovered, blinking rapidly as a blush climbed her cheeks. "Sorry. Right. Yes, here you are. Let me just . . ." she dropped the menus on the floor and then scrambled to pick them up before finally leading us to a table in the back of the restaurant. As we moved through the space, I had the strange sense of causing some kind of commotion, but guessed it was just the frazzled hostess that people were looking at.

Only, my gut was telling me that wasn't it.

When we were finally seated, the hostess promised a server would be right over, and then scurried away. I glanced around, wondering why I felt like I had a spotlight over my head, but most diners had turned their attention back to their own tables.

Penny was staring fixedly at her menu, practically using it as a shield.

"Hey," I said, using a finger to push it lower so I could see her face. "Sorry. Small towns aren't known for fine dining experiences."

She stared at me for just a second, and then nodded. "Right. I'm sure that's all it was." Penny glanced around her, as if she thought the other diners might be about to attack, and a hard knot of worry formed in my gut. Why did she look so rattled?

"You okay?"

She looked back up at me, those dark eyes scanning my face. "Truth?" she asked, surprising me.

"Please."

"I feel safe with you."

Safe? I frowned at her for a second. Why would she need to feel safe? "Did something . . ." I shook my head, searching for words. "Back in LA, was there . . .?"

Penny reached across the table and dropped her hand on mine. "Nothing like that."

"Good." Relief wound through me, but something had shifted, and I wasn't sure I could make any sense of it. I wanted to protect this woman. To shield her from whatever had put that fear in her eyes.

The server appeared just then, and Penny pulled her hand back and kept her eyes down, flicking them up just once to order a glass of wine.

Whatever odd atmosphere had accompanied us into the restaurant dissipated as we sat and sipped our drinks.

"Are you ready for the resort to open in a couple weeks?" Penny asked.

I felt the frown tug at my lips. "Honestly? No. I know it's completely not the point, but I've gotten used to having the whole place to ourselves. Like a secret clubhouse or something."

Penny grinned at that.

"When the guests come, suddenly we'll all be staff. There to serve them." I didn't like the idea much.

"I guess that's kind of how hotels work though, right?"

"It is. I just don't look forward to being at the beck and call of a mass of wealthy, overprivileged jerks from all over the country."

"You'll be in charge, though," Penny pointed out.

"Which means I'll be the one they want to talk to when things don't go right."

Penny smiled at me and sipped her wine, putting it back on the table and then looking back up at me with those stunning eyes. "Anyone ever call you grumpy, Harrison?"

I should have been grumpy about her question, but in reality, I felt seen. And like it was okay to be myself with her, to let her see the side I often tried to keep hidden. "It's come up."

"I'm not exactly cut out for customer service either," she said. "That's why I'm working in the back office, hidden away from curious eyes."

"They're missing out," I said, the words darting out before I'd had a chance to make sure they were the right ones. "I just meant, you're gorgeous. No wonder people were staring as we came in here."

"Maybe they were staring at you," she said, but I could hear the tease in her tone. "You're not so bad to look at," she went on. "In fact, I could see some of those wealthy socialites and movie stars requesting you personally for their private ski lessons."

I felt my nose wrinkle in distaste.

"Maybe they'll tip really well." Penny wiggled her eyebrows suggestively, and my stomach threatened to turn over.

"I didn't go through OCS and flight school and then risk my life for the Navy so some prissy ski bunny can belittle me with a wad of cash. I'm really only here to help Ghost." Though I felt a little disgusted at the thought, I delivered this without coloring it with the emotion swirling through me.

"Help Ghost, and then off to take the job you mentioned?" The question was innocent, but it sounded like she was invested in my answer.

I nodded, though Gator's offer sounded somewhat less attractive now that I knew Penny would be here.

"Probably a better fit," Penny said, sounding thoughtful.

The server returned then and we ordered food and more drinks, but Penny's last words had rubbed me the wrong way.

"You don't think I'm a good fit here?" Did she mean for her? Or for Kasper Ridge?

"You're brilliant and accomplished," she said. "If you haven't spent all those years working and dreaming about running away to the mountains to be a ski bum, then it's not the right thing for you. I have a feeling you're one of those guys who'd much rather be using your brains than your brawn." Her eyes dropped to her wine glass. "Though the brawn is . . . impressive."

"You like my brawn?" I teased, leaning in until her eyes met mine, sending a hot jolt of fire straight through me.

"I might." She took a sip of her drink, and I did the same, needing to relieve a bit of the tension that seemed to be building around us. "I'm just saying, if you wanted to be the debonair, ski-bum playboy, you look the part. I'd cast you."

"Oh yeah?" I grinned at that, at the idea of her choosing me to play the hero in some movie, like James Bond or something.

"Definitely."

We talked more about the upcoming opening, and I couldn't help the current of sadness that accompanied the thought of giving up the resort to strangers, but I knew it was what Ghost needed. It was the whole point. This place wasn't my home, or my playground. It was just a stopping over point. One that had held a surprisingly compelling extra attraction in Penny.

As dinner was cleared, I took the last sip of the drink I'd been nursing most of the night. "Dessert?"

Penny's face dimmed as if she was about to say no, but then her chin tilted up. "You know what? I would like that."

"For a second you looked like you were going to say no."

"I've just spent a lot of years worrying about what I look like." She waved this statement away, but it struck me as odd.

"You're beautiful. I can't imagine you any other way."

"You're kind."

"Just objective," I assured her. She ordered dessert and I ordered coffee.

"Watching your figure?" she teased when our orders

arrived. The chocolate cake in front of her was a towering slice of deep dark deliciousness topped with thick frosting.

"I think I'll be happy just watching you eat that." Maybe I shouldn't have said it, judging by the way Penny's eyes snapped to mine and dilated slightly. She got my meaning. And she didn't look at all put off.

"Really?" She asked, picking up the fork. And then she dug it into the frosting and brought it to her lips slowly, purposely pulling my attention to her mouth. As she met my eyes, the tip of her sweet pink tongue darted out and tasted the frosting, and I shifted in my seat, immediately hard.

I watched her openly, and a tiny smile lifted one side of her mouth as she toyed with the forkful of cake—and with me. Finally, she pushed the morsel between her full, lush lips and her eyes dropped shut as her head tipped back slightly. I watched her savor the bite, nearly leaping out of my seat when she let out a soft moan, just for me.

"Penny," I said, my voice rough and low, even to my own ears.

Her eyes popped open, and a sexy smile pulled across her lips. "So good," she said, lowering the fork for another bite.

"If you do that again, you're not going to get to finish the cake." It was a warning. Or maybe a promise. I'd wanted her before the little tease, but now I was struggling with self-control. I was a gentleman first, but there was another guy just below the surface who had a lot of opinions and ideas about what he might like to see happen next this evening.

"Just a few more bites," she said, and she proceeded to test me by eating the cake in the most seductive way possible, offering me a bite, which I accepted mostly to try to distract myself from the iron length in my jeans, which made continuing to sit politely rather difficult.

When the server returned with the bill, I made her wait

while I slipped my card into the portfolio and practically cried with relief when she returned quickly.

Penny put her fork down as I slid the signed receipt back into the folder.

"Are you done?" I asked, my voice belying my internal struggles.

"With the cake?"

"Yes."

"Yes, done with that." She smiled sweetly at me. "But do we have to be done with our date?"

I didn't think things could get any more uncomfortable down below, but those words turned my already stone dick to titanium, and I fought the urge to drop a hand to it to try to relieve some of the tension.

"We're definitely not done," I managed. "Let's go."

Penny rose, and I followed her from the restaurant, my hand finding her low back and relishing the curve that swept down to her perfectly round ass, which was on display in the tight white jeans she wore. She was gorgeous, and I found myself wanting her more than I could remember wanting anyone before. From her banter, I was pretty sure this attraction was not one-sided, and that hope had my dick straining painfully against my fly in a way I hoped wasn't obvious to the entire restaurant.

I opened Penny's door and helped her up into the car, and was about to walk away when she caught my hand and tugged me back. She sat sideways in the high car, her legs still hanging out the door, and she pulled me between them. Her hands fell to my shoulders as I stepped close between her thighs. She was at eye level in this position, and there was a playful glint in her pretty brown eyes that made promises about what she might be like if we had a bit more privacy.

"Harrison," she said quietly, her face just inches from mine, my senses filling with the scent of something floral and a hint of spice, her shampoo maybe?

"Yes?" I managed, my hands falling to the outsides of her thighs and sliding up ever so slightly to capture the round firmness of her hips where she sat on the seat of the SUV.

"Would it be all right if I kissed you?"

"Fuck yes." I didn't give her time to change her mind, closing the distance between our lips immediately and kissing her more forcefully than I'd intended to. Penny didn't seem put off by my assault, her arms wrapping around my neck and her body melding immediately to mine as I pressed into the delicious heat between her legs.

The kiss started desperate and hot, lips warring for control, and my tongue asking as politely as I could manage for more access. She granted it, and as I slid my hands up her back, loving every inch of her beneath my palms, the kiss turned languorous, sensual. Her tongue teased mine, and her hand slid into my hair, sending a raft of sensations through my body all at once as she toyed with me.

I stepped back with something that was more like a grunt than I would have liked, but I was teetering on the brink of control. "I'd better take you home," I said, testing myself to make sure I was steady on my feet.

"I guess so," she said, and she pulled her legs into the car and reached for the seatbelt as I closed her door. I moved around the back of the vehicle so I could adjust the ache in my jeans without her seeing, and then climbed in beside her.

"Truth?" she said softly.

I turned to meet her gaze. "Always."

"I had a great time tonight. I don't want it to end."

Neither did I. But it didn't feel right to do all the things I wanted to do to her on a first date. She deserved some time to think about it, to decide if she really wanted to get into whatever this might be. I was leaving, after all, and she wasn't exactly a permanent resident of Kasper Ridge, either.

"Maybe we can do it again," I suggested, pulling out of the parking lot and onto the highway.

"I hope so," she said.

I walked her to the door of Bennie's house and on the doorstep, she gave me another incredible kiss, wrapping her arms around my neck and pressing her body into mine.

I saw her inside and waited there until I heard the deadbolt click. Then I drove back to the lodge and took the longest shower of my life.

Chapter 9
One of the OGs

PENNY

That week at work I saw Harrison often. At first, he made excuses to come to the back office, pretending to be looking for Aubrey or to have a question about one of the ski instructors he'd hired. But after a couple visits, he began to drop the pretense.

"Knock knock." Harrison stood in the doorway of my office at lunchtime Thursday.

"Hey," I said, turning my attention away from the spreadsheet I'd been working on with Aubrey to manage the many hires that had been made over the last few days.

"I brought you a piece of chocolate cake from the Fox." He pulled a plastic container from behind his back.

The chocolate cake. I'd thought about my behavior several times since our date, and was equal parts shocked at myself and turned on when I reflected on it. Harrison had brought out something in me I hadn't really felt before. And whatever it was, it was a little bit wild.

"Thanks," I said, feeling the blush climb my neck at the memory. I dropped his gaze.

"Thought we could grab lunch and then maybe I could watch you eat that." A tiny smile lifted one side of his sculpted lips.

I didn't know what to say about the cake, so I put it into the little fridge at the side of my office and turned to face the man I hadn't stopped thinking about since our date. "Yes to lunch for sure."

His smile widened. "No cake today?"

"We'll see," I said, flirting even though I hadn't really intended to.

We left the back office and walked together toward the restaurant, where one side of the huge space had been built out into a one-way traffic buffet line so skiers and boarders could grab a tray, select what they wanted, and move through to the registers quickly. As we moved, our hands brushed and a little spear of want lodged deep inside me as the warm heat of his skin brushed mine.

I picked up a sandwich and a drink, and the new employee at the register gave me a broad smile when I stepped in front of her. A few of the new staff had recognized me during the interview process, so Aubrey had made it clear that up here, no mention should be made of my former life. But this girl, Emma, definitely knew.

"I'd get yours, but now that we've got this whole staff

system . . ." Harrison said, stepping close as he slid his tray toward Emma. We'd recently installed the accounting system that tracked to inventory for pre-packaged food. It included a unique staff identifier for each of us, so the resort could track employee meals, but we didn't have to pay for them.

"Thanks," I said, picking up my tray.

We headed out to the patio, which was gloriously sunny beyond the overhang where we chose a table. The weather was still warm, but there was an intangible shift in the air, something I could practically smell that told me on an instinctual level that cooler months were near, though I'd never lived anywhere with real winter. I looked forward to it.

"You have the ski school all set up?" I asked, lifting my sandwich up for a bite.

"Pretty much. We're already booked for lessons the first month. It's nuts."

We both looked around at the nearly empty space that had become so familiar, probably each imagining it filled with guests.

"That's good news for the resort," I reminded him.

"So many people though," he grumbled.

I shared the worry over what would be different with the resort full of guests, but I hadn't been here in the early days like he had. I was only here because guests were coming soon. And my worries about what having lots of people around would mean were very different from Harrison's.

"Hey guys, mind if we join?" Archie, Aubrey, and Wiley stood next to the table holding trays in front of them.

"Of course," I waved toward the empty seats at our table. I had no idea if Harrison had shared with his friends that we'd gone out, or that we were . . . whatever we were, but it didn't change much about us having lunch together either way. Maybe

I just wouldn't indulge in dessert. I loved feeling like part of this group, being so readily accepted.

"I cannot believe we open in two weeks!" Aubrey grinned around the table at us all and then punched her brother in the arm, causing him to drop the French fry he'd been about to put in his mouth. "Arch! We did it!"

"Ow." Archie scowled at his sister.

"Take it easy, slugger," Wiley said, smiling at her with a warmth that might as well have announced his feelings to the entire mountain.

"It wasn't that long ago this whole place was a shambles," she said. "Arch and Wiley and I were the first ones up here, and things have really changed in the most incredible ways. It's so amazing."

"And we still haven't gotten any closer to finding the—"

"Do not say treasure." Harrison sounded stern, and I could picture him as a fearsome professor at the front of room full of students suddenly. It was kind of hot.

"Booty," Archie said, grinning at his friend.

"I found some booty up here," Wiley said, dropping his arm around Aubrey.

"Please remember that this is my sister," Archie said, his voice flat.

"Anyway," Aubrey said, smiling up at Wiley. "We definitely need one more staff celebration before we're invaded."

I wasn't so sure. The new staff was young, less subtle, and might be tempted to take videos or post photos of me if they knew who I was.

"Definitely," Wiley said.

"After staff week?" Aubrey asked the table. "Friday night?"

"We cannot trash the place," Archie warned.

Aubrey rolled her eyes.

"It's not us I'm worried about," he said, nodding his head

past us to a table full of college-aged staff that had been hired in the past few days.

"Oh, we have to include them?" Aubrey asked, pressing her lips together as her brow wrinkled.

"Maybe we keep it to the OGs," Wiley said.

"OGs?" Harrison asked.

The entire table stared at him.

"You really did grow up in a hole, didn't you?" Archie asked him. "Original gangsters, man."

Harrison seemed to be considering this and potentially concluding that he was not a gangster of any kind, but he let it go.

"OGs only," Aubrey said. "And Penny, of course. And invite Bennie and CeeCee if you want."

"Thanks," I said, relief sweeping through me. I suppressed a grin at being included this way.

The man they called Sasquatch came bustling out the back door of the resort then, managing to cause enough of a commotion by just existing to draw all of our attention. "Joining you," he announced, dropping his tray and taking an empty seat at the table.

I hadn't spent much time with the guy, but he took up a lot of space. I wasn't sure quite how he did it—he was huge, for one thing. But it was more than that. It was like the air around him behaved differently than it did for other human beings, kind of rearranging and shifting to accommodate his existence. He was loud and boisterous, and if I was being honest, I avoided the guy when I could. Something about him made me worry I'd get in his way, or he'd out me in front of Harrison, or . . . I couldn't put my finger on it.

"Listen," he began, after taking a huge bite of his burger and essentially talking around it. "I needed to talk to you, Ghost, so I'm glad I found you. It's about my emotional support dog."

Archie spit out the sip of the drink he'd just taken, then cast an apologetic glance around the table as he wiped the soda from the tabletop. "You don't have an emotional support dog."

"Right. Getting one. Just letting you know."

"Wait," Aubrey said, leaning in. "What do you mean? Like, you'd have a dog with you everywhere you go here? Like inside the luxury resort we just finished renovating and which will soon be accepting very fancy guests?"

"Yup."

"No." Archie dipped a fry in mustard and pointed it at the big man. "No dogs inside."

"Some of your fancy guests will probably have purse pups, you know," Sasquatch pointed out, his tone becoming suddenly reasonable and measured.

Archie turned to Aubrey. "Have we talked about this? Are we allowing pets?"

"We have two designated rooms for pets." Aubrey shrugged.

"No one tells me anything," Archie complained. "No dogs for staff."

Sasquatch made a clicking noise and shook his head. "The VA would beg to differ, my friend."

I had no idea where Sasquatch was going with this, but the banter was definitely entertaining.

Harrison rubbed a hand over his face. "What does that mean?"

"They're the ones who got me the dog. Or they would if I went through the whole process with them. But my way is quicker." Sasquatch shoved the rest of the burger into his mouth.

"Is this a properly trained service animal?" Archie asked.

"Will be." Sasquatch said.

Aubrey and Archie exchanged a look.

"We can talk about this later," Archie told Sasquatch.

"Good. Roscoe will be here tomorrow. You can meet him then."

"Roscoe is . . .?" Harrison asked.

"My dog." With that, Sasquatch, having somehow cleared his entire tray during the course of this short conversation, rose and headed back inside.

"That guy is a loose cannon," Harrison said, shaking his head.

"You think?" Archie said.

"I'm sure it will be fine." Wiley seemed always jovial, happy to give people the benefit of the doubt. I liked him a lot.

"I'm sure it will not be fine," Harrison said. "But it will probably be entertaining."

"Great," Archie muttered, shoving another fry into his mouth.

The easy banter and air of latent amusement that flowed around these new friends of mine made me want to sit with them enjoying the sunshine and patio forever, but my phone buzzed in my back pocket.

"Excuse me," I said, rising. "Be right back." I took the call at the edge of the patio. It was Paul. I didn't want to talk to him, but I'd been thinking a lot about the reunion show he'd emailed about and I couldn't dodge him forever.

"Have you let the producers know you're coming to the reunion show?" he asked without preamble.

"I haven't decided for sure yet," I told him. I did not want to go, the thought of going back to that life made my stomach turn. But I'd begun to think that the reunion event might be a good place to officially announce my retirement from show business. I was moving on, mentally and physically, and maybe the right thing would be to properly close that door in some kind of official manner.

"It's good money, a way to relight your star a bit, Penny."

"Paul, don't be mad, but I don't think I want to relight my star."

"What does that mean?" He sounded confused, like it would never occur to him that I wouldn't want the constant scrutiny and scandal that my life had been for years.

"It was your metaphor."

"So you're not doing it?"

I took a breath and suggested the idea I'd come up with. "What if I just do the reunion event? Not the show?"

"Those aren't the terms."

"Can't you renegotiate?" He was my agent, after all. Wasn't that what he was for?

"I'm supposed to act in your best interest. That's why I got you this kickass deal to do the show."

"Without talking to me first. My best interest at this point is to walk away. But I'll make an announcement at the event. If you'll negotiate it." I felt someone walk up behind me as I finished speaking and spun around to find Harrison standing nearby, smiling. The rest of the table remained where they were, laughing about something. I lifted a finger to let Harrison know I was almost done, hoping he hadn't heard anything that would make him suspicious.

"This isn't the right choice for you," Paul said, sounding disappointed. "You'll regret it." Paul had used this tactic on me my whole life, acted like he knew my mind better than I did.

"Maybe," I told him. "But I don't think so."

Paul sighed loudly. "Have you told your mom? I just spoke with her about an audition—"

"Not her call," I said, trying to keep my words short since Harrison was nearby. Irritation rose in me, threatening to make my voice higher, but I tried to push it down. I was tired of Paul and Mom running my life. "Send her if she wants to go. She was the one who really wanted all this in the first place."

"You're my client."

"Am I? Or maybe is she?" I'd never spoken to Paul like this before, never really stood up for myself. Maybe because I'd never really known what I wanted. I'd been too young to consider that there were even any other options when Mom had pushed me into television.

"I'll let you know what they say." Paul sounded suddenly exhausted.

"Thank you." I hung up and shoved my phone back into my pocket.

"Everything okay?" Harrison asked, smiling. I could see a question in his eyes, but he clearly didn't intend to pry. I was glad, but in a weird way I was beginning to feel like I was lying to him.

"Fine," I said. "Just wrapping up some loose ends back in LA."

He nodded as if this made perfect sense.

"Walk?" Harrison's gaze moved to the trail that led away from the back patio of the resort. I knew that there were a few trails back there, one of which was a nice loop through the yurts and around the resort property. Aubrey told me another led to the back country cabins that were miles from here at the top of the ridge.

"Sure. If you don't intend to climb the ridge."

He grinned. "Though I wouldn't be too upset if you and I got snowed in like Mateo and Monroe did," he said, "I was thinking the loop. I have more interviews later."

We turned to the trail and started out at a leisurely pace. When we were far from any curious glances, sheltered by the thick branches of the pine trees between the resort and the trail, Harrison took my hand and a full-body tingle went through me.

"I've been thinking about kissing you again," he said, his voice low and serious.

God, I wanted that too. I hadn't stopped thinking about the way he'd kissed me in the car. I stopped walking and turned to face him. "Yeah?"

"Can't think about anything else," he said.

The man's eyes were dark, the slate blue turning almost stormy as he looked at me, dropping to my mouth before tracing back up my face. There were little crinkly lines around them, and the steel and sable at his temples did something to my tummy, flipping it this way and that. He was so handsome. So mature. So unlike any of the men I'd been involved with before.

"I'd like that," I told him.

Harrison's hand found my cheek then, tracing a line downward until his fingers cupped my jaw lightly, tilting my chin upward. The scent of pine around us, the hushed quiet of the forest, and the touch of Harrison's fingers on my skin had every one of my senses heightened, yearning for more. I stepped closer, my hands finding his shoulders.

When he leaned in, I had the urge to pull him closer, to wrap myself around him. I'd been thinking about kissing him again too. I'd been thinking about a lot more. I'd also told myself I didn't need the distraction of a fling up here. I had enough to iron out in my life without introducing new wrinkles.

But when Harrison's lips touched mine, softly at first and then slanting against my mouth hard, his tongue tracing my bottom lip, my mind went blank. All the things I'd told myself about taking it slow, about being careful, they all shimmered into invisibility, replaced by a hot fiery need for the man in my arms.

Chapter 10
Tango on a Trap Door

HARRISON

I kissed Penny in a way I was pretty sure I'd never kissed anyone. Even being around her had nerves firing in places inside me I'd had no idea I had nerves. She inspired . . . feelings. Things I honestly hadn't experienced before, and the best I could figure was that it was chemical. Something in my cellular makeup responded chemically to something in hers.

But I wasn't thinking about any of that as I pulled her soft body into mine, one of my hands threading into her soft wavy hair while my tongue pillaged and took her mouth.

Penny kissed me back, and the fervor with which she did assured me this was not a one-sided lab experiment. There were chemical reactions happening on both sides, and as our bodies pressed together, a faint worry in the back of my mind asked about what would happen if we let loose together. Could things ever be too hot?

I was willing to find out.

There was something mysterious about Penny. Even as I held her in my arms, her tongue teasing mine in a way that made me wonder what that tongue might be capable of in other situations, I felt like there was part of her I didn't know. And god, I wanted to know her.

Penny moaned into my mouth, and my rational mind ducked into whatever dark space it occupied when I wasn't using it. Lust and desire were in charge now.

One of Penny's hands had found its way beneath the waistband of my jeans, and as I kissed her, I could feel her hot center pressed to the top of my thigh, grinding into me in the sexiest possible way.

I dropped my mouth to trace a line down her jaw, to taste her throat, delve into the hollow at her clavicle. Her hands scrabbled more frantically with my clothing, and I felt desperate to get her somewhere I could explore her properly.

Penny moaned again as I scooped her into my arms and plowed off the trail and into the dense trees past the trail. It was quiet back here, there was no reason for any staff to be near, and there was a clearing next to an enormous tree trunk and a boulder that provided a bit of cover, should anyone wander by on the trail. I set Penny down for a moment, immediately missing her warmth in my arms.

"What are you—" Penny's words trailed off when I whipped the button-down flannel from my body and spread it on the ground, then reached for her hand. I laid her down softly onto the fabric, which was big enough when spread out to keep her hair and torso off the bed of pine needles that carpeted the forest floor.

Penny's eyes were glued to my chest.

"You're incredible," she said in a hushed voice, and her fingers began to explore my body in light feathery touches that were driving me insane. "You look like you're carved out of stone. Shit." It was possible I could come just from the way she was touching me, aided by the look of pure desire in her eyes.

"So are you," I reminded her, capturing her mouth again as I covered her body with my own. I kissed my way down her throat again, moving lower and accessing what skin I could through the loose collar of her blouse. After a moment, I slid her shirt up, exposing her gorgeous belly. "Is this okay?" I asked her.

Penny's eyes were dark and hooded with desire as she watched me move down her body. "Yes," she whispered.

I kissed a trail across her belly, relishing every centimeter of soft smooth skin, until Penny began to writhe beneath me, her fingers kneading the skin of my back.

"Harrison," she breathed, and it sounded like a prayer. "Please."

My body heated, hearing her say my name that way, and the hard length in my pants began to demand attention. My hands found the button on her jeans, and I opened it slowly, following every move of my fingers with my lips as Penny's breathing increased, sounding rough in the dense close quiet of the forest.

I paused as I began to push the fabric of her pants down, glancing up to make sure this was what she wanted. Penny didn't have to say anything, instead, she reached down and shoved her pants and panties lower, exposing her center to me.

"Beautiful," I murmured, struggling for control. She was so beautiful. And I loved her like this, desperate, pleading for release. God, I wanted her in my bed, I wanted to bury myself inside her, to see what she would feel like beneath me, around me . . . But this would be enough for now.

I began by tracing the tip of my index finger across her lower belly, then down the lines of her thighs, teasing circles on her inner thighs as I let a hot breath wash over her center. She groaned and thrashed, and though I'd planned to tease her much longer, I was on the brink of losing control. I dropped my mouth to her soft mound and licked a line up her center, pleased by her rough gasp.

"More." It was a command, and as I moved down farther to give myself better access, everything in me responded to it. Penny's legs spread, and I spent the next few minutes teasing and tasting her soft center, finding the bundle of nerves between her folds and finally pulling it into my mouth hard.

"Oh god," she cried out, and when I added a finger, and then another, the beautiful woman spread out before me on the forest floor let go. She moaned her release, breathy and desperate, and I nearly came myself. That would have been a little bit embarrassing to explain as I returned to work, however, so I managed to hold on by a thread even while Penny let the most incredible sounds out as her body pulsed around my fingers.

"Fuck," I whispered when she'd relaxed beneath me again. "Fuck me, that was so hot."

A lazy smile spread over Penny's face, and her eyes blinked open to watch me scoot back up her body to press a kiss to her soft lips. "Wow," she said.

"I'll take wow."

She glanced around, her expression slipping suddenly. "Was I loud?"

"Not at all. You were so fucking sexy. Breathy and hot."

"But not loud?" She frowned.

"Very quiet. And we're pretty well hidden out here. No one has any reason to be nearby."

"We didn't have any reason to be out here either," she pointed out, reaching down to pull her pants back up.

"I had a pretty good reason to bring you back here."

"It was a good reason," she agreed, grinning, reaching for me. "Your turn?"

God, I wanted that, but knew we probably shouldn't press our luck. We hadn't been caught so far, but I hated the idea of Penny being found in a compromising situation, didn't want anything that might embarrass her to taint things. "I can wait," I told her.

"Are you sure? That doesn't seem fair." Penny's hand was rubbing through my hair, and it felt so good, but I could wait for a more private moment.

"It's okay," I told her. I wanted very much to keep Penny beneath me, to feel her body release again and again, and to drive myself into her . . . but there would be time for that. And I wanted to take my time when it happened, not rush because we were worried about someone strolling by. Or about bears.

We got up, brushing ourselves off as we grinned at one another like two kids who'd just gotten away with something. I picked up my shirt and shook it out, and something heavy went flying and thudded against the base of the enormous tree trunk to one side of us.

"Shit, my phone," Penny said, going after it.

I buttoned up my shirt and adjusted my jeans, hoping I didn't look like a man so desperate for a woman he could barely control himself—because that was exactly what I was. Penny was everything I'd been looking for, at least in a sexual partner. What scared me was how much I believed she was everything I'd been looking for in general. But we were heading different directions, so I wasn't going to let myself think about that. Not now.

"Hey, Harrison?" Penny was squatting down a few feet away by the tree. I moved to join her.

"Yeah?"

"What do you think this is?" She was clearing dirt and needles from the ground at the base of the tree, brushing away years of cover to reveal a wood plank of some kind. We'd been almost directly on top of it.

"I don't know," I said. We were close to the depression that had been noted in the topo survey, and I wondered again what it could be. As we used our hands to brush away decades of dust and forest debris, we revealed what looked like a trap door, complete with hinges and a handle.

"Oh my god," she said. "What is this?"

"It's a door," I said, stating the obvious for lack of anything better to add.

Penny reached for the handle.

"Wait," I said, stilling her hand. "Should we get Ghost?"

"Maybe we should see if there's anything to tell him first. I'd hate to get his hopes up. He seems fixated on this whole treasure thing."

I nodded. She wasn't wrong. "He is. I'm just not sure this is totally safe. We could come back with some of the others."

"You seriously want to walk away without opening this?" Penny's eyes were wide with disbelief.

"Okay fine. Let's take a look."

Together, we pried open the heavy wooden door, which was about half the size of a regular door, and which opened to reveal stone stairs leading down into darkness. The second the door was opened, a chill blasted through my body, partly from the cool dank air that rushed out of the space, and partly something else.

Penny pulled her phone from her pocket and switched on

the flashlight, illuminating a few feet more than we could see from the daylight shining in. "Should we go in there?"

It didn't feel like the right choice, how would we know if it was safe? "No. We have no idea what state this tunnel might be in, things shift and move. It's too dangerous."

Penny's lower lip jutted out. "Let's just take a quick peek."

I crossed my arms, considering. I wanted to see what was in there, but I did not want Penny down in a potentially dangerous dark hole in the ground. "You wait up here."

"Hell, no."

"What if the door shuts and we both get trapped in there?" I felt like we were suddenly in a teenage mystery novel.

"I'm not letting you go in there alone," she said.

I looked around and after a moment spotted what I was looking for. "Okay," I said, moving to lift a big rock and drop it onto the open door, which was now lying on the ground next to the open hole. "I go first though."

She sighed, rolling her eyes. "Fine. Be the hero."

I lit my own phone's light and carefully stepped onto the first step, testing it for strength. Who knew how long this had been here, or how sound it might be?

Slowly, we made our way down the creaky steps into the still cool air below. It smelled musty and felt damp, the darkness ahead complete outside the small arc of my phone light.

"A tunnel," I said, illuminating a passageway ahead of us. It was cut into the earth, the walls made of hard-packed dirt, but supported like an old mine shaft might be, with timber supports and planks lining the ceiling and walls and pressing from the earth to the ceiling in some spots.

"I don't like this," I said.

"If it's held up all these years, it's probably fine," Penny pointed out.

"No offense," I told her, "but you're not an engineer, are you?"

Penny made a face.

We were whispering, as if the inherent quiet of the space demanded silence.

"Where does it go?" Penny asked what we were both wondering.

"It's long," I said, seeing no end to the shaft my light was illuminating. "It descends." The floor sloped gently downward, back in the direction of the resort.

We followed the tunnel, everything inside me screaming that it was a bad idea, but eventually, we reached the end. A thick metal door blocked our way. I tried the handle. "Locked."

Penny pushed past me, and I tried to suppress my smile as she pulled and prodded at the door. I probably weighed at least seventy-five pounds more than her and was certainly stronger. But she wanted to try it herself. I liked that. "Or stuck," she said.

"We should let Ghost know. It wouldn't be good for guests to find this."

"Oh, I didn't think about that." She nodded, and then her eyes glanced around at the walls of the long tunnel we were in. "We should get out of here." Now that the excitement was fading, Penny seemed to realize we probably shouldn't have taken this risk.

"After you." I followed Penny out of the tunnel and back up the stairs into daylight, and for a moment we just stared at one another, trying to catch our breaths.

"What the hell did we just find?" she asked, a smile playing at the corners of her mouth.

"No idea." I moved the rock and swung the door shut over the hole, placing the rock in the center of it to mark the space. Without discussing it, Penny and I both worked to scatter dirt and pine needles over the planks again, hiding it.

When we stood, the door camouflaged once again by the forest floor, we stared at each other. Then Penny stepped forward and wrapped her arms around my neck.

"Truth?" she said.

"Always," I replied.

"You are a fantastic adventure."

I chuckled at that. I had very little to do with what we'd just discovered, but I felt it too—Penny and I together were magic.

* * *

Telling Ghost what we'd found was what I imagined it would be like to tell a kid they could open all their presents the day before their birthday. At first, he looked wary when I said I'd been walking the lines of the runs and had checked on the depression the topographical survey had discovered.

"Is this going to be bad news, Brainiac?" Ghost scrubbed a hand over his face. "I'm ready for it."

I laughed, part of me wishing I could tell him the truth about how we'd found the door, but Penny had asked me not to. We'd decided that this story worked better for now.

"It's not bad news," I assured him. We stood in the lobby near the front doors, where I'd found him after quite a bit of searching around the resort. "It could be really good news actually."

Ghost's dark red eyebrows climbed slightly. "Oh yeah?"

"Might even relate to booty," I said, emphasizing the word.

"Really?"

I had his attention now. "Remember I told you there was an odd depression on one side of the main run that the guys found in the topo survey?"

He nodded.

"I know what it is."

"What is it?"

"A tunnel." I told him about the trap door, the tunnel and the locked door at the far end as his face went from wary to surprised to downright jubilant.

"You're fucking kidding me," he said, his voice as excited as I'd ever heard it. "Brainiac, this is it!"

I didn't want him to get too excited. What if this wasn't it? "But the weird thing is that it isn't like any part of the hunt led us to this door."

"Maybe we just missed that clue. It doesn't matter."

"Could be unrelated."

"Doubt it." Ghost was actually rubbing his hands together as he absorbed the news. "Let's go take a look."

I showed Ghost the trap door, but it was growing dark by the time we got there. He wouldn't be talked out of going in to see for himself, but he promised not to hammer on the door at the end of the tunnel or to shake things up in there too much. I was worried about the tunnel's stability, and this seemed to make sense to him.

"Tomorrow," he said, grinning at me as we closed the trap door over the hole again.

"You're the boss," I said, happy to have made Ghost happy.

Chapter 11
Couples Therapy for Sass and Roscoe

PENNY

I let Harrison tell Archie about the door we'd found. Telling him together would have potentially required an explanation of how the two of us happened to be rolling around on the ground in that exact spot, and I wasn't sure I was ready for that.

I spotted him, Ghost, and Will heading that way with a bunch of tools after I'd checked into work the next day. I loved the huge window that let me watch the world while remaining hidden in my office. Work had gotten busy, fast. Suddenly there were actual employees, real payroll to begin handling.

But back here at this desk, ensconced in the relative quiet of my office and handed the trust and expectations that came with a real job, I was happier than I'd ever been. This felt like the real world. My life before now seemed like some kind of mirage in which I'd been mired for years, always grasping at illusions, constantly working to hold myself together as each thing I depended on shimmered out of existence or exploded into bits.

And there was Harrison.

It was temporary, whatever this was. I knew that. I wasn't telling myself anything different.

But even if I couldn't have it for longer than the season, I'd take it. Being with him was one more part of this "real" life I was discovering. He didn't know who I was, and he didn't care. And I sensed that even if I told him about my past, about *Our Girl Chrissy*, he still wouldn't care. Which was why there was no point dredging it up with him. He liked me for who I was now, and I liked very much having only a present and maybe a future. I'd been only my past for too long.

Harrison was finishing up some ski instructor interviews as Aubrey and I took trays outside for lunch. I moved to sit far away from where he was in conversation with a kid who looked like he couldn't have possibly been over sixteen, but Aubrey grinned and plopped down at the next table over from him, studiously looking anywhere but at the interview happening. She wanted to listen in. I shrugged and joined her, forcing myself to keep my eyes off Harrison. It was nearly impossible because he looked so hot playing the role of stern hiring manager.

"But Professor Ketcher," the kid was saying. "I'm still tripping that you ended up here at this random resort, like, running a ski program. You're an engineer, right? You were, like, this badass pilot fighter pilot—"

"So you've been snowboarding your whole life, Teague?"

Harrison's voice was a razor, effectively separating the kid's line of questioning from the present moment.

"Uh, yeah. I don't even remember not knowing how to shred."

"And you've taught lessons?"

"I mean . . . I taught some of my friends."

"No formal teaching experience? Even off the snow?"

"I worked at a summer camp last summer at my college. I mean, well, your old college." The kid chuckled nervously.

"So your motivation for applying here was . . ."

"Check out the newest Colorado mountain, mostly. My folks have a place in Crested Butte, so if this doesn't work out, I'll go see if I can scrape up something there."

"And you graduated from Archer?"

"Not quite."

"But you're taking the year off?"

"Promised my folks I'd go back for summer session if they let me bum around for the season."

"Still an engineering major?"

"Uh, switched to poly sci." The poor kid's tone was apologetic.

"I see." Harrison was quiet for a long moment, and Aubrey and I exchanged wide-eyed glances. I was glad I hadn't had to interview with Harrison. He sounded like he was barely tolerating the kid, and I kind of worried he was just going to sigh, stand up, and walk away.

"Staff training week starts Monday. You have CPR and first aid already, so that's good."

"Wait, so, Professor Ketcher, I'm hired?"

"Probationary hire. This is a luxury resort. The people coming here pay top dollar for an experience they won't have anywhere else. Every aspect of this mountain is absolutely impeccable. Including the staff."

"Totally."

"Work on your vocabulary."

"Sorry?"

"Pay and benefits are all listed here. Check in Monday at eight-thirty. Here's a list of properties for rent in town and a link to the discord group of other instructors looking for roommates."

"Cool, okay."

"Keep the partying to a minimum."

"Yeah, tot—I mean, of course."

At that point, without saying another word, but after issuing a mighty sigh, Harrison stood and walked back inside, leaving his new hire looking confused and elated.

"Dude," Teague whispered to himself, clearly needing a second to recover from his interview.

"Congratulations," Aubrey offered, leaning over and smiling at the guy.

"Yeah, thanks."

"I'm Aubrey Kasper. My brother and I own this place."

"Oh, cool." He paused and looked contrite for a flash. "I mean, that's really impressive. It seems like an amazing resort." Clearly, Harrison's suggestion about vocabulary had already sunk in.

"Thanks. Looking forward to having you here."

Teague stood and glanced between us, his gaze lingering for just a moment too long on my face. I held his questioning glance, hoping he wouldn't ask. Finally, his face cleared and he let out a held breath, looking back at Aubrey.

"Well, that interview was pretty intense. I'm gonna head out."

"See you Monday!" Aubrey waved to him as he departed. "Wow, Brainiac is taking this pretty seriously, huh?"

"Guess so."

Just then, the man in question returned, a tray in his hands. He set it down on our table and looked between us. "Join you?"

"Please," Aubrey said. When he was settled, she leaned in. "I thought Teague there might cry for a second."

Harrison gave her a stern look, but then his face softened. "I'm not good at these interviews."

"No, it was fine, it was just intense."

I wanted to reach over and give his hand a squeeze. He looked so desolate suddenly. But we hadn't talked about what we were just yet, not as far as others at the resort were concerned.

"This was part of why I was let go from the university." He said the words quietly, like a humiliating secret he wasn't sure he wanted to share.

"I thought you were on a sabbatical?" Aubrey asked. I watched as she realized he'd been keeping up a pretense, part of me honored he'd told only me about the real reason, and part of me aching for his fragile pride that felt this lie was needed.

"Easier to tell you guys that than to tell you the truth, I guess. But that kid, Teague, he was in one of my classes. And he knows."

"Figured you should tell us before he outed you?" Aubrey smiled, but her voice had softened. And her words lodged inside me. Should I be telling Harrison before he found out about my past?

The situations were completely different. Besides, I already knew about Harrison's job. He hadn't been keeping it a secret, not really.

"Nah." Harrison took a moment to take and swallow a bite of his sandwich. "Just getting tired of pretending I might go back to teaching."

Aubrey nodded, though she threw a quick glance at me as if this whole line of conversation had surprised her. It felt like she was telling me to come clean, to share my own secrets. I dropped her gaze.

"Well you're going to have some pretty straight-laced ski school instructors," I said. "I think you scared the crap out of him."

"Good," he said. "The last thing you guys need is a bunch of kids up here thinking this is just a great excuse to ski for free and party their asses off." He nodded at Aubrey when he said this.

"Isn't that the whole point of working a season as a ski instructor?" she asked, smiling.

"Not at Kasper Ridge." He was so stern, so serious. It was doing something to me, and I wanted to climb into his lap and see if he'd be willing to play angry professor with me a little later today.

Aubrey rose and headed back inside after saying goodbye to each of us, and Harrison and I were left alone on the big patio in the sunshine.

"You sticking around tonight for happy hour?" he asked me, and his clear indication of what answer he hoped for made my heart warm.

"Definitely. Last chance to enjoy the bar before it belongs to the guests, right?"

"Right."

"I think Bennie and CeeCee are coming too."

"I'm only interested in you." The words sent a bolt of desire straight through me and I practically melted where I sat from the intensity of Harrison's gaze.

"Me too," I whispered. I wanted to tell him then. To take down whatever wall my past might hang between us. Seeing him be honest with Aubrey had made me rethink letting him remain clueless. It was nice being a regular person, but I doubted Harrison would care at all about *Our Girl Chrissy.* "Hey, I wanted to—"

"No!" A stern admonition came from behind us, and we both turned to see Sasquatch fending off what looked like an attack from a large German Shepherd.

Alarm flared through me, stopping my words and stealing my thoughts as Sasquatch struggled with the dog. Was he okay? Was the dog on the loose, rampaging around and attacking people? A tiny prick of fear threatened to expand inside my chest.

"Sass, you need help?" Harrison called, standing.

The dog was hanging from his arm by its jaws, and Sasquatch was red-faced and sweating, but the altercation seemed to have come to a standstill.

"Nah. Me and Roscoe just have a little work to do on our relationship, that's all." Sasquatch grinned at us, then turned back to the dog hanging from his arm.

Now that the dog wasn't actively attacking, I could see it wasn't a full-grown dog. Maybe an adolescent—closer to a puppy than an adult.

"That your support dog?" Harrison asked him.

"Yep. Meet Roscoe." Sasquatch detached the dog from his arm and bent down, petting the animal, who now seemed fairly benign.

"Is the attacking part of his support service?" Harrison asked.

"Funny. No. We're just getting to know each other a bit." The dog had bent low, and seemed to be attempting to disassemble Sasquatch's hiking boot while it was on his foot. "Quit it. No!"

"Looks like it's going well. I thought those dogs came pre-trained?"

"Yeah, he would have, but Roscoe here didn't quite make it through the program." Sasquatch tugged on the leash and the dog plopped into a sit. "Good boy."

"What does that mean, Sass?" Harrison seemed somewhat amused by this situation. I doubted Ghost would be amused by a barely trained attack dog wandering the resort.

"He failed out, okay? But he can be rehabilitated. Like the Six Million Dollar Man. I'm gonna make him better. Stronger. Faster."

"You know that makes no sense at all, right?"

"I know what I'm doing. Just because Roscoe here didn't want to bend his principles to fit in with those other pansy support dogs or be told what to do at the police academy doesn't mean he won't be a perfectly suitable support animal for me."

"Wait, he failed out of two training programs?" Harrison was barely suppressing a chuckle and I hid my smile behind my hand as Sasquatch attempted to lead Roscoe around the patio on his leash. Roscoe refused to get to his feet, and was allowing himself to be scooted along slowly by Sasquatch tugging the leash.

"He's a late bloomer," Sasquatch said. "Aren't you boy?" He bent down to pet the dog, who immediately attached his jaw to Sasquatch's hand.

"And Ghost knows you have an attack dog here?" Harrison asked.

"I told him Roscoe was arriving today, yes."

"Keep him away from the guests, man."

"He'll be fine." Sasquatch had finally gotten Roscoe to his feet, and they disappeared together around the side of the resort.

"That has bad idea written all over it," he said, chuckling. "Pretty much a reenactment of Sass's entire time on active duty."

I laughed. "What is his job here, anyway?"

"That's a good question. I thought he was doing some kind of event planning, but then Monroe came back. And Antonio is helping her, so I'm not sure what Sass does. He helped out getting the lifts running. But he doesn't ski, so . . ."

"Maybe he's just here for emotional support," I suggested. "Like his dog."

"Or comic relief," Harrison said.

We rose, picking up our trays and heading inside. When we'd dropped off our dishes, Harrison turned to face me, glancing around before planting a swift kiss on my cheek. "I'll see you tonight."

"Bye," I said, watching him walk away. The man looked good from every angle. My stomach twisted as I considered what he might look like with all those clothes off. His chest had been chiseled perfection, and I suspected the ass beneath those dark jeans was also pretty damned impeccable.

So much for telling him the truth. I'd leave the past where it was. For now, I was going to focus on the present. Maybe there'd be a good chance to tell him tonight.

* * *

Everyone was in the bar when I arrived back at the resort after heading home to Bennie's to change clothes and pick up my friends. We all rode together in CeeCee's car, and the girls were as excited as the staff about the resort season kicking off. Big changes were coming to the little town of Kasper Ridge, and the whole town felt personally involved.

"So next week is all training?" Bennie asked me as we parked outside the imposing resort, which was lit up against the dark sky, glowing merrily and looking impressive and welcoming all at once.

"Yep. Hiring finished up today, and we've got a full staff now."

"That was quick," CeeCee said.

"A lot of recent graduates seem to want to take a year before they head out for their real lives, I guess," I told them. "So many kids in their early twenties."

"Kasper Ridge is about to be a party town," Bennie said, sounding depressed.

CeeCee's business depended on tourists, so she was somewhat more upbeat about the impending influx of strangers. "We need it," she said.

Wiley waved to us from the end of the bar, and Aubrey ducked around to get drinks for us, and then we settled on three stools next to Lucy and Will. I didn't see Harrison in the wood-paneled space, and tried not to let disappointment flood my happy mood.

"You guys hear about the door Brainiac found?" Will asked us, grinning widely as he draped one arm around Lucy.

"Um, yeah," I said, calling on my acting skills not to give me away. I'd already told Bennie and CeeCee about it, and about how we discovered it. "Did they get it open?" I asked.

"Not yet," he said. "Ghost says they'll probably have to break the door down, and he didn't want to start beating on it until they've shored up the tunnel to make sure smashing the door won't collapse the whole thing."

"Can't they like, pick the lock or something?" Bennie asked.

"Sounds like it's probably sealed by years of dirt and the earth settling, more than by the lock," Lucy said. "Ghost is all giddy about what must be behind it, though."

"I bet," CeeCee said.

The mood was different than it had been other nights when we'd hung out together in the resort bar. There was a note of anticipation in the air, a kind of unspoken awareness that this was it, the threshold of everything we'd been working toward. Even though I was a new addition to the Kasper Ridge crew, I felt it too.

I was in conversation with Archie and his sister when I felt Harrison enter the space. I didn't even have to look, I could tell he was nearby just by the way my body reacted, shifting into high alert, humming in a way it never had before. If there was such a thing as chemical attraction, Harrison and I had it. I wanted him on a molecular level, if that was possible. It was something I would have laughed at if anyone else had said it, but I knew it was true. My very essence wanted him.

"Hey." It was almost a whisper, a gruff acknowledgement just off my left shoulder that sent a thrill of liquid heat through me.

"Hi," I said, turning slightly to let him slide closer to the bar at my side.

He leaned in a bit, focusing on Archie. "Figure out how to brace the tunnel around the door?"

"Maybe," Archie said. "I mean, we've got like six engineers up here, right? We ought to be able to get this done."

"We have to," Aubrey said. "It's not like we can hire someone from town and expect them to keep it quiet."

I wondered if she was right. People in Kasper Ridge had certainly identified me, and so far it'd been kept on the down low.

"Doesn't everyone in town know about the treasure hunt at this point anyway?" Harrison asked.

"Maybe," Archie admitted. "But with the staff starting tomorrow and lots of younger kids around all the time, I just think we're going to need to be more careful. Especially as we get closer to the actual treasure."

"You think this is the end?" I asked. "The treasure's behind that door?" It was an exciting idea.

"I've thought we were close before," Archie said. "But this feels monumental." He was quiet a minute, and we all followed suit, sipping our drinks.

"You planning to stabilize the whole tunnel, or just around the door?" Harrison asked.

"Definitely around the door," Archie said. "But it would make sense to be diligent, do this right. The last thing we need is someone trapped down there, and I'm not sure Uncle Marvin had the tunnel dug right in the first place, you know? He definitely wasn't an engineer."

"Are all fighter pilots engineers?" I asked, the question suddenly occurring to me.

"A lot are," Harrison said. "Most have some kind of scientific degree at least. Or math. There's a lot to know about physics and math if you're going to fly a jet."

"Sasquatch?" Aubrey asked, her voice carrying a skeptical tone that made me hide a smile behind my hand.

"Believe it or not," Archie said, grinning. I was surprised, but also suspected the guy they called Sasquatch had hidden depths he didn't show just anyone.

"You met his service animal yet?" Harrison asked.

Archie's grin faded. "I have."

"You okay with this?"

"Not even a little bit," Archie said.

"Are we going to make him get rid of the dog?" Aubrey asked, sounding sad.

"I don't know what to do. He's being very Sass about the whole thing, acting like there's nothing to see here, hoping we'll all just move along." Archie replied.

We all turned to look at the big man in question, who was holding court at the other end of the bar, CeeCee and Bennie practically falling down with laughter at whatever he was saying. His service animal, Roscoe, did not seem to be with him. I wondered where he was.

"He's good at peopling, though," I pointed out.

"Someone has to be," Harrison replied, in a voice so low I doubted anyone but me heard it.

We stayed in the bar another hour, rotating around the space and laughing together in a way that made me feel like I was really part of something for the first time in a long time. And Harrison stayed at my side, not in a possessive way. It was as if his body yearned for me as much as I was pulled to him.

"Any chance you want to get out of here?" he asked me after a while, leaning in close so his breath danced hot across my throat below my ear.

"Every chance," I told him, taking a moment to turn and meet his eyes, my body flashing with fire at the desire I found in his gaze.

I let CeeCee and Bennie know I'd find my own way home, and then quietly left the bar behind Harrison, warmth flooding me as he took my hand in his the second we were out of sight. He led me to the elevator at the side of the lobby, and as soon as the doors shut and he'd pressed the button for his floor, I was in his arms, our mouths coming together hungrily.

Chapter 12
Just Yes Please

HARRISON

Penny's body pushed against mine as I pulled her to me in the quiet confines of the elevator, and I suspected she'd wanted me every bit as much as I'd wanted her from the first second I'd entered the bar. She'd been sitting with her back to the door, the pendant lights overhead catching flares of gold in her dark auburn hair. She wore a fitted blue sweater that hugged her curves, and dark jeans that left little to the imagination about the wonder that was her ass.

I'd never wanted anyone this way before.

Sure, I'd had flings, even relationships, though I was not

adept at maneuvering through the complex web of interaction that most of those required. I hadn't tried in a long time, but with Penny it was different.

She was open, accessible. I didn't feel like I was constantly on the verge of offending her or saying something wrong. It was easy.

We tumbled out of the elevator when the doors opened, breaking apart regretfully, our chests heaving as I pulled her by the hand toward my room near the end of the hall.

There was no one around, but we maintained our distance anyway, at least until I got the door open. And then it was as if we'd stepped into an alternate dimension, one where words weren't necessary and we each knew instinctively what to do.

My hands found Penny's waist beneath the soft drape of her sweater and slid up her sides, lifting the fabric from her body. Her arms lifted, and I pulled the sweater over her head, revealing a silken tank top beneath it. She wore no bra, only the close-fitting silk, and something about this discovery had my body pulsing with desire.

I walked her backward, kissing her throat, my arms bracing her back, until we reached the bedroom. When her knees hit the edge of my bed, I released her, our eyes meeting for a long moment that was filled only with the sounds of our breathing.

"Yes," she said, and it was all I needed.

I pushed her gently back onto the bed, and her hands reached for me, pulling me to climb over her, resting my arms on either side of her head, our lower bodies pressed together. Penny wrapped a leg around my waist, pulling me into her center, and the delicious heat I felt there, even through our dual layers of denim, had rational thought threatening to slide from my mind altogether.

I rolled to one side, both to buy myself some time—the direct contact in certain areas wasn't helping my self control—

and so that I could free up a hand to explore the miles of soft skin below me.

Penny's hands were unfastening the buttons on my shirt, and then sliding to the waistband of my jeans, and soft huffing noises of impatience were coming from her, as if she couldn't get me undressed as fast as she'd like. I loved it.

I pulled my shirt off, and shucked my jeans to the floor before peeling the silky fabric from Penny's torso slowly, following the movement of my hands with my mouth. I traced a soft trail around her navel and then up to her perfect, full breasts, loving the way they spilled from the fabric as I removed it, pulling it off her body over the cascade of her soft hair.

Penny's eyes were half closed, and those little huffs of want were still issuing from her lips, ratcheting up my need for her with every tortured moan.

I slid lower, my hands finding the button on her jeans, and once again, I met her eyes, pausing just to make sure we were on the same page. When Penny's hips bucked beneath my hands, egging me on, I knew that this was going to be it. I was going to have the chance to bury myself inside her, and the knowledge nearly drove me to explosion right there. But I wanted to do better than that for her, so I forced myself to focus on unfastening her jeans, pulling them carefully down her legs.

Penny's skin was pale and beautiful, every inch of it worthy of worship. But I definitely didn't have that kind of self-control. I wanted to feel her, to be inside her, to get as close to her as I possibly could. Because there was something about Penny that drew me near, that I couldn't resist.

I stepped back, removing my boxer briefs and standing before her, appreciating the expanse of beautiful silken skin laid out before me. Penny scooted herself up the bed, resting her head on the pillows near the headboard and waiting, her eyes never leaving mine.

"Come here," she said softly.

And those two words erased the last vestiges of self-control I had.

I climbed back up her perfect body, worshipping every centimeter until I took her mouth again, our tongues meeting in a hot cooperation that felt practically choreographed.

Penny's hands explored my body, and when her fist wrapped itself around my cock, stars threatened to explode behind my eyelids, heat sparking into fire inside me.

"You're perfect," she whispered, stroking me, her fingers slipping over my sensitive crown and then her palm pumping downward again. I knew I would need to stop her before things got completely out of control, but I couldn't bring myself to do it.

"Fuck, that feels good," I heard myself say. I was in some other world, pleasure and sheer instinct guiding me forward.

"I want you inside me," she whispered, her fingers and her voice threatening to send me to pieces at any second.

I rolled to the side and slipped off the bed, knowing I had a condom or two stashed somewhere, but it wasn't something I had a need for on the regular. "I'll find a condom," I said, wishing I'd thought to do this earlier.

Penny smiled, her face flushed and blissful. As I headed for the attached bathroom, I glanced back at her to see her peeling off her panties, and I thought I might lose it right there. Finally, with some digging, I found two condoms in my shaving kit, and returned to her, rolling one down my length and trying hard not to look as eager as I felt.

I laid to her side and let my hand caress her, her greedy mouth finding mine once again. My hand drifted lower, tracing small circles on her breasts, her stomach, and then finally, coming to glance over the soft heat of her center.

Penny let out a breathy cry, which I captured in my mouth.

And when I increased the pressure a bit, using three fingers to tease her folds, she bucked under my hand.

"More," she moaned.

I let my index finger delve into her soft wetness then, and her moans pushed me forward until I was circling her clit, using long strokes and then smaller firmer ones to bring her close to the edge.

"God, I want you," she moaned, reaching for me.

I slid a leg across her hips, looking down at the beautiful woman in my bed in something that felt a lot like disbelief. This was not what I'd come to Kasper Ridge to find, but I wasn't going to walk away, either.

I notched myself to her slick entrance and Penny encouraged me, lifting her knees to open herself to me. Bracing myself above her shoulders, I slid home as slowly as I could manage. The breathy gasps and moans coming from Penny's lips made it difficult to practice control, and when I was fully seated in the most delicious pleasure I'd ever felt, a groan issued from deep inside my chest.

"Good?" she asked, her voice vulnerable, young sounding.

"So good," I told her, taking her mouth once again as we began to move together.

Penny's legs trapped me against her, holding me tight in a way that had me fighting for every bit of friction, and causing a glorious kind of want to bolt through me with every eked-out movement. She was like a vise, her body clamping to mine, her channel pulsing and fluttering around my cock and driving me to the brink.

When I couldn't take any more, I drove forward, setting a rhythm that worked with her tight hold on me, but one that had me inching toward paradise at the same time.

Penny's soft voice issued an ongoing string of soft moans, gasps, and muttered expletives that had long since driven any kind of rational thought from my mind. I wanted her like I was dying and she was the cure, and when we came—within seconds of one another—it was unlike any orgasm I'd experienced before. Subtle at first, but long, and undulating until it exploded into something that left me feeling as if my mind and body had separated completely.

When I returned to myself, Penny was there, holding me close and smiling up at me, her eyes bright and happy, and I wondered absently if this might be the thing I was put on Earth to find.

Chapter 13
Superstitious Snow

PENNY

I found it difficult to leave Harrison's bed, and soon, my hands had begun exploring the hard planes of his body again, and leaving was the last thing on my mind. We talked and enjoyed one another, and by the time the second condom was gone, it was late.

"I should go," I said, stretched out in the circle of Harrison's arms and finding exactly zero motivation to actually get up.

"Or you should stay," he said, his voice sleepy and rough.

I rolled to face him, and his arm tightened around my side, a comforting possession I loved. "If I stay," I said, trying to verbalize the question I felt but wasn't sure how to phrase, "isn't it just . . . soon?"

"I don't think there are any official rules," he said, his eyes popping open to look at me.

He was right. People cited arbitrary rules about the progression of dating and sex, but no one's emotions or desires ascribed to these. Mine certainly didn't.

Harrison's eyes dropped shut again and he pulled me closer to him. "Stay," he whispered, and I let my eyes fall closed, enjoying his soft breathing in the darkness and the feeling of the huge resort around us, dark and silent in the night.

The next time I opened my eyes, sunlight was streaming in through the crack between the curtains, and Harrison was sitting up, a laptop on his legs and a frown on his handsome face.

For a moment I allowed myself to stretch, to simply be. But then I had a flash of fear. What was he doing? Was he online? Had he somehow learned who I was?

I blinked, trying to wake up more fully, and tested my voice. "Good morning."

The frown disappeared, and Harrison's eyes met mine. "Morning sweetheart."

The endearment lodged in my chest and made it hard for me to talk for a second. No one had ever called me sweetheart. Not even my mother. I liked it. A lot.

Harrison slid the laptop to the side table and moved over, taking me in his arms. "How'd you sleep?"

"Well," I said. "Really well."

"Good. I'd take credit but it was probably just the mattress."

"No, it was you." I could feel his smile against my neck as he hugged me closer. "What were you doing? Work?"

Harrison sighed and released me so he could look into my face. "Email. I accepted that position in Sacramento my buddy hooked me up with. I was just checking out the company a bit and trying to understand exactly what I'll be doing there."

I didn't like thinking about Kasper Ridge without Harrison here. I hated it, actually. "But you don't leave yet, right? Not for a while."

"Not until spring." His smile softened. "We have time."

I had to go back to Los Angeles before that for the reunion event anyway, though I wouldn't be gone for good. Paul had left a voice message, letting me know he'd renegotiated and while the network wasn't pleased, they'd accepted the offer as long as I didn't make any announcements anywhere else first. I hated the idea of being here at Kasper Ridge without Harrison, but spring was a long way off. And he was right—we had time. For whatever this was.

"Are you looking forward to the new job?" I asked him.

He sighed, each of us snuggled into the covers, our hands linked between us as we faced one another. "Not really."

"You could probably stay here." A tiny light of hope flickered inside me. He could, couldn't he? Couldn't we both stay here and just do this, whatever this was, forever?

"I probably could," he said. "But I'm not sure being a ski bum was the life I was created for."

"Even if it makes you happy?"

Something like a smile crossed his face, but disappeared just as suddenly as it had appeared. "I know it's popular to say that as long as we're happy everything else is good," he said. "But I don't buy it."

"What do you mean?" Wasn't happiness all that really mattered?

"I can do more," he said. "I don't want the measure of my success to be that I managed to get an ancient ski lift running and reinvigorate a resort full of spoiled rich people. I guess I just feel like my legacy is meant to be a little more notable."

That made sense, and I felt like his statement gave me real insight into what made this man tick. "Is that why you were a professor?"

"Yes, partially."

For a minute we were quiet, and I let his words roll through my mind. In his world, I'd done nothing of value at all. What was my legacy going to be?

"Life is pretty short," I said, thinking as I spoke, the words coming slowly. "Shouldn't we try to be as happy as we can be while we live it?"

He looked at me, the line appearing between his brows once more. "It sounds nice," he said. "But I think financial security and meaningful contributions to humanity are equally important."

He was right. And I had neither of those things. This job though, it felt like a start.

"So the job . . . the one in California. You'll be doing something important?"

"I'll be in the lab, working on building the kinds of things the military will need to stay viable in the future, to keep us safe, to protect freedom and democracy."

"Those things sound pretty important," I agreed. A hell of a lot moreso than playing a silly kid on television. Still, something in the way he said these big words made me feel like even he didn't really believe them.

"It's what my dad did," he added, his voice softer.

"You said he was a diplomat, right?"

Harrison grunted an agreement, his fingers tracing a line down my shoulder, his touch light and feathery. "He worked all over the world, negotiating with other people to maintain our freedom, ensuring basic human rights, helping other governments do good for their citizens."

"That's a lot." I thought about my parents, doing little

beyond exploiting their only child, and was glad Harrison didn't ask about them. I didn't want to let their legacy wreck what he'd just said about his own father.

"He was so impressive," Harrison said. "I just don't want to think about him being disappointed in me."

"Is he disappointed? You were a military officer. A fighter pilot. That's pretty impressive."

"He's proud," he said, sounding thoughtful. "But I think he's worried about what I'm doing now."

I nodded, understanding that at least. My mom was worried about what I was doing now too, only because if I stayed out of show business, the odds of me funding her life were very slim.

"The other side of it," Harrison said, his slate blue eyes on mine as if they were looking for something specific, a reaction maybe. "Is that I want to make sure I have the security I'd need to have a family someday."

A tiny thrill shot through me—something in the way he was looking at me, like he was asking a question. But of course, he wasn't.

"I'd like the same thing, maybe," I said. Only I wasn't sure I'd had any valuable training in how to be a mother. I'd had a terrible example. At least I knew what not to do.

Harrison kissed me softly then, and we spent another hour in his big bed, exploring one another's bodies. The knowledge that we didn't have another condom made it somehow better, as we found other ways to tease and delight each other. I wasn't sure our goals were aligned, but our bodies seemed to be perfectly in synch.

"Would you mind if I use your shower?" I asked him, stretching deliciously but aware that it was definitely time to get up.

"Of course not. Help yourself," he said, reaching for the laptop again.

I let the warm water sluice down my sore body—enjoying the gentle aches that would remind me for days of the night I'd spent in Harrison's arms. And when I stepped out, clad in the same clothes from the night before, Harrison was standing at the window, a pair of jeans slung low across his hips, shirtless. I moved behind him to wrap my arms around him and let my hands dance across the muscles of his chest.

"It's snowing," he said. His voice was full of disbelief and amusement.

"What?" I had only seen snow a couple times in my life. I ducked around him to stare out the window.

He was right. It wasn't exactly heavy, but flakes were drifting lazily from the overcast sky above, which had darkened slowly from the morning sunshine as we lingered in bed.

"I guess we're going to be all set when the resort opens in a week."

"Will one snowfall cover the mountain?"

He smiled and tucked me into his chest as we both looked back outside. "No, but we'll make snow on the main runs until we have enough. This will help."

We stared at the flakes, which were falling faster and thicker, with more determination now. "I didn't even know snow was coming," I said, pulling my phone from my pocket and pulling up the weather app. "It's supposed to snow all week!"

Harrison smiled and kissed my cheek, moving to pull a T-shirt over his glorious chest. "Ghost knew. He was ecstatic, but he told me he wasn't going to talk about it in case he ruined it."

"Superstitious, huh?"

"Surviving something like he did does that to a guy."

"What happened to him?" I asked. I'd heard people hint about a terrible end to Archie's military career, but I didn't know what it had been. I wasn't sure if asking the question might be overstepping, but I felt safe with Harrison.

"It's not really my story to tell," Harrison said, his face grave. "There was an accident and a couple civilians were killed. Archie was tried and cleared, but it ended his career."

"Oh god," I whispered. I couldn't imagine the guilt he must be carrying, and though I longed for the details out of some twisted human curiosity, I understood now why everyone here seemed a little protective of him. "Poor Archie."

"He's okay," Harrison said. "We all look out for him a bit now. It's why we're here."

"That makes sense." I was touched by the idea that all these former fighter pilots were so bonded that they'd manipulate their lives in a way that they could stay close, make sure their friend was okay. I'd never had friends like that.

I thought about how that same group of people had welcomed me with open arms, no questions asked. How had I gotten so lucky?

I glanced outside again, and a twinge of worry struck me. "I'd better get home before this gets too thick to drive in."

"I'll take you," Harrison said.

Soon, he was delivering me safely to Bennie's house, the big SUV he drove handling the swirling flakes on the ground with no problem.

"I'll see you Monday," I said, leaning across the console and wishing we weren't saying goodbye.

"See you then," he agreed. "Thanks for staying." He kissed me softly, and let me go, waiting until I'd closed Bennie's door behind me to back out.

Chapter 14
Time to Dig

HARRISON

I arrived back at the resort to find Ghost waiting for me in the lobby, pacing and looking worried.

"What's up?" I asked, glancing around for any obvious issues.

"You said you'd help me get to work on that tunnel this morning."

I had said that. A vague memory of the night before resurfaced. But seeing Penny had suffused any rational thought and practical promises as surely as too much of Wiley's Half Cat Whiskey could do. And I'd had a bit of that last night too.

"Sorry. I'm here now." I didn't like the idea of letting Ghost down.

"Since when are you a late sleeper?" He frowned at me. This was the side of Ghost I worried about, the anxious and grumpy side, which was all we'd seen for about a year after his discharge.

"Sorry." I rubbed a hand over the back of my neck. I wanted to tell him what I'd been busy with, but it wasn't my place to share what was going on with Penny. Not without mentioning it to her first.

He raised an eyebrow and scanned my face, looking for something. "Aubrey says you and Penny are friends."

I didn't give him the reaction he was clearly waiting for. Telling him anything seemed like it would be an invasion of Penny's privacy, and while I would have liked to skip around the lobby singing about the night I'd just spent with the most beautiful woman I'd ever met, that wouldn't have been fair to her. I kept my mouth shut.

"Whatever, man. I've got a bunch of stuff to take up there on the four-wheeler, and tools are already there. You ready?"

"Fake Tom and Sass coming?" I was tired and would have liked to go back to bed for a bit, but I'd made a promise. I just hoped there'd be some other hands to help with the work.

"FT's there now. Sass begged off, saying he needed to take Roscoe to therapy today. That guy is seriously driving me nuts. Antonio's up there, though."

"So Sass is useless, but he brought a proxy to do his work while he fucks off." I shook my head. Sasquatch hadn't changed. His antics in the squadron were legendary.

"Pretty much. Let's go."

I followed Ghost out the back to the four-wheeler, and we spent the bulk of the very cold day in the tunnel Penny and I had found, shoring up the dirt walls with sheets of plywood and bracing them to make sure the tunnel wouldn't cave. By the time darkness fell, we were almost done, and Ghost's clear excitement was almost enough of a reward to make up for my freezing fingers.

"Finish tomorrow?" Fake Tom suggested, his hands and face streaked with dirt as he looked at the rest of us. We were all filthy and freezing. The snow hadn't let up all day, and while our own exertions in the tunnel warmed the air slightly, it wasn't the most pleasant of environments.

Ghost looked over his shoulder in the gathering darkness at the metal door, still sealing whatever secrets it obscured behind its dark, aged lock. "Yeah. Okay." His teeth actually chattered as he said it.

"So you really believe there will be a room filled with gold behind that door?" Antonio asked me as we walked back to the resort, having let Fake Tom and Ghost take the four-wheeler.

I chuckled. "I don't know what I believe. There's something back there, for sure. But what's important is keeping Ghost focused and managing his expectations."

Antonio was quiet for a minute, and then he said in a voice I could only characterize as excessively neutral. "You guys all treat Archie like a delicate vase. You really think he is so close to breaking?"

I cast a sideways glance at the former soccer star. "It's happened before."

"He doesn't seem fragile to me."

"You don't know what he's been through." I didn't say it argumentatively, but Antonio was new here. He didn't understand.

"I know that people change and grow. That the scars we bear are the toughest parts of us."

I thought about that. Maybe we did treat Ghost with kid

gloves, but it was only because we cared. I didn't offer an answer, and didn't need to as we stepped through the big lobby doors off the patio into the blessed warmth of the resort.

The scent of something delicious wafted from the kitchen, and my mouth watered, but as soon as I stepped foot inside the restaurant, followed by the other guys, Aubrey blocked my path.

"Nope. Showers first." She crossed her arms and stared up at me ferociously.

"Seriously? We're starving." I looked around at the three other filthy faces at my side.

"You guys look like you've been flinging mud at each other all day. Don't bring it in the restaurant. We have guests arriving in a week!"

"They're not here now," Ghost pointed out.

She glared at him, giving him what I could only assume was a meaningful look between siblings, and Ghost let out a mighty sigh. "Fine. But there better be food left."

With that, we all turned and headed upstairs to do as Aubrey directed.

* * *

I woke the next morning to find the view out my window completely transformed. The snow had continued all night, drifting high around the patio below and blanketing the central ski run with a thick layer of white. The temperature had dropped noticeably too, and I crossed the room to tap at the thermostat, feeling a ping of jealousy for the renovated rooms in the opposite wing. They had gas fireplaces installed. We were lucky the HVAC updates had included this wing and that the heat was working.

Renovations in what we were calling the "staff wing"

weren't planned until the following summer. But the room I had, while outdated perhaps, was still nicer than many places I'd stayed on active duty. And I wasn't picky. In fact, the longer I stayed here, the more at home I had begun to feel. Having my friends around . . . and Penny. It was comforting in a lot of ways. I didn't let myself think about the fact I'd be leaving it all soon.

I picked up the book I'd been reading: *Empathy for Assholes*. If this book couldn't help me, I figured, nothing could. I knew I needed to work on this part of my personality. It was what had gotten me let go from my previous role, and I didn't want my lack of people skills to screw anything else up. I was beginning to suspect that I'd lost much more in my life than the job I'd previously had due to my shortcomings. Relationships and friendships as far back as I could remember had cited my inability to relate as the biggest reason why people walked away from me.

In fact, the only people who'd stuck around were the guys I was up here with now. Them and my dad, of course, but he was currently disappointed with me. Telling him I'd been passed over for someone younger and less experienced was one of the hardest things I'd done. Telling him the reason they gave me was even harder.

You just don't seem to care about these kids, Harrison. You project a cold and unapproachable front, and we need someone who can relate to them, who can really connect with other people on a human level. That's not you.

It was not me.

But maybe it could be. If John Andrews, author of *Empathy for Assholes* had anything to say about it.

To be honest, though, most of the book seemed like common sense to me. That or sheer stupidity. "Ask people about their interests, even if you don't really care at all."

Was that empathy? Or was that just pretending to be empathetic? If nothing else, at least I was genuine. If I didn't give a shit about your pickle ball obsession, at least you knew it.

I put the book down and stood. Ghost would be desperate to get back to that door today, and I could picture him in the lobby sighing dramatically and wondering where I was. I pulled on a warm coat, hat, and gloves, and headed downstairs.

When I got there, Ghost was pacing around, but he wasn't in a hurry to go.

"We can't get it open," he said the second he saw me geared up and ready to go. He'd already been in the tunnel today?

"Why not?" I didn't love the idea of Ghost going down there without me.

"Well, because it's an old metal door that's been sealed for who knows how long, and the thing won't budge."

Sass was standing nearby, with Roscoe actually sitting rather obediently at his side.

"Did you try throwing Sasquatch at it?" I asked.

"He tried throwing himself at it, but the thing opens out, so that's no good. Plus, his attack dog had a fit the second he started in on it."

I glanced over at Sass, raising an eyebrow.

"Roscoe has become very protective. He was worried I'd get hurt." Sass bent down to pet the dog, who growled menacingly at him. The big man straightened back up, smiling. "Still working on some things."

"Okay, well, there's gotta be a way," I said, thinking about the handle and keyhole below it. "There's a key to it somewhere."

"There was a key to it somewhere," Ghost said, sounding frustrated. "But we don't have it. And it didn't turn up during renovation."

"So it must be in the staff wing," I said. Those were the only rooms construction crews hadn't been in and out of.

"I got a buddy with a lead on some pretty good fireworks," Sasquatch said, stepping closer. Ghost and I both moved a few steps away as Roscoe moved with him. Sass frowned at us and then shrugged, standing still. "We can blow the thing open."

"By good fireworks, do you mean dynamite?" Ghost asked, his voice wary and tired.

"Maybe."

"That will collapse the tunnel for sure," I said. "A few sheets of plywood and two-by-fours are not going to hold up to TNT."

"We've got staff arriving, we can't blow a hole in the mountain," Ghost said. "Plus, just . . . no."

Sasquatch shrugged as if to indicate we were morons for not deciding to blow up the resort.

"Let's all search our own rooms to start. Uncle Marvin was sneaky, but he wanted us to solve this thing. So it's probably hidden in plain sight. Or taped to the underside of a table or something simple."

"Pretty strong tape to hold up this long," I said.

"We have to start somewhere." Ghost looked so disappointed, Sasquatch and I both assured him that we would search our rooms thoroughly. "And we'll get to the empty rooms one by one as we have time." He shook his head and wrapped a hand around his neck, looking at the polished lobby floor. "I almost wish we had a few more weeks before everyone gets here."

"We'll find it," I said, feeling exactly zero confidence that it was true, but wanting to keep Ghost positive. "And once this place is hopping, it's going to change everything. People will come here from all over the world. Look at this place." I waved an arm around the impressive lobby, and the three of us gazed around at the paneled walls, the chandeliers sparkling overhead, the massive reception desk and the dual staircases curving away from it up to the second level.

"Yeah," Ghost said, his tone lightening. "We did good here. It'll be great."

Roscoe barked as if to indicate that he agreed with us.

Chapter 15
Moving In

PENNY

It snowed all weekend, and Bennie and I watched it from the windows of her little cottage, curled up on the couch with coffee in the morning and wine at night. It felt like being in some cozy holiday movie.

But when Monday rolled around, I realized that snow was going to make getting to and from work a terrifying endeavor. I'd been relying on Bennie for a ride in the mornings, and her brother often drove me home at night. I'd actually looked at a couple of used cars online, but with the drifts of slippery snow piling up, I was second-guessing the idea. I had no idea how to drive in snow. All I knew was that it was dangerous. And that scared me.

Bennie's car seemed to do fine as she took me in to work all week, but I couldn't stop myself from gripping the sides of my seat until my fingers ached, an uncomfortable fear lodged in my throat. It was worse all week as Jepson drove me home. I would have preferred Harrison's big SUV (with Harrison in it, of course), but with staff training this week, I hardly saw him at all, except in glances out my big window and a couple of quick lunches in the restaurant. We texted, of course, and talked.

On Thursday night, I cradled my phone against my ear as I lay in bed, Harrison's deep sexy voice filling my head.

"I don't like the idea of you going back and forth with Jepson," he said after apologizing for being too busy to drive me again.

"I don't have a lot of options until I buy a car."

"Do you want to buy a car, Penny?"

I sighed and rolled to one side, letting my gaze rest on the window beside my bed, which was fogged on the inside with a thin layer of condensation. "I did, when it was nice out. I'm not a terrible driver, but I've literally never driven in snow. It freaks me out. I know that's stupid . . ."

"It's not. It takes a while to get comfortable driving in these conditions, and even when you're comfortable it can be danger-ous." His voice was reassuring, soft.

"Thanks for that reassurance," I laughed.

"I just don't like you hurtling around in that little death mobile. Have you taken a look at Jepson's tires?"

"Not my usual M.O. when getting into a car."

"They're practically bald. It's not safe."

Hearing Harrison repeat what I'd already known about my

carpool provider made me worry. My insides turned over at the thought that Jepson was just tempting fate, driving around on bald tires. One would think that since he was the one Uber driver here, his car would be up to a high standard. Maybe his affinity for collecting roadkill and keeping it in the car's built-in cooler should have been a tip off that this was not your usual Uber. "I guess I better buy something." I had money saved and could certainly afford a car, but I honestly hated the thought of driving the twisty highway in the snow.

"Or . . ." Harrison's voice stretched out the word, and I could picture his handsome face, the eyes darkening as he thought about something.

"What?"

"There are plenty of empty rooms in the staff wing here."

The thought of living at the resort, with Harrison just a few doorways away, had me clenching my thighs together. What would it be like? To be with him full time? To spend nights together whenever we wanted?

But just as quickly as the warm rush of enthusiasm for the idea swept through me, a cold rational tide followed it. What if something happened to end whatever this thing was between us? What would it be like being forced to be so near to him then?

"You're quiet," he said.

"I'm thinking," I told him. "Plus, wouldn't Archie or Aubrey have to make that offer?"

"I guarantee they'd be on board."

I rolled to my back again, staring up at the low ceiling above me, more grey than white in the dark room. I thought about living with all my new friends, really being part of that group. I loved the idea. It would be like the family I never had. But it was complicated. "What would that be like, though?"

"Short commute," Harrison said, a teasing note in his voice. "Nice accommodations. Excellent company." The last bit was delivered in what was practically a growl.

"You'd get tired of having me around." Maybe I was fishing a bit, but only because I was so unsure what this thing between us actually was. He was leaving at the end of the season. He'd been clear about that. Plus, if we saw each other constantly, I'd definitely run out of excuses for not telling him about my past. My identity.

"Would you get tired of me?" he asked.

"No." My answer was immediate.

"I feel the same," he said, reading whatever subtext I'd spoken too quickly to conceal.

"But . . ." How did I phrase the question I needed to ask?

"Penny." The rough timbre of his voice sent a shiver through me. I would never get tired of hearing him say my name.

My answer was a loud breath as I tried to tamp down my feelings. Feelings for him. Things I shouldn't be feeling for someone I barely knew, someone who'd promised me nothing. Someone who was leaving.

"I don't know what this is between us either," he said, his voice pulling and scraping at things inside me, in my heart, my core. "I don't think everything needs a label, though. Whatever it is, as long as we're both in, it doesn't matter. I love seeing you, spending time with you. The thought of having you in my bed whenever I want . . ." A low groan sent a rush of warmth through my low belly.

"Me too."

"It would be good," he said. "And maybe we just let it be whatever it is."

"You're leaving," I said, unable to keep myself from voicing the one thing that was always there, in the back of my mind.

"I am," he said, his tone careful. "But we don't need to think about the future first. Let's focus on now. We're both here, we can be together, and we know it's good."

"Okay." He was right. And focusing on the present felt right too.

"I want to be sure you really mean that. I don't want to lead you on or deceive you and I'm not in a place to make promises about the future." He said this softly, like he was trying not to hurt me.

A little lump of dread threatened to expand in my gut, but I ignored it. He was right. I couldn't say what the next year would bring in my own life, why should I expect him to make me any promises about the future? "I'm not either."

"So we enjoy the time we have. Even if it's just the season." Did I hear a note of uncertainty in his voice, or did I just let myself imagine it because I wanted to believe there was a part of him that wished for more too?

"Yes. We enjoy the time we have."

"So you're moving to the resort."

"Um. Is that what we were talking about?" I laughed.

"I'll talk to Ghost. You move tomorrow. I'll pick you up at seven." His commanding tone made my blood heat.

"You're serious? You're going to talk to him right now? It's eleven o'clock at night."

"One thing I know about Ghost. He doesn't sleep. See you at seven."

"What if he says no?"

"He won't. Be ready."

"Okay," I said, feeling like I'd just been swept into some kind of whirlwind and was being tossed around, out of my own control.

"And tomorrow night," Harrison said, his voice taking on that sandpaper roughness again, "I'll help you get settled."

The promise of his words pushed warmth through me, sweeping away the uncertainties I felt. "Good night, Harrison."

"Night, Penny. Sleep well, sweetheart."

I put the phone aside and stared into the darkness around me. It felt right—everything with Harrison felt right.

And that was what scared me.

* * *

Harrison texted me at six the next morning, assuring me that there was a room ready for me and that Ghost had no issues with the idea and agreed it was safer than commuting during the season when the roads might be treacherous.

"You're leaving me?" Bennie said, seeing my suitcase next to the door when she came out for coffee.

"Only to go stay at the resort."

She raised an eyebrow. "Oh really? Moving in with your boyfriend so soon?"

"I'll have my own room. It just makes more sense than commuting through the snow." Was Harrison my boyfriend? A little thrill shot through me at the idea.

Bennie poured herself a cup of coffee, doctoring it with sugar and half and half before turning to face me again. Her curly hair was piled on top of her head, and she wore a sweatshirt that said "Kasper Ridge, hard to find, hard to leave."

"You sure that's the reason you're moving over there? Transportation concerns?" One of her eyebrows crept higher.

"Stop that. It's safer, that's all."

"There's definitely more sex over there." She sipped her coffee after delivering that zinger.

My face wouldn't cooperate with my desire to be annoyed by her comment, and I cracked a smile. "That is one upside."

"What's going on there? Between you guys? Serious?"

I shook my head and picked up my own coffee, mostly to give myself time to figure out how to put whatever it was into words. "Not serious."

"Think it's gonna get serious though? If you're living like, next door . . ." the implication of her words was clear.

"No. It's just fun for the season. He's leaving in the spring." I pretended this was not a big deal.

"What about you?" Bennie looked sad for me.

"I don't know. I'm going down just after the new year to do the reunion show."

"I thought you said no."

"I said no to the series. I'm doing the event. I'm going to announce my retirement." Saying this out loud made me even more certain it was the absolute right choice.

"And then you're coming back."

"Yeah." I had a job now. A place to be.

"Good. I like the idea of you being here long term. I guess you would have moved out eventually anyway."

"You would have kicked me out."

"Never. Even if you do leave Diet Coke cans everywhere."

I grimaced at the two cans I could see from my seat at the table. One on the coffee table and another on the low entryway wall. "Sorry."

"I'll miss you. This has been so fun." Bennie smiled at me and I knew I'd miss her too. It had been like an extended slumber party.

"You'll be glad to have your place back. Thank you for letting me stay here."

"Of course."

I stood and walked around the table to hug Bennie just as a knock came at the door.

I opened it to find Harrison standing there in a barn jacket, dark jeans, and boots that made him look like some kind of rugged mountain man with style, and I had to repress the urge to swoon. He was almost too handsome to be real.

"You ready?"

"Yep." I pulled the door open wider to reveal my suitcase.

"Hey there," Bennie called, still leaning on the counter, coffee in her hand.

"Hi Bennie."

"You take care of her, okay?"

Harrison paused, putting my bag back down as he straightened to look at my friend. "I will."

His tone was so stern it made me suck in a quick breath and really pause to look at him. What if he could? What if Harrison and I were serious? It would feel so good to believe that he was always going to be there, to take care of me.

But of course, it was just something to say. Bennie didn't mean it like that, and neither did Harrison. And I needed to take care of myself. That's what being up here was all about – well, that and hiding out a little bit.

"Bye friend." Bennie moved to the door to give me a hug.

"You coming to the grand opening?" I asked. There was a party planned the following week, but it was on Monday night, so I wasn't sure Bennie would be up for it.

"Wouldn't miss it. Can't wait to see the first guests at Kasper Ridge."

"Okay. See you then."

Before I knew it, Harrison and I were pulling up in front of the Kasper Ridge Resort. My new home.

* * *

Harrison told me he'd picked out my room himself.

"I didn't want to assume you'd enjoy sharing a connecting door," he said as we walked down the hallway his room was on.

"I would have," I said, an edge of playful longing in my voice.

He chuckled and smiled at me with a glint in his eye that came close to melting my clothes right off my body. Of course it was seven thirty in the morning, and that would have to wait - we both needed to get to work.

"I looked at all the vacant rooms on this floor. Ghost had us searching all the vacant rooms for the missing key to the door in the tunnel anyway," he went on, stopping in front of a doorway across the hall and a few doors down from his. "And this one was in the best shape."

He handed me an old fashioned metal key. The guest rooms in the other wing had updated locks, but this side still sported the antique locks and keys that were original to the resort.

The lock turned with a couple of hefty-sounding clicks, and the door swung open. The room was a lot like Harrison's: an old floral couch, a low dark wood table in front of it, a table and chairs next to a low, long buffet table against the wall where someone had plugged in a modern coffee machine and a little refrigerator that sat beneath it. The bedroom was through another door, and featured a queen-sized bed topped with a soft-looking white duvet, a dresser and two night tables with charming curved legs and old fashioned lamps with pink bases. There was a bathroom, a closet, and a gorgeous view out the window overlooking the front of the resort. Today that view was of soaring sturdy trees wearing blankets of white along their branches, and of the recently plowed road into the resort.

I loved everything about it. Being part of the "OG" crew here at the resort, and being right down the hall from Harrison too.

"This is great," I told Harrison, turning from the window to find him watching me expectantly.

"It's not as nice as a modern place would be," he said, sounding as if he felt responsible for this.

"It's amazing," I said. "It's nicer than my apartment in LA, and it's better than being in Bennie's way all the time at her place. I love it. Plus," I said, stepping near enough for him to slide his arms around my waist. "You're right down the hall."

He grinned. "That is a bonus."

Harrison leaned in, the smell of his soap and aftershave filling my senses and twisting up my insides. His firm bottom lip brushed against mine, as if he was testing to see if I'd resist. I let my head fall back slightly, my lips answering his, and his arms tightened around me as he deepened the kiss. When his tongue teased the center of my top lip, tingles shot through me, and I met his tongue with my own, chasing the pleasure his skillful kisses brought to every single part of my body.

Time dipped and swirled around us as we kissed there in front of the big window, and for those moments I thought of nothing but how happy I felt in Harrison's arms. Protected and taken care of, cherished, respected. Harrison had me feeling things I wasn't sure I'd ever felt before. None of my previous relationships had felt so equal, so open. The other party was always trying to get something from me, something they could use. Even my parents had used me. But Harrison's expectations weren't about what I could do for him, they seemed to revolve around me instead. Was I safe, was I happy? He cared about me, and I could feel it in the soft press of his body to mine. I could see it in the way he looked out for me, even in the little things.

"Thank you," I said, my voice breathy and quiet as I broke the kiss to catch my breath.

"For what?" He smiled at me, keeping me tight against his broad chest.

"For everything." I wanted to say more, to explain why it was a big deal that he was looking out for me, tell him about my life before this, but he was kissing me again before I could continue, and I was practically powerless to stop. And when we finally did break apart, each of us flushed and panting, we were already late for work.

"We'll continue this tonight," he said.

Chapter 16
She's Not Our Girl

HARRISON

Staff training week was a mix of classroom work and time spent out on the slopes. The ski patrol had their own training program, and everyone intersected during meals, so the resort was suddenly full and busy, and probably rowdier than it would be the following week when actual guests came. At least I hoped so.

Penny spent most of the week in the back office, which I supposed was normal. I wished our paths crossed more often in the course of a regular day, but she had a tendency to get to meals very late, after almost everyone else has cleared out.

After moving her into her room this morning, I'd been fighting an almost giddy desire to see her all day. It was a strange feeling, and I knew there was something there I should probably investigate a bit more deeply, but for now I was enjoying it instead.

"Professor?" The kid, Teague, stood next to the table where I was having lunch on my own after a very long morning reviewing the procedures for group lessons with kids on skis.

"What's up, Teague?" Two of the other instructors stood next to him, looking slightly uncomfortable, which was how all my students had always looked when they'd had to come speak to me. *Empathy for Assholes* was clearly not making an impact yet.

"Yeah, so, we just wondered. You said something about staff discounts on passes and stuff, and like, for our families?"

I squinted up at him. "Was there a question in there?"

One of the other kids, a tall, thin kid who'd been quiet through most of the training week, spoke up. "Yessir. Does our staff discount extend to family members or friends?"

Adam. That was the kid's name. Adam was direct and articulate. I liked Adam. "I'll need to ask, Adam," I told them. "But I'll find out for you when I'm done with my lunch, okay?"

I looked from face to face, but none of them was looking at me now, their eyes were all following Penny as she picked up a tray and went through the food line.

"Is that Our Girl?" The other kid asked, his voice almost a whisper.

"Chrissy," Teague said, as if confirming something.

"That's Penny," I told them, wondering why the hell they'd refer to her as their girl. She was my girl if she was anyone's. "She's the one who makes sure you get paid, so you better be respectful to her."

Adam shook his head and looked back at me. "She looks just like the girl from that show."

"You guys have more questions?" I asked, picking my sandwich up again.

"No sir," Teague said, finally looking back at me and away from Penny, which was good because something in me did not react well to these three young guys drooling over my . . . my what?

The ski instructors departed, and Penny came to join me with her tray.

"Made quite an impression on my staff there," I told her.

"I did?" Penny looked worried—more concerned than I would have expected her to be.

"I think they're just not used to seeing gorgeous women up close," I said, pulling her chair out for her.

"Thanks," she said settling, but her face did not clear.

"You okay?"

Penny took a second, and then her expression returned to normal. "Yeah, of course. Just busy today." She smiled at me, and I had to fight an overwhelming urge to pick her up and carry her up to my room, but I valiantly fought that urge down and just smiled at her instead.

"How's your day?" she asked.

"It's been long and it's only half over," I said. "Spending my days trapped in a room with a bunch of ski bums is exhausting."

"Isn't it a bit like your previous job?" She lifted her sandwich and took a bite.

"Turns out that was exhausting too."

"But you liked it." She spoke around her sandwich in a way I found oddly adorable. It was kind of a question, kind of a statement.

"I'm not sure I liked it. Or that it was actually a good fit. One of the things I'm learning in this book I'm reading is that some people just aren't cut out for jobs where you interact with other people. I'm not good at the people part."

"Are you reading a career guide or something?"

I frowned. I didn't really want to admit that I was so inept with people that I'd turned to a self-help book. But Penny already knew why I'd lost the tenured position at Archer. "It's supposed to teach me to be more empathetic."

Penny chewed, her big eyes watching me thoughtfully. Then she straightened, as if deciding what to say. "I think you are empathetic," she said.

She was being nice. But I knew the truth. "I'm not. It was why they let me go. I can't relate well to people, people don't trust me, so they aren't comfortable talking to me."

"I'm comfortable with you," she said, a tiny smile hiking up one corner of her full lips.

I sighed, both to try to stifle the urge to lean in and capture those lips with my own, and because she was just wrong. "That's probably different. You know me. I know you."

"But what I'm saying is that you do have empathy, but maybe you just don't waste it on lots of people you don't know well. Maybe you reserve it for a few that you really care about." As soon as she said the words, she dropped my gaze. "I mean, I didn't mean to imply that—"

"I do really care about you, Penny," I told her, knowing it was true. I'd been thinking about it a lot, and figured she might as well know.

The little smile took over her pretty mouth again and she looked up at me through thick dark lashes. "Oh you do, do you?" Everything about her was teasing me, and I was desperate to respond, but we had half a work day still to get through.

"I do. And I plan to show you just as soon as we're done with work. Text me when you get off."

She raised an eyebrow at me.

"I mean. If you want to." Maybe I'd assumed too much?

"I want to," she whispered, and I wished I could take her right there, on the table in the center of the restaurant.

"I'll see you later," I said, pushing my chair out and rising. My cock had decided to involve itself in our conversation, and I needed to distract myself before it was impossible to walk away. It was uncomfortable enough as it was.

"See you," she said, and all I wanted was to hear that lilting voice whispering and moaning in my ear, in private. Later.

* * *

When the day was over, I took a quick shower and was just toweling off when my phone chimed.

Penny: Come over?

I responded, pulled on clothes in record time, and practically bolted from the room after stuffing a few supplies into my pocket.

Penny cracked the door open when I knocked.

"Oh, hello there," she said, her voice higher than normal. "Can I help you, sir?"

Her smile told me we were playing a game, and my blood heated immediately. "Hello, ma'am. Is the man of the house around?"

She shook her head. "I'm all alone," she said, playing along. But then she frowned. "Why does there have to be a man of the house, anyway? It's my house."

"Do you want to get into a conversation about gender roles right now?" I asked her, still standing in the hallway.

"No," she laughed, opening the door wider. "Please, sir, come in and tell me more about the encyclopedias you're selling."

"I have to be an encyclopedia salesman in this scenario?"

"Vacuum cleaners? Knives?"

I stepped inside and closed the door behind me, moving close to Penny so she was looking up at me, our chests nearly touching. "Maybe I'm not selling anything," I suggested. "Since you're such a renaissance woman, maybe I'm just the guy you call when you're looking for a little—"

"Wait, like a hooker?"

"Penny, this role-playing isn't going especially well." I lifted my hand to capture her jaw, loving the way her mouth formed a soft O as her eyes softened at my touch. "Maybe we can just try something else."

She nodded gently, her arms coming around my waist.

I dropped my head to hers, slanting my mouth to her lips, and though I'd intended to be gentle, to take it slow, it was like the simple contact unleashed a hurricane. The heat between us spiraled out of control, and soon hands were gripping and pulling at clothes, each of us panting and gasping.

When Penny was left in nothing but her panties and a simple grey bra, I broke away, taking her hand and pulling her toward the bedroom, but she resisted. I stood, waiting to see what she had in mind, every cell in my body screaming for her, to touch her, to feel her around me. I wanted to bury myself in her again—it was all I could think about since the last time we'd been together.

Penny moved to the window that looked out over the snowy front of the resort, and lifted her arms, bracing one on either side of the scene through the glass. Then she turned her head and smiled at me over her shoulder, pushing her gorgeous ass backwards. Was she teasing me? Or was it an invitation?

I didn't waste time asking. I stepped close and took her hips in my hands, pressing myself into her as she threw her head back into my chest and moaned. I let my hands roam, exploring her soft belly, sliding up her ribs to cup her breasts through the soft fabric of her bra, and finally dipping down to trace the line of her thighs just below the tiny patch of silk covering her pussy.

"You don't want to move to the bed?" I asked her, nipping at her earlobe as my fingers teased their way closer to her center. Penny was pressing into me, wiggling her perfect ass in a way that made me want to pound into her right here. But I had more empathy than that.

Maybe my asshole book was working.

"No," she moaned. "Right here. I want to watch the snow fall."

It had begun snowing again this afternoon, and the scene outside was quiet and serene as darkness fell. The day staff had departed, and this was one of the few quiet nights we'd have left here.

I peeled Penny's panties from her body and retrieved a condom from my jeans, rolling it onto my steel-hard cock before retaking my place behind her at the window. I hoped there was no one out there in the woods, watching us, since there was one light glowing in the far corner of the room, but I didn't actually care much if there was someone out there. Nothing could distract me from Penny's perfect body.

I teased her some more, rubbing myself between the cheeks of her butt as my fingers circled and dipped into her soft wet folds, dancing over the sensitive nub of her clit.

When she was gasping for breath and shivering with need, I bent my knees and notched myself at her hot entrance as she arched her back to give me access. She braced her hands on the windowsill as I slid into her, centimeter by centimeter. This would be the only part of this that was slow, I knew. I could feel my self control slipping further and further away.

"Oh god," she moaned, the desperation in her voice matching my own.

I pulled out and then thrust into her, holding her hips

between my hands to give me better control. I thrust again and again, trying to keep the rhythm smooth even as Penny gasped and moaned in a way that made me want to lose every rational thought and just pound relentlessly until I found my release. But I wouldn't do that.

Because again, empathy.

When I was so close to the edge that my spine was tingling, my vision was beginning to fade and my balls were so tight I thought they might either disappear or explode, I reached one hand around to circle Penny's clit. And it sent her over the edge.

And hearing Penny's voice like that? Broken and desperate and needy as she ground out her release on my cock? That sent me right along with her.

Stars exploded against my eyelids as I let go, thrusting into her until I heard my own voice match hers, until my release pulsed out of me for what seemed long minutes. Until Penny was limp before me, still impaled on my twitching dick, beautiful and vulnerable and spent.

"Holy fuck," she breathed, bracing herself with her hands on the windowsill. "God, that was amazing.

I still had no capacity for words, but let my hands slide smoothly over her back, trying to tell her I felt the same. My knees were shaking and I thought there was a chance I'd collapse. "Should we move to the bed now?"

"Yeah," she breathed. But then she stiffened. "What. What's this? There's something here."

"There's definitely something here," I assured her, feeling slightly cocky about what we'd just done and the fact she seemed a little off balance too.

"No," she said, turning to look at me with wide eyes. "Here. Under the windowsill. I can feel it. There's something here."

Chapter 17
Sticking Pointy Things in and Wiggling Them Around

PENNY

My fingers, which had been gripping the windowsill for dear life a few moments before as Harrison took me to a level of pleasure I hadn't even thought existed, were now brushing against something on the bottom side of the sill that definitely shouldn't have been there.

"What is it?" Harrison asked, moving his glorious heat away from my back so he could step around me to squat down next to the window.

"I don't know." I joined him, dropping low and trying to look under the old wood frame.

Harrison was tracing his fingers where mine had been, and I heard him suck in a quick breath. "It's wedged in there good."

"That's what she said," I muttered, earning a chuckle from Harrison as he leaned down to look.

We both angled ourselves to see beneath the sill, and our simultaneous gasps would have been comical—especially since we were both squatting on the floor completely naked and probably fairly disheveled from our last activity.

There, cut roughly into the wood beneath the sill and wedged into the opening, was a big, metal key.

"You think that's the one?" He'd told me about the failure they'd had trying to break down the door and the all-out search for an old key.

"Only one way to find out," Harrison said. "Let's get it out."

"Maybe if we stick something kinda pointy in there we can wiggle it out."

Harrison looked at me with barely suppressed amusement on his handsome face. "That's what she said."

"Ha ha. Hold on." I dug through my bag and returned with a metal nail file, handing it to him.

Harrison worked for a few minutes, trying to pop the key from its snug hiding spot, and finally managed to pry it loose. The old key hit the wood-planked floor with a clang. I picked it up, the old thing cold and hefty in my hands, and we both stared at it in awe, as if we'd just discovered the Holy Grail or a place in Maryland that didn't cover every shrimp with Old Bay seasoning. (According to Wiley, these didn't exist.)

"Let's go see if it works," he said, pulling his pants back on in a rush.

"No."

He stopped. "No?"

"It's cold and snowy out. It's dark. And I'm guessing Archie probably wants to be there when that door gets opened."

"But we could go see if the key even fits. I don't want Ghost to be disappointed."

"He's a grownup, and he'll want to know what we found. He can handle the disappointment. And I'm not ready to leave this room just yet," I told Harrison, stepping close to him and pressing my chest against his.

"You don't play fair." His voice had dropped to the low, sexy growl I loved.

"We'll show him the key in the morning." I took the old key from his hand, laid it atop the big wooden desk near the window, and then returned to help Harrison out of his pants again. "You don't need these." I led him to the bedroom, and for the rest of the night, neither of us talked about keys or doors or treasure.

We didn't rush off to find Archie in the morning either, though part of me knew he'd want to know right away about the key we'd found. We had agreed not to be too explicit about just how we'd found the key, and we'd also agreed that it might be nice to stay in bed for a little while, considering the Saturday mornings for the foreseeable future would undoubtedly be workdays, at least for Harrison.

"I kinda wish we could stay in this moment forever," he said, his chest reverberating beneath my cheek. "Just curled up and hidden from real life."

"That's what she said?"

"Doesn't work there."

We were quiet a long moment as I thought about how much my life had changed, how dramatically things had shifted from the place I'd been when I left Los Angeles. I hadn't thought about the scandal, not really, in weeks. And I'd never expected to find myself in the arms of a handsome man, one I could actually imagine a future with—even though we were definitely not thinking about that. We'd agreed that this was whatever it was for now.

But something in me wanted more. Wanted to see past the end of the ski season.

"Truth?" I said quietly, my voice as tentative as I felt.

"Always," Harrison answered, his hand rubbing my shoulder reassuringly.

"I wish you weren't leaving at the end of the season. I wish we could just stay like this forever, in this in-between phase. Together." Even though he'd just said something similar, my heart lodged in my throat as if I'd just admitted something big.

"In between?"

"Where we just are. Where I'm so happy, and we don't have to name this. Where we can just be."

His hand pulled me closer and rubbed big warm circles on my back as I breathed in the woodsy scent of him. "Me too," he said softly.

Did that mean he was thinking about more than just the season? About what it would be like if we could stay together somehow?

We didn't say anything else about the future, or about us. We lounged in my bed, exploring one another until we had certainly missed whatever breakfast Aubrey and Annalee had organized downstairs, and finally we got up and showered.

"I guess we should find Archie," I said, pulling on a long-sleeved T-shirt.

"Yes," Harrison said. "And then we should go skiing."

I laughed at the idea. "I don't know how to ski. Like, at all."

"Perfect time to learn. You have all season to get the hang of it, and today there's no one else on the mountain."

I glanced out the window, as if I could find some excuse not to do it out there, in all that snow. "Um."

"So that's a yes."

"It was an 'um.'"

"I'll teach you. It'll be fun."

"It sounds terrifying, actually."

"You can't live at a ski resort all season and not even try." He came close and pulled me against his chest, bringing his soapy clean manly scent with him. I was powerless against the sensory assault of his body and his scent and his handsome face smiling down at me.

"Fine."

"Great. Get your ski clothes on. We'll talk to Ghost and then head out."

"I have no ski clothes, Harrison."

"Good thing there's a ski shop downstairs. Put on some of those sexy tight leggings, and we'll get everything else down there."

"Great." I did as I had been ordered, and then followed Harrison from my room. I'd never really thought about skiing, but it turned out I was willing to follow this man just about anywhere. He pocketed the huge key, and together, we went downstairs to find Archie and Aubrey.

They were sitting, along with Annalee, Mateo, Mateo's daughter, Lily, Lucy, Will, and Wiley in the lounge off the far side of the lobby, a fire blazing in the big stone fireplace. I hadn't been in this room a lot, but it was the kind of place you'd want to bring a book and just spend the day. The room was filled with overstuffed chairs and leather couches, low tables and little poufy ottomans, and dominated by the two-story stone fireplace we'd gotten cleaned out and certified for use only this week.

"Wow, this place is amazing," Harrison said, looking around. It had been locked for much of the time we'd been here, mostly to prevent any of us from getting good ideas about lighting the fire, since we were fairly sure there'd been something living in the chimney. Now that it was ready to go, I imagined we would be in here a lot. Or the guests would, at least.

"Right?" Aubrey asked. She sat on Wiley's lap, her arms comfortably around his neck. I had a pang of jealousy at their easy love for one another. I wanted that. But we were different. We were temporary.

"So, Penny found something in her room," Harrison said.

Archie's spine straightened, and he leaned forward, his expression eager. "Found what?"

"I think it might be the key to that door out back," I said, holding my hand out to Harrison. For some reason, I wanted to give it to Archie. It had been in my room, after all.

He handed it to me and I held it up for everyone to see.

"Holy shit," Annalee said loudly, glancing at Mateo and Lily and mouthing "sorry." Lily held her hand out and Annalee stood up, digging in her jeans pocket. She pulled out a dollar and handed it to Lily. "Damn swear jar."

Lily held her hand out again.

"Damn is not a swear word," Annalee cried.

"Can we get back to the damn key?" Archie asked, holding his own hand out.

I handed him the big metal key. "Holy shit," Aubrey said, then glanced around quickly. "I'm not part of the jar thing. I'm exempt."

"If everyone was in on that, Lily would have her college education funded in two weeks," Will said.

"Good plan," Mateo said. "Everyone's in."

"Like fuck we are," Harrison growled.

Lily held out her hand, but something in Harrison's face made her put it down again. Poor Lily. Harrison's grumpy face could definitely be scary.

"Let's go see if it fits!" Aubrey said, jumping out of Wiley's lap to examine the key.

Archie stood. "Get geared up. We're going treasure hunting."

"Aubrey?" I interrupted, pulling her bright gaze up. "Would it be okay if I grab some snow gear from the ski shop? I'll keep the tags and take it out of my next paycheck."

"You should have ski gear," Archie said. "And if there's treasure behind this door, we can afford to outfit everyone here."

"Take what you need," Aubrey said. "We'll figure it out later."

The bookkeeper in me still planned to take it out of my paycheck, but I appreciated the spirit of generosity. "Thanks."

"Meet out back in twenty," Archie said, putting the key into his own pocket. "And we'll see what Uncle Marvin left us."

"Think this is really it?" Will asked as everyone stood and got ready to go put on their snow gear.

"I hope so," Archie said. "I don't know how many more wrong turns I can take."

Chapter 18
The Door

HARRISON

Aubrey and Penny disappeared into the darkened ski shop, which lay at one end of the resort, beneath the finished guest wing. Twenty minutes later, they rejoined the group, which was gathered on the patio outside, standing around the inactive fire pit, as if hoping it might spring to life and take the cutting chill from the air. The first snow was early, and winter seemed determined to stick.

Penny was decked out in hot pink ski pants and a jacket with a pink stripe across the front, a pair of black gloves, a hat with pom-pom on top of it, and snow boots. She looked adorable, and I had to fight the urge to get to work on the zipper, which she had pulled up to her chin.

"What do you think?"

"I won't lose you on the ski hill," I said. "Not in those pants."

"Too much?" She did a little turn in front of me, grinning.

"Never."

"Fashion show complete," Ghost said, his barely contained excitement channeling into the pilot persona I remember trusting more than almost any other. Serious, focused, commanding. "Let's go." He turned and led the group off toward the trail.

Toward the treasure, we hoped.

Part of me wondered if it would be as exciting being here without the promise of Uncle Marvin's booty suffusing the place with a kind of lingering magic. Though as she marched ahead of me, I thought that maybe the promise of Penny's booty could be even more motivating.

When we arrived at the spot where the big rock marked the trap door, it was little more than a lump in the snow thanks to the endless flakes that had been falling.

Fake Tom got to work with the shovel he'd been carrying, and the rest of us watched.

"Will looks good performing manual labor," Lucy commented to Monroe as they observed.

"Funny," Fake Tom shot over his shoulder.

Monroe shrugged and bumped Lucy with her shoulder. "All yours. He'll always be Fake Tom to me. Just a little too . . . something," she said.

"I can hear you, you know," Fake Tom said.

"Then you're not working hard enough," Monroe said.

I missed our squadron days a little bit just then. The easy

camaraderie we'd all shared, the quick wit and sharp tongues, the complete trust in each other. Real life had proven to be somewhat less reassuring, and I'd never felt as capable as when I'd been in the cockpit with these guys on my wings.

"Good to go," Fake Tom said, backing away from the exposed wood of the trap door.

"I'll do the honors," Aubrey said, stepping in to lift the door. It was heavy, and as soon as she lifted a corner, bending down awkwardly in the thick snow, it slipped from her hands. "Little help?"

"I thought you wanted to do the honors," Wiley said, moving to the other corner of the door.

"Just need a hand, that's all."

"Hang on, I need to make a note of the first time in life you've ever admitted you need help," Wiley said, smiling at her.

"Would you guys please just open the door?" Ghost didn't seem amused by the banter. Or foreplay. Whatever it was.

The big wood plank was slowly raised to reveal the stairway, and within a few minutes, we were all heading down into the tunnel, phone lights illuminating the path ahead of us. It was less anxiety-inducing being down here this time, with the walls and ceiling shored up a bit, but it still wasn't completely comfortable. The tunnel smelled like damp earth, and there was a musty, ghostly feeling to it near the door at the end. The whole tunnel was probably fifty feet long, long enough that the light from the open trap door was impossible to see when you stood at the other end, in front of the locked metal door.

I suppressed a shiver, and Penny stepped close, pressing her side against mine in the tight space. I wanted to put my arms around her, but we hadn't made anything official, not with the rest of the crew, and I didn't want to push her into anything she wasn't ready for.

"Here goes nothing," Ghost said, pulling the key from his pocket.

He pushed the hefty metal key into the hole beneath the knob on the door, but it didn't quite go in. He squatted in front of the door and shone his light on the hole. "It's kind of blocked up with some dirt and crap. Anyone got a bobby pin or something?"

We all turned to look at Monroe, who lifted her hands and looked around apologetically. "It's just a call sign. I'm not actually a pinup girl or a movie star. No hairpins here, sorry."

"I've got a toothpick," Wiley said, handing it to Ghost.

"My hero," Aubrey said softly.

"Yeah until you sit on my lap and get that thing poking you in the ass."

"Please, let's not discuss my sister getting poked anywhere," Ghost shot out, working the toothpick into the hole and clearing out years of dust and grime. "Okay, here we go."

He lifted the big key to the hole again, this time sliding it in all the way. And when he turned it, an audible clank could be heard within the door as the lock let go.

"Yes," he murmured, standing and dropping a hand to the knob. "Ready?"

Anticipation built around us and I felt a palpable excitement rising inside me, even though if there was treasure beyond the door, it certainly wasn't mine.

There were sounds of agreement, and Ghost turned the knob, pulling the heavy door toward us slowly. Whatever lay beyond the door was dark, and the musty smell that had suffused the tunnel was stronger now, years of still air mixing with the fresh air we'd let in when we'd opened the trap door.

"What's in there?" Aubrey practically shouted through the group, the narrow tunnel forcing us to enter the space ahead in an almost single-file line.

"You're not gonna believe it," Ghost called back, his voice practically giddy. "This is it!"

Surprise bolted through me at his words. There really was treasure?

Soon, we all stood gathered in the room, peering down at a chest. I stared at an actual ancient looking treasure chest that was almost as big as the coffee table in my hotel room. The locked room turned out to be fairly large, and there was another door at the opposite end, the walls made of concrete instead of dirt. It looked a lot like the basement storage rooms at the resort.

"Where does that door go?" I asked, pointing, but the rest of the group was focused on the chest.

"That thing better not be locked," Monroe said. She meant the chest, but I moved to the back of the room to the other door.

"It's not," Ghost said, as he and Aubrey knelt next to it, slowly lifting the lid.

I pulled open the opposite door, which was thankfully not locked, and found myself staring at vague chinks of light through piles of paper towels, toilet paper, towels, and other supplies. I was behind a storage rack in the basement of the resort. This tunnel connected to the resort. Through an unlocked door!

"I think we took the hard way here," I told them, but no one was listening to me. I smiled to myself and shut the door again, turning back to see what treasure we'd finally found.

"Um." Lucy did not sound excited about whatever they'd discovered. Oh no, I didn't want to see Ghost disappointed after all this.

"Seriously?" Ghost's tone assured me that it was definitely not a chest full of money.

"What is it?" I asked, trying to look over the crowd on the floor.

"A photo album," Aubrey said. "Uncle Marvin and Lola's wedding. And some stuff after."

"Oh, and these look earlier," Lucy said, flipping pages in the album, which had been spread open on the floor.

"Is there anything else?" Fake Tom asked.

"Wait, yeah," Ghost said, working at something in the chest. "This thing has a false bottom. Or a shelf. Whatever. Help me move it out."

Fake Tom reached down and I joined them on the opposite side, and together we lifted out a surprisingly heavy shelf that was wedged into the top of the chest. I set it aside, as Ghost made a noise that was somewhat more appreciative than the one he'd let out on discovery of his uncle's album.

"This could be something." He pulled a wrapped item from the bottom of the chest. It wasn't big, but had been carefully wrapped in tissue, and when Ghost unrolled it, a faint gleam caught one of the flashlight beams, silencing the group. Ghost removed the rest of the paper to reveal a necklace, wrought in shining gold and studded with very large red and blue stones.

That looked like real treasure to me.

"Costume," Aubrey said. "Let's assume it's costume jewelry."

"Even costume jewelry from a certain era is worth a lot of money," Penny said. "And those stones are huge. Real or not, that's gonna be valuable."

"Huh," Ghost said, setting the piece down gently on the tissue he'd put next to him.

Aubrey was unrolling another piece, and within seconds we were all reaching into the chest, pulling out more jewels. I unwrapped a tiara while Penny discovered a handful of huge rings. All in all, there were at least twenty necklaces, several rings and bracelets, and a few hair pins and combs, all of them studded with what could be real jewels.

"Think this is the treasure?" Aubrey asked her brother, smiling widely.

"I guess so," he said, sounding disappointed.

"I have some news," I told them, now that the excitement over the chest had abated some. "We could have gotten in here a whole lot more easily."

"What?" Ghost turned around, his attention on me now.

I moved to the door and pulled it open, punching a stack of toilet paper rolls out of the way and shining my light into the basement of the resort.

"Holy shit," Aubrey said. "How did we miss that door?"

"It's behind a storage shelf," I said. "We didn't really look for hidden doors."

Ghost laughed, but the sound held little humor. "So it's over," he said. "We spent a summer and a ridiculous amount of money, and we've got some dress-up jewels and Marvin's photo album."

I felt a little let down too, though part of me was relieved we could finally move on.

"There might be more to it," Aubrey said hopefully.

Ghost shook his head, staring into the now empty treasure chest. He let out a hefty sigh. "Maybe it's for the best. I was becoming obsessed."

"No, really?" Fake Tom said. That was followed by an "oof" when Lucy elbowed him in the gut.

"Papa will be excited to see the photos," Lucy said. "Maybe we can take a look at the album a little more closely inside."

"I'll go around and clear the shelf," I told them. "We can push the chest through and give it a once-over in the light."

"Okay," Ghost said.

Penny and I headed back out the tunnel and up the stairs. As soon as we were back in daylight, she grabbed my hand.

"That was exciting," she said.

"How do you know about costume jewelry?" I asked her, impressed.

"Oh, just random knowledge." Her voice sounded strange, but I chalked it up to the biting cold air, which was making us both gasp a bit after the warmth of the tunnel.

We went inside and found the shelves blocking the open door, removing all the supplies and then pulling the shelves from the bracers, which were fastened to the wall. Once the bottom few shelves had been removed, Ghost pushed the chest through and the others followed.

"I guess we should lock this door again," Aubrey said, pulling it closed behind her.

"It wasn't locked," I reminded her.

"I don't like having an open route into the resort," she said.

"Give me the key," Wiley said. "I'll re-lock the first door and then head up."

Ghost handed him the key and Wiley disappeared. Aubrey and Ghost collected the jewelry, planning to have it appraised down in Denver somewhere, and Monroe picked up the album.

"I'll put this in the bar, okay Ghost?"

"Sure."

"Mind if we look at it a bit, or do you want us to wait?" she asked.

"Go ahead," he said, sounding deflated.

Monroe headed out with the album, Lucy and Fake Tom with her.

"You okay, man?" I asked Ghost.

"Yeah," he said, staring into the treasure chest at his feet. "I might just stay here a second. Kind of thinking, you know?"

"Sure." I glanced at Penny, who nodded at me. She thought we should leave Ghost on his own for a minute. Aubrey had followed the others up to the bar, and Ghost looked sad and alone standing there, the empty promise on the floor, revealing nothing he'd hoped for. "We'll see you in the bar later."

"Yeah," he said.

Penny and I left, heading back into the main resort, the removal of the hope of treasure making the whole place glow just a little less brightly around us.

Chapter 19
Pizza, Pizza, French Fry

PENNY

I'd planned to head into the bar with the others, hoping to get a look at the photo album. It might not have been treasure by standard definitions, but it was exactly the kind of thing I loved—ties to the past. It wasn't something I had, since neither of my parents had kept in touch with their own families, and here I was, continuing the cycle of family estrangement.

As I followed behind Aubrey, our snow pants making soft "schwick, schwick" sounds in the silent lobby, Harrison caught my hand.

"Not so fast," he said, tugging me over to one side of the huge space.

"What do you mean?"

"Ski lesson. Remember?"

"Truth?"

His eyes softened and he inclined his head, as if to hear me better.

"I'm scared."

The little wrinkles at the corners of his eyes formed, as his sexy lips pulled into a reassuring smile. "I've got you, Penny."

Something about those specific words put my fears to rest. No one had ever really "had" me, had they? I'd been looking out for myself most of my life, and those who should have "had" me were actually using me. But Harrison? The way those steely blue eyes held my gaze, the way his firm grip secured my hand . . . he did have me.

"Okay," I whispered, and we headed back to the ski shop.

Soon, I was outfitted with skis and boots, poles, a helmet, and goggles.

"You can go without the poles if you want," Harrison said, causing me to grip them even tighter as we stood on our skis at the very top of an enormous mountain, which he'd referred to several times as the "bunny hill." Whatever bunnies tackled this hill were braver than I was, that was certain.

There was a conveyer belt coming up the middle that he'd switched on, and I'd stood on it to get to the top. Harrison called it a magic carpet, but I thought of it more as the highway to Hell. Probably not an appropriate name to use when they taught little kids to ski, though.

"These poles are the only thing keeping me attached to my nerve," I told him, gripping them tighter still as I stood sideways to the hill below me, certain a painful fall was in my very near future.

Harrison talked for a while, and demonstrated a few of the things he talked about, sliding slowly and easily down the hill, his skis in a wedge. He came back up on Hell's highway and skated gracefully over to where I stood completely motionless for fear of falling without even moving. "Ready to try?"

"Not at all."

"It's physics, sweetheart. Putting the tips together will add enough resistance to keep you going nice and slow, and we're not going straight down. Just an easy slide to one side to start."

"Sure. Right." I wasn't exactly terrified, but suddenly I was questioning the intelligence of humans as a race. It was cold and there was snow on the ground. We should have been inside reading books or having sex, but instead, we'd decided to stuff ourselves into padded suits, put sticks on our feet, and see if we could hurtle down a mountain without dying. Smart.

"Hey," Harrison said, stepping close and peering into my eyes through the goggles. He lifted his own goggles and smiled at me. But something about my expression stifled the smile and he looked uncertain. "Hey. If you really don't want to do this, we don't have to. I know I'm not exactly the most perceptive when it comes to other peoples' feelings. Am I forcing you into this? Not being empathetic enough?"

He put a strange emphasis on the word "empathetic" that caught my attention and distracted me from the fear roiling inside me. "You're always attentive to my needs," I told him. "No one has ever treated me like you do—carefully, thoughtful-ly." His smile returned. "This right here?" I waved my pole at the drop of death in front of me. "This is just simple fear of death or dismemberment. That's all."

"Do you want to try?"

I sucked in a deep breath and steeled myself. People skied every day. This was not life or death. And Harrison was here.

"Well, I don't want to give up without trying. But I don't want to be dismembered, either."

He grinned. "I've got you, Penny. I won't let you get hurt."

I believed him. And so when he motioned me to angle my skis toward the far side of the hill, reminding me to wedge them into the shape of a pizza slice and bend my knees into a kind of squat, I followed directions. And soon I was sliding slowly toward the side of the hill.

It was terrifying.

"Great!" Harrison called, skiing backwards in front of me, watching my every move.

Showoff.

"Now shift all your weight to that downhill foot and think about turning the tips to face a little uphill."

"It's hard to think about anything when I'm moving at death-defying speeds like this!" I yelled, trying to follow his advice.

I managed to slow down, but kept sliding forward until Harrison moved himself to catch me in his arms, his skis angled outside my own and his big body providing a firm but soft resistance to stop my slide.

"That was good!" He said, hugging me and grinning.

I waved the poles out to my sides. "What are these for?"

"They help some people balance. Like I said, you really don't need them. If we do moguls later, you'll want them."

"Moguls? What's that?" I imagined wealthy businessmen chasing me and possibly fending them off with the ski sticks.

"Little bumps in the slope. We only have one mogul run set up right now and it's a black diamond."

Harrison had explained the colors to me. I was not going to be visiting any black diamond slopes. Probably ever.

"No moguls please."

"Let's go the other way," he suggested, and soon, I was

wedging my skis together and sliding toward the other side of the mountain. We went like that, back and forth, repeatedly. In between slides, we rode the hellish highway back to the top, and before too long, I was feeling a bit more confident on my skis, getting on and off the conveyer with more ease, and less convinced I was tempting death with every slide across the bunny hill.

Harrison showed me how to turn, and gave me so much praise that I almost believed him when he told me I was a natural.

By the time he suggested we take the lift up to an easy run, I was eating up his praise like jellybeans.

"If you think I'm ready," I said, exhilaration filling my body. I was beginning to understand why people liked to do this.

The ski lift was a horrific contraption of constantly moving chairs, but Harrison had called Antonio and Sasquatch out to help (and potentially to watch me fall down). Sasquatch stopped the lift for us to get on and then Antonio stopped it again at the top, where I promptly fell off the stupid thing.

Antonio and Harrison helped me up, but the bottom of the lift was a slope, so I started sliding down immediately, toward a snowbank at the back of the area that had a huge picture of the resort standing there on a couple big posts. It was big enough to catch me when I slid into it, crumpling to the ground in a heap.

"She okay?" Antonio called.

"I'm fine!" I called from my pile. But every time I tried to get up, my skis slid out from under me.

"I got you," Harrison said, lifting me to my feet and standing close enough to keep me from sliding away. "You okay?"

"You know how I said I was ready for this?" He nodded. "I'm not ready for this."

"Once we get to the top of the hill, it'll be less scary."

"This isn't the top?" Fear made my voice sound a little screechy.

"This is just the unloading area for the lift. I think we made it a bit steep. I'll get the guys up here with the bobcat to level it a bit."

"On it," Antonio called back. "Cool if I download?"

"As long as Sass is still at the bottom," Harrison told him. Antonio set the lift running again, radioed Sass at the bottom and then hopped onto one of the descending chairs. By the time the lift stopped again, telling us he'd unloaded below, we'd managed to get to the more level area at the top of the hill.

"Here we go!" Harrison skied a little ways below me, and I found the courage to follow. Soon, we were slowly moving back and forth across the gentle slope, the wind and sun and land-scape pasting a perma-grin on my face. I didn't fall again, not until we reached the bottom, and I decided that one day I might become a skiier. Harrison called to me as we went down, "Pizza, pizza, French fry," to help me remember how to wedge my skis and when to straighten them out. It made me hungry.

"That was exhilarating!" I told Harrison, who skied over and pulled me into his arms.

"I'm so glad you like it! You really are a natural. I've seen people spend an entire season on the bunny hill."

"Thanks," I told him. "For teaching me, and for being patient."

"Any time. We can come out again tomorrow if you want."

"Definitely!" I was proud of myself for facing something scary. Now I wanted to do it again.

We popped off our skis and headed inside, storing them in the staff lockers in the back office. I left my parka in there too, along with my helmet, gloves, and goggles.

"I need a shower," I said. It was surprising how sweaty you could get when trying to defy death in freezing temperatures.

"Your shower or mine?" Harrison asked, his voice practically a purr.

I raised an eyebrow at him, and then glanced around to see if anyone was nearby. "Mine," I told him, and soon we were clean, wet, and very satisfied.

* * *

That evening, everyone gathered in the bar, along with CeeCee and Bennie, Lucy's grandfather Ernie, and Lily, Mateo's daughter. It was the last Saturday night we'd have the bar to ourselves before guests invaded.

The photo album we'd discovered lay on the bar, open to a wedding photo of Marvin and Lola. I stared down at the couple. It was an informal wedding, from the looks of it, Marvin and Lola dressed up but not in traditional wedding attire. She held a bouquet, and they stood in front of a chapel with a sign above it that said "Kasper Ridge Worship."

The smile on her face kept pulling me back. It was serene and certain, and something about it told me she loved the man at her side unquestioningly. The thought gave me chills. Would I ever feel that certain about another person?

"She's so pretty," Bennie said over my shoulder.

"I guess that's why she was so famous," I said. "Annie Lowe gave up an incredible career to come up here."

"Why?" CeeCee asked, leaning in. "Why would she leave all that behind?"

"Look at her face," I told them. "She was in love."

"Women do stupid things for love," CeeCee declared, stepping back. Sasquatch was leaning against the wall behind us, Roscoe sitting calmly at his feet as the enormous former pilot sipped a beer and watched the scene before him. CeeCee approached, and I heard her ask, "Can I pet your dog?"

"Roscoe is a working dog, you probably shouldn't—ah, okay sure."

CeeCee was already kneeling before Roscoe, and he was licking her face as she put one hand into the ruff on either side of his neck and talked to him in a baby voice, saying something unintelligible.

"He likes you," Sasquatch said, sounding mystified. "I really thought we'd be making a trip to the ER in a minute."

CeeCee glared up at him. "You might have mentioned it if you thought he was going to bite me." She returned her attention to the dog. "Besides, this guy wouldn't hurt anyone, would he? He's such a sweetie."

Sasquatch reached down to pet Roscoe, and the dog let out a low growl, making CeeCee peer up at the man. "Maybe I'm wrong."

"We're still bonding," Sasquatch told her, returning to his casual lean against the wall.

We'd been flipping through the pages of the album and came to one of the first pictures, which showed Lola and Marvin with another man, the three of them posed with their arms around one another, looking like a group of friends about to get into some kind of mischief.

"Who's this guy?" Harrison asked, pointing at the stranger.

Aubrey had joined us and she smiled, looking between our faces. "Rudy Fusterburg. Says so on the back."

"I thought your uncle hated that guy," Harrison said. "He named the bear after him, right? Didn't he leave some kind of note about him on Rufus's paw?"

Aubrey nodded. The note said, *"Rufus was named for Rudy "the traitor" Fusterburg. May he rot in hell."*

"Well, that's cheery," I said.

"But at one point, they were friends," Harrison pointed out.

"But if anything, seems like Rudy must've hated Marvin,

because Uncle Marvin stole his fiancée. Aunt Lola. This all means something. The mystery isn't over," Aubrey said, smiling at us while she bounced a little on her toes as she leaned over the bar. "And look at this." She flipped to the very last page of the album, where a list was scrawled in a shaky cursive hand.

"What are these?" Bennie asked. The written statements said things like, "Carefree in Chicago," and "Down and Out and Off Their Rockers."

"Movie titles," I supplied. I recognized a few old Annie Lowe movies I'd heard of or seen.

Aubrey grinned at me. "That's what I thought!" She pointed to the ones at the bottom of the list that were marked with an asterisk. "Why do you think these are marked?" She was asking me, but I didn't have an answer for her.

"No idea."

"Well, that's what we need to figure out next." Aubrey was practically glowing.

"You really think this is some kind of clue?" Harrison asked.

She nodded. "But don't tell Archie. I don't want to get his hopes up again."

I exchanged a glance with Harrison. He wouldn't like keeping a secret from his old squadron mate. But he said, "Maybe that's a good idea. Let us know if you need help."

Aubrey thanked us, and we spent the rest of the evening with our friends, enjoying the resort they'd created one last time before it became something else entirely.

Chapter 20
Let Me Get a Little Sniff

HARRISON

Penny and I agreed to get up early because she wanted to do a ski run before the all-hands staff meeting at ten. It was hard to convince myself to wake her up, though.

We lay in my bed, Penny curled against my chest, her dark hair spread across the pillow. Her breathing was soft, steady, and as I lay there with her gathered in my arms, I was reluctant to move. The moment felt suspended in time, precious and still, and the longer I lay awake watching Penny sleep, the deeper the twisting and longing inside my chest seemed to become.

Penny didn't ask for anything from me, she didn't point

out all the ways I was insufficient, something I'd experienced in every relationship I'd ever had. Women, in my experience, had been dissatisfied in my presence, leading me to feel repeatedly inadequate for the complex interpersonal requirements of intimacy. I had concluded that relationships were something I was not very good at. After all, they required empathy.

But Penny made it easy.

We were only together for the season, I knew that. We'd agreed upon it, and it made sense. I was leaving. But if I was the one driving us apart, wasn't it within my power to keep us together? She had said she wished we could stay like this too. If we both wanted to be together, why couldn't we be?

I pushed my nose against Penny's soft neck, inhaling the sweet scent of her. She didn't smell like flowers, or like sugar, but like something I couldn't identify, something that was unique to Penny. It was deep, comforting, and held a hint of something herbal and intriguing. It was Penny, and I couldn't get enough of it.

"Are you sniffing me?" Her sleepy voice pierced my contemplative bubble and time resumed its forward march.

"Of course not," I said. "That would be odd."

She rolled over in my arms, and I pushed her hair off her face, feeling the startling jolt that hit me every time I met her dark eyes with mine. Her cheeks were flushed, her lips slightly swollen and pink. My heart lurched. She was so beautiful.

"Truth?" she asked, her voice still thick with sleep.

"Okay."

"Sometimes when I'm close to you, I purposely smell you."

I felt the smile pull at the corners of my mouth. "You do? What do I smell like?"

She made a soft humming noise and leaned her head in, inhaling as her nose touched my collarbone. "The woods," she said. "The wind. The mountains, and something that's all you. Manly."

"I smell like trees and man." I liked her assessment.

She nodded and inhaled again. "It's my favorite smell." Her chin tilted against me, and her lips were on my collarbone then, her tongue leaving a trail of heat that had my lower body jumping to attention.

"If you keep doing that, we might not have time to ski this morning," I warned her.

"I can be quick," she said, and a moment later, her sweet softness was covering me as she rolled on top of me, her mouth finding mine as my hands filled themselves with her skin and my senses flooded with Penny.

She kissed me slowly, but the heat in the contact exploded within seconds, moving from a sleepy early morning encounter to something fiery and urgent. She was grinding against me as she kissed me, my cock trapped between us and stiffening rapidly with the friction of her body against me.

I let my hands explore, gliding along the smooth firm skin of her back, slipping down to the round fullness of her ass. I was torn between closing my eyes and letting the feeling and scent of Penny surround me, enjoying it all on a sensory level, and keeping them open so I didn't miss a second of her taking control and demanding her own pleasure.

She pressed her palms against my chest, pushing herself up slightly, and one hand slid between us, grasping my dick firmly and causing me to suck in a sharp breath.

"I love it when you touch me," I told her.

"I love touching you." She moved me between us, positioning me so that her wetness slid up and down, her hand braced beneath my cock, creating a pressure so glorious I never wanted it to end. But when it did, I didn't mind, because Penny was slipping me into her body, notching me against her slick, hot entrance and taking me in slowly.

It was almost too much - feeling her around me, her soft silky wetness inviting me inside, it was the closest thing to heaven I could imagine.

Penny answered my desire by moving her hips gently in an undulating motion, each forward roll taking me in a little more, each outward motion pulling away. It was the sweetest torture I'd ever endured, and I could feel my body demanding more, more. My hands found her hips again, and I forced myself to simply feel her motion, to let her guide us toward that beckoning cliff's edge.

Penny held herself up, her back arched and her perfect breasts jutting out before her, bouncing softly with every undulation of her hips. Her eyes had slipped shut, and her chin was lifted, her lips slightly open.

It was absolute fucking torture.

And I never wanted it to end.

It felt like years before she finally let me slide home, all the way inside her, deep and warm and hot.

"Fuck," I ground out, extending the word like a prayer asking both for this to be over immediately and for it to never, ever end.

Penny held me inside her and lowered her body to mine, her eyes meeting my gaze as her hands moved to trace my jaw. She kissed me then, and the twin sensations of being welcomed into her pussy and her mouth at once sent me spiraling, and my hips bucked into her without my intention.

She started to move then, a gentle glide that was like nothing I'd ever felt, her body clenching every inch of me as she pulled back and then releasing for the briefest second as she brought me back home, that clamp activating again when I was so deep inside her I could barely breathe. She repeated it, over and over, as my mind departed, and our voices began to fill the quiet morning.

"Oh god," she moaned, ratcheting my desire and the frenzy inside me higher and higher.

"Fuck, yes," I groaned, doing my best to hold on until I was certain Penny was right there with me.

"God," she said, repeating it like a chant to the rhythm of our bodies. When the chant began to break down, her voice cracking and the rhythm of her motion stuttering briefly, I knew she was there. As Penny's body clenched and released me, my hands found her hips and held her close, and when I was sure she'd gotten her release, I let go, my hips hammering up into her as I held her against me, and everything inside me focused on that singular connection between us. When I came, it was the sweetest, most incapacitating feeling I'd ever known, and I heard words coming from my lips that I'd never considered giving voice to before.

"You're so fucking good, so beautiful, so perfect. You're everything I've ever wanted."

Penny stilled when the words came out, and I wasn't sure at first if I'd said that out loud. But when I managed to regain consciousness and was able to pop one eye open, she was looking at me questioningly.

"Hi," I said, feeling a little embarrassed.

"Hi," she replied, the look still on her face, one dark eyebrow higher than the other. "You were saying some things there at the end."

I could play it off. I could act like I had no idea what had been coming out of my mouth. But that wasn't the guy I was.

"I know," I said. "I surprised myself too. But . . . truth?"

She nodded, a soft smile on her lips.

"I meant it. I didn't even know I was looking for you. And here you are. Perfect."

Penny stared at me and I watched emotions flit through her eyes one after another, though I couldn't really tell what they were. I tried to reassure her.

"We haven't known each other very long. Just a month." She said this softly, like she was still contemplating things.

I could feel our hearts beating in rhythm as the energy between us faded and settled back into the warm cozy morning. I felt dizzy and lightheaded with a happiness I didn't know I was capable of.

"But I feel the same," she said, her voice a whisper now.

I didn't think hearing words like these would have any effect on me. They were just words. But they were words that conveyed something I wasn't sure I'd ever find. And they changed something deep within me. And in a gruff assertion from my dad now and then. And that, of course, was very different.

My heart pumped inside me and my skin felt electric. Was this what everyone was talking about? Was this what life was supposed to be? This intimate connectedness with other people? With one other person I could no longer imagine living without?

I had a terrifying impulse to cry, something else that hadn't happened aside from maybe a few times in my life, and I stuffed it down urgently, my arms tightening further around Penny as I struggled to control my breath.

"Are you okay?" she asked, peering into my face, a little smile hooking up one side of her mouth.

"Yeah," I said. "I'm just . . . I've never felt this way before. I'm trying to figure it out."

"I don't think there's anything to figure out."

The emotions inside me began to calm. "I feel so lucky to have found you," I said, mystified at the truth of it.

"Me too," she said, hugging me and dropping her head to my chest.

After a while, we rolled out of bed, the whole world feeling different than it had when we'd gotten into it the night before. I felt changed. Like I understood something about life I'd never known before.

I let Penny use the bathroom first, and she came back out, wearing a long T-shirt she'd brought over for sleeping, but it had become unnecessary within minutes of getting into bed.

"I don't think we have time to ski," she said, glancing at the clock by my bed.

"Probably not." I didn't care in the least. The morning had been better than any time spent on the runs could have been.

"I'll go get ready. Meet you downstairs?"

"Okay," I said, kissing her again, pulling her against me and feeling that same sense of awe that she really loved me. That this was real. "See you soon."

Penny pulled on her leggings and disappeared, and I showered, letting the hot water slide over my skin, feeling like I was about to step into a whole new world.

Chapter 21
Time for a History Lesson

PENNY

Downstairs, the resort was almost unrecognizable for all the people wandering around. Over the last weeks, staff had been hired to manage every aspect of the place, and suddenly, there were people everywhere. Harrison and I exchanged a wary glance.

The warm glow inside me that had felt inextinguishable just moments before suddenly dimmed as one woman about my age watched me approach the entrance to the restaurant area where we were having the all-hands meeting before guests began arriving this afternoon.

"Hey!" she said, stepping in front of me and blocking my progress. I felt Harrison's attention on us, protectively hovering at my side. "I know you!"

"I don't think we've met," I said quickly, hoping to stop her from saying more. "I'm Penny. I handle bookkeeping for the resort."

The woman's brows pulled together for a second, and then her face smoothed. "I'm Bea. I'll be running housekeeping." She reached out and shook my hand. "You must get that a lot," she laughed. "You look so much like the girl from that television show. God, I can't remember what it's called. I'll think of it later."

I shrugged and chuckled like this was the most outlandish thing I'd ever heard. "No idea," I said. My smile felt falsely bright as I led Harrison through the rows of chairs that had been set up in the space to a spot in the far corner at the back.

"I see you're one of those," he murmured as we sat.

I turned to peer at him, worried he might have gotten more out of the encounter at the doorway than I'd wanted him to. I hadn't told him about my past, and now? It just felt too late. It was irrelevant anyway. One day I'd tell him, in the same way I'd probably tell him about having had a puppy. Except I never had one of those. "One of what?"

He grinned, his sexy eyes dancing. "I used to watch where kids would sit in the lecture hall the first day of class. I could tell what kind of student they'd be by where they chose to sit. You're hiding back here, hoping you won't get called on. You're probably planning to slip out early, ditch the next couple classes and stare at your phone when you are here."

"Well that's pretty judgmental." I raised an eyebrow at him and feigned offense.

"Anecdotal maybe. But there was a definite pattern."

"Maybe you should publish a study."

"Not my field," he said.

"And I'm not hiding. Just figured the new folks should sit closer. We've been here a while. We know where things are."

"We're all new now," he said. "This whole place is about to change."

I frowned and looked down at my hands, folded in my lap. Harrison's thick thigh was pressed against mine as we sat together, and I studied it—tight muscle wrapped in dark denim. He was so solid, so reassuring. I didn't want anything to change —not this place, not my ability to sigh and press deeper against his sturdy presence when I felt worried. And I was worried now. How many of these new people would recognize me? And what might they say? If they knew Chrissy, they might also know about the latest scandal I'd been hiding from. And I didn't care if Harrison knew about Chrissy, but what would he think about the other stuff? Would he believe me when I explained what had happened? That I'd trusted the wrong people, over and over again?

I didn't want him to think of me that way, and I sat in the back of the meeting, absorbing his warmth and reassurance, even as I realized it all had to change at some point. He was leaving. And I couldn't hide my past forever.

"Welcome to Kasper Ridge Resort!" Aubrey stepped up onto the raised area at the front of the space, bouncing with excitement as usual. "I'm Aubrey Kasper, and this is my brother Archie."

A smattering of applause followed this, along with a loud "whoop!" from Sasquatch, who stood to one side, Roscoe at his feet. The dog tilted his head to look at the gathered crowd, but didn't seem bothered by the sudden influx of strangers.

"This place has a long and storied history," she went on. "Archie's going to tell you a little bit about its past, and then we're going to talk about its even more glorious future, which begins today with all of you!"

More applause followed this, and Archie stepped up beside Aubrey.

"Kasper Ridge was built in 1919 originally, but it wasn't much like it is now. It started as a camping destination with a central kitchen building and platforms scattered around the hillside for camping. Sometime in the thirties, the back country cabins were built. Those are the ones you saw featured on Douggie Masters' YouTube Show, *Out and Out There*, if you watched."

Some hoots and hollers indicated that there were a few Douggie fans in the audience.

I'd heard of Douggie Masters, but hadn't seen the show.

"The whole place got rebuilt in the 1940s, and officially named the Kasper Ridge Motel. That was when running water and electricity were brought in, and the main building sat on this spot. There's a lot of legacy up here—our family's certainly, but the family that managed the motel back then was the Dale family. And today, Ernie Dale and his granddaughter Lucy are part of our resort family. Ernie lived onsite here as a child, and he was friends, or maybe we should say co-conspirators, with my Uncle Marvin."

Ghost motioned to where Ernie sat in the front row, Lucy at his side.

"In the 1950s, the place fell into disrepair. It was still owned by the Kasper family, but there was no one here to look after it. The Dale family moved on to found their construction business, and the property sat, mostly abandoned, until the early 1960s.

"During that time, my great-uncle Marvin, our father's uncle, was in Hollywood, where he worked for a little while as a screenwriter without much success. He had a big personality though, and he made a lot of friends out there—stars and celebrities, sports personalities and musicians. And he made enough money that when he came back up here, he was able to buy the property around the motel, including the ski mountain and the backcountry areas that weren't part of the national forest. He rebuilt the motel into the first version of the Resort, which looked a lot like it does today, and for thirty years, he ran the place with his wife, hosting those friends he made down in LA."

"Check out the pictures on the walls in the bar when you have a chance," Aubrey said, grinning.

"My uncle closed the place down when our Aunt Lola died in 1990, but he kept living here. It was during those years that Aubrey and I came to visit, and at first we just thought our uncle had the coolest, craziest, biggest house of anyone we knew. But over the years, we came to understand the history of the place, and to know what it meant to our uncle. And when he died, he left it to us, stipulating that we should get it up and running again.

"And that's why we're here today."

There was light applause from the crowd.

"All of you will be part of the new legacy of Kasper Ridge, and part of our family. When guests begin arriving this afternoon, we can't wait for them to see everything we've done and all the wonderful things you are going to do going forward. Don't hesitate to find us if you have any questions, or any of the crew that's been here for months, helping get this place ready to go."

Aubrey looked out at the crowd. "Guys, stand up. Lucy, Will, Wiley, Antonio, Sasquatch, Harrison, Annalee, Mateo, Penny." She waved her hands toward the gathered crowd, and those of us who'd been here a little while all rose. I felt eyes on me, and tried to keep my spine stiff, even as someone in the crowd called out, "Chrissy!"

Aubrey ignored the interruption, and went on. "These are

the OGs up here, guys. If you need anything, find one of them. But soon, every one of you will be one of the real originals, getting Kasper Ridge on its feet again, and putting this place on the map!

"There's likely to be a decent amount of press around these first few weeks, so please—best behavior everyone! Represent the resort in the way a place with this kind of legacy deserves to be represented. Help us make Uncle Marvin proud!"

I cringed at the mention of press, but hoped I'd be out of sight back in my office. It would be good for the resort, I knew. Necessary, even. There was heavy applause after Aubrey finished, and people began to rise and move in all directions, everyone preparing for their specific roles. A few people looked my way, but I kept my face turned to the back of the room, sticking close by Harrison's side.

"Rousing speech," he said, low enough that only I could hear it.

"I thought it was good," I told him. "I didn't know all the history."

"He left out the hunt."

I looked up at him, chuckling. I could only imagine what would happen if every staff member up here spent half their time looking around for treasure.

"Maybe it's over anyway."

"Not if you ask Aubrey."

Harrison took my hand quickly and dropped a kiss on my cheek. "I need to go get the ski school staff set up," he said. "See you tonight."

It was the first time Harrison had kissed me where others could see, and I felt a blush climb my cheeks. Still, I was proud to be with him, and I liked the feeling of him proclaiming his feelings for me in this small way.

I headed for the door to the back offices, eager to be in my quiet space, away from the crowd of staff. Soon, I was behind my desk, checking to be sure I had all the information I'd need to run the first big payroll at the end of the week, and then sorting through billing issues for a few of the incoming guests.

I didn't leave my office, but I could feel a shift when guests started arriving, as if the resort itself was sighing at the feeling of being busy once again. Strangers began appearing out on the patio visible through my window, drinks in their hands and smiles on their faces.

The door to my office swung open late in the afternoon, and Aubrey stepped in. "Hey," she said, sinking into one of the chairs across my desk.

"Hey," I said. "How's it going?"

We both watched the crowd around the fire pit on the patio. The guests looked happy, the mountain behind them beckoning with its pristine snow. The ski operation would officially open in the morning. Just as I was about to turn back to Aubrey, Harrison strode by outside, three ski instructors at his side. I watched him pass, entranced by his confident stride and commanding manner. My belly did a little flip as I thought about what it felt like to be next to him in bed.

"Yeah," Aubrey said, following my gaze. "How is THAT going?"

I snapped my head around to look at her, realizing too late that I'd been staring. "What?"

"You and Brainiac. Everyone's wondering."

"Everyone?" My voice revealed more worry than I'd intended. I didn't like the idea of everyone saying anything about me.

"The crew," she said. "You guys have been spending a lot of time together." She waited, and when I didn't respond, she went on. "I used to think he had a thing for Monroe, but since you've gotten here, he's only got eyes for you."

He and I had talked about his relationship with Annalee, and I wasn't jealous, though I might have been if we hadn't discussed it. I had no doubts she was right about him now. Harrison wasn't the kind of guy to stray. "He's a good guy."

Aubrey wiggled her eyebrows and grinned. "How good?"

I felt the blush climb my cheeks and wished I could think it away. "That's not what I meant."

"So pretty good, huh?"

"Did you come in here for something?" Diversion probably wouldn't work, but I wasn't sure I was ready to admit my feelings for Harrison. They were deep. And scary. And he was leaving soon, and I knew I'd be nursing a broken heart if he didn't suggest we stay together somehow.

"Yeah, to say hello and to hide. I forgot how exhausting it was, interacting with people all day."

"Long road ahead then, given your chosen occupation. I get the hiding part though."

"Yeah." Her brow wrinkled and she tilted her head at me. "So we're keeping the whole TV show thing a secret?"

"I mean . . . not a secret. Just not announcing it."

"What does Brainiac think?"

The blush drained quickly from my face. "He doesn't know. He never saw the show and has no idea who I used to be."

"You didn't mention it?" Aubrey sounded surprised, maybe a little accusing even.

"It hasn't come up." It felt lame to say. Why hadn't I told him?

"I can't believe he has no idea." The wrinkles were back and she leaned in. "Do you think it'll be a problem when he finds out? Like, will he think you were keeping it from him for some reason?"

That thought had occurred to me more often than I wanted to admit at first, but lately I'd decided he wouldn't care. We both had pasts. What mattered was the future. I had an answer ready. "I just feel like keeping it quiet is the right move. The last thing we want is for this place to attract the paparazzi, right?"

"I suppose." She didn't sound convinced. "I mean, there's some press here already. A couple photographers showed up today and there's a food critic staying!"

"Wow." I didn't want to bump into the photographers. I could only imagine the headlines that might follow if one of them figured out who I was and connected my presence here to my sudden disappearance from Los Angeles. Or worse, connected the dots to the reunion show, which would soon be announced. "I'm glad I work back here. I wouldn't want to distract from the resort opening with all the stupidity around my old life."

Aubrey was quiet a moment. "I guess you're right," she said. She leaned back in the chair and tipped her head back. "Can I just hide here forever?"

"You'll probably have to go out there again soon. You sure you picked the right job? Seems like one afternoon of peopling has been enough for you."

She laughed. "I'll get used to it. I'm just missing having the place to ourselves, but this is what we had to do. A resort is meant to be . . . resorted?"

"That's definitely not a word."

"Full."

"Right."

Aubrey stood, stretching her arms over her head. "Wiley's slammed in the bar. I guess I should go help him."

"Things going well at check-in?" I asked.

"Thanks to the system we put in, yeah. Everything's smooth."

I was glad to hear it. "Good."

"If you guys are still up, we're all gonna meet in Archie's room for a drink around eleven. Like old times."

"I wasn't here back then."

"But you're here now. See you then?"

"Sure," I said, knowing I'd check with Harrison and we'd do whatever we both felt like, even if it meant missing the rest of the crew.

Aubrey left and I turned back to the window, my mind fogged with warring thoughts and emotions. Warmth and happiness when I thought about Harrison—fear and worry when I thought about everything else. Had I built myself a house of cards by keeping my secret? It was bound to fall, so . . . the question was just when.

Chapter 22
Dad Muddies the Waters

HARRISON

Once we were spending our days and nights dealing with guests at the resort, the season picked up momentum, time seeming to accelerate in the rush of unfamiliar faces and constant motion. I was too busy to pay attention to the reporters and photographers who'd come up for the resort's opening season, but the reviews were phenomenal, and I was glad for that.

Kasper Ridge Resort Makes Its Mark!
New Rockies Playground is the Place to Be This Winter!
Kasper Ridge is the Next Aspen!

Thanksgiving came and went, not much of a holiday since the resort was open and therefore hosting families celebrating their own holidays. I'd invited Dad to join the little dinner we'd had as a staff team, but he had plans with friends in Greece, and didn't plan to be back in the states in time.

"It's funny," Penny said as she lounged in my arms late that night after we'd spent the evening helping out in the kitchen, thanks to a staff shortage. "I think that was maybe the nicest Thanksgiving I've ever had."

I stared at her, unsure what to make of that. "How could that be true? You were washing dishes most of the night."

She chuckled, and I felt her about to brush off the question, so I tightened my arms around her, hoping to convince her to open up. "Just . . . that wasn't what my life was about when I was a kid," she said. "My parents were focused on other things, I guess."

"No big family gatherings? No turkey?"

She sputtered a laugh, as if I'd suggested something so outlandish she could hardly imagine it. "No," she said.

"What about Christmas?" I asked her, my mind ticking forward. We'd be here for that holiday too, but Ghost and Aubrey had planned that one ahead. The resort wouldn't be open to guests that week, only to the families of resort staff. They'd discounted the rooms by a ridiculous amount and encouraged everyone on staff to invite their families and join us here for a holiday celebration at the resort.

"Presents, yeah," she said.

"Santa? Stockings? Having to kiss weird aunts and uncles you barely knew?"

Penny laughed, and the sound warmed me. I wanted to make this woman laugh as much as possible, to make her smile whenever I could. Penny hadn't shared a lot about her childhood, but I'd gleaned that it wasn't especially happy, and I hated the idea of her being sad.

"Yeah," she said. "I had a little of that." It felt like Penny was saying the words she thought I wanted to hear. But I wasn't sure if they were true.

That was why when we finally shut down for Christmas, four days before the actual day, I had a plan.

The lobby of the resort had been transformed, and the center of the space held an enormous tree, at least fifteen feet tall and nearly touching the paneled ceiling overhead. It glowed with white lights and silver and gold decorations that managed to evoke the resort's 1920s roots in a kind of Art Deco style. The space was quiet that week, comparatively anyway, since much of the staff had gone home for their week off.

The rest of us enjoyed having the resort to ourselves again, plus a few family members. Monroe's parents and sister and Mateo's former mother-in-law had come to stay, and Mateo's daughter was doing her best to entertain her two little cousins, the three of them filling the common spaces with laughter. Monroe's sister was beautiful, just like her, but in a more typically Southern way, and it was amusing watching her attempt to maintain her demure composure as she chased twin six-year-old boys through the space.

Fake Tom's father had come to stay, and he and Ernie Dale spent a lot of time side by side in the bar, sipping scotch and exchanging construction stories.

Wiley's brother was visiting too, bringing more alcohol than might be legal to transport across state lines, since he was now running the Half Cat Distillery back in Maryland. His fiancée, Veronica, brought several cases of wine.

I'd invited my father to join us, but he had some other plans in Washington. Though he was retired, he still rubbed elbows with influential people, and I suspected it was his way of staying busy.

"I'd love to get up there soon, Harrison," he said on the phone when I spoke to him a couple days before Christmas. "Sounds like my time to visit is running out though."

"It is. Planning to head down to California as soon as the snow clears." I was sitting in the desk chair in my room, facing the window, my stomach churning as I said the words aloud. I didn't want to leave. Penny was moving around the room behind me, having just gotten out of the shower. We had a staff dinner tonight—it was Christmas Eve, and Aubrey had a whole party agenda planned out.

"That's going to be a good job, Son. Good company. Solid resume builder." Dad sounded proud, which always made me feel good.

"Yeah," I agreed, pushing myself for enthusiasm I didn't feel.

"You sure it's the right move, though?"

That got my attention. Dad had always pushed for experience, resume building, important work. "What do you mean?"

"You don't sound enthusiastic about it."

"You've met me. Enthusiastic isn't really in my repertoire." Behind me, Penny snorted, and I turned to give her a squinty-eyed look. I'd handle her when I hung up. She grinned and moved into the bedroom, and I heard the hair dryer fire up in the connected bathroom.

"Maybe you're in the right place now," Dad said.

"Being a ski bum in Colorado?" Did Dad think I wasn't equipped for the job I was taking on?

"You're running the whole ski program at a major resort. That's not nothing."

"It's not what I was trained to do, either."

"You were trained to fly a multi-million dollar jet at speeds that make most people pass out. I don't think you're going to find that again anywhere, Son. What I'm saying is, you might want to look at aspects of the job beyond whether it's a match on paper for your skillset and degree."

I shook my head. Where was this coming from? "This doesn't sound like you, Dad."

Dad sighed, and he sounded tired suddenly. "I know, and maybe that's been my mistake. I know I've pushed you, Harrison. What I'm saying now is that it's just as important to focus on the other stuff in life. Are you happy? Do you get a chance to have some fun now and then?"

"Fun?" It was like I was talking to a stranger.

"Listen, son. I don't want you to worry."

Immediately, worry rampaged through my veins and I sprang to my feet, unable to sit. "What's going on?"

"I'm fine. Just . . . I had a health scare. I didn't want to tell you until I knew one way or the other. But it made me think a bit about where I'd spend the time I had left if it came to that." Dad delivered these words in his usual straightforward tone, but I thought I heard an edge of wistfulness behind it.

"But you're okay?" I imagined Dad being scared for his health, realized he hadn't chosen to call me to share the fear. Did even my own father believe I wasn't capable of handling emotional issues? Was this another empathy ding?

"I'm okay. For now. But none of us have guarantees."

"I know that. But your health . . . it's all clear? It's not . . ."

"I'm fine, Harrison, I promise. It's not anything chronic or long term. Just had a little wake up call and realized I'm getting older, that's all." He paused, and I could hear him taking a deep breath. "So do what makes you happy. That's all I'm saying." In the background of Dad's call, I heard a female voice asking a question. Dad's voice came back, muffled as if he had a hand over the phone, and then he returned to the call. "Sorry."

"Who's that?" I asked, my curiosity overriding my need to be polite.

"I'm following my own advice," Dad said. "Spending the holiday with an old friend. Samantha Dowell. You met her a long time ago. We've been . . . dating."

I didn't remember Samantha Dowell, and I couldn't think of a single time my father had gone on a date, not when I'd been with him, anyway. In the twenty years since my mother had died, I'd never even considered my father in that way. But here he was, choosing to spend his holiday with a woman, even though I'd invited him here. The realization loosened something in my chest that I hadn't known was tight until that second.

"That's great, Dad."

"Yeah," he laughed. "It is."

For a moment we were both quiet, something unspoken passing between us.

"Merry Christmas, Dad. I hope you'll get a chance to get up here soon."

"Let's plan for the new year," he said. "Merry Christmas, Harrison."

I hung up and spent a few minutes staring out the window at the snow-covered mountain beyond. Dad was different . . . the man who'd been stern and scary most of my youth suddenly sounded human. And his advice had been strangely emotional.

"Hey, everything okay?" Penny's voice came from behind me, and I turned to find her standing in an emerald green dress that made her eyes stand out and sparkle, her dark hair in curls over her shoulders. Her cheeks were flushed and those rosy lips made my body coil in desire.

"You look incredible," I told her, standing to step closer. "Will I mess you up if I kiss you?"

She laughed and her arms slipped around my neck. "Of course not."

I kissed her, carefully so I didn't smear her lipstick, letting my eyes drop shut so I could breathe her in. Something in my chest flipped as I held her. I didn't want to let go.

"You know," I said, my voice low as I held her to me carefully, like a delicate treasure. "Spring is just around the corner." She stiffened slightly in my arms at the reminder of our impending separation. "And I was just thinking, well, talking to my dad, actually. About the job, about how it's a perfect fit for my experience. He called it a good resume builder." I was about to continue, to tell her that I was thinking about calling Gator and telling him I didn't want it after all, but Penny stepped away, her arms falling to her sides and the brightness in her eyes dimming.

"I know," she said. "And it's fine. We're temporary. I get it. That was the deal from the very beginning."

It didn't feel fine. My chest constricted at the thought of her absence from my arms being permanent.

"I meant that I really enjoy your company," I started again, sounding like I was in a board room, not trying to convince the woman I loved that I wanted her to ask me to stay.

"Good," she said lightly, poking me in the chest. "It's mutual. Now we'd better go, or we'll be late for dinner."

"I . . ." I was at a loss for words, and I cursed John Andrews silently. His stupid book hadn't covered this situation. Or maybe I hadn't gotten to this part yet. "It's just—"

"Harrison, it really is fine. I have to go back to LA for a bit after the holidays anyway. It'll be good practice for when you leave. We can still talk, you know."

"Right." I hated the idea of her leaving, of us being apart at all. She'd mentioned going back to Los Angeles once or twice, but I knew she'd be back. I wanted to address the bigger issue with her, my job. But she was already heading for the door.

"Let's go."

I followed Penny out the door and down to the lounge, which had been set up with tables and place settings in front of the massive fireplace. Stockings hung from the mantel, one for each of what Aubrey now routinely called the "OGs." The one that said "Brainiac" hung next to Penny's, and the sight gave me a strange feeling. What would it be like to have stockings hanging like this in a smaller place? A home? Our home?

"Penny," I said, taking her hand and pulling her aside. "What if we stayed here? What if neither of us left?"

"That would be a lovely fairytale," she said, smiling brightly. "But we live in the real world. And we both have commitments." Her eyes held mine for a moment, and I couldn't sort through what I saw there. Was she telling the truth? She was fine with the idea of us separating? Was I the only one who felt this way? I didn't believe it. These confusing feelings were mutual, but somehow, Penny was handling them better than I did.

"Let's sit," she said, pulling me to join the others at a round table off to one side.

And we did, joining our friends for the evening and celebrating the holiday.

But the brightest spot of my holiday was at my side, and I was going to lose her. I kicked myself for failing to communicate what I meant. I'd just worked up the nerve to suggest we could stay, that this could be something real, and she hadn't understood. I replayed the conversation in my head as we ate, trying to understand how I had botched it so badly.

Chapter 23
Christmas Eve - Ho Ho

PENNY

Harrison was quiet through dinner, which was fine since others more than made up for it. Wiley's brother and his fiancée kept everyone laughing with stories about the strange little place they lived and worked, where the Half Cat Distillery and attached bar actually straddled the lines of three counties. Evidently, the bar had to abide by some pretty outdated laws, thanks to the county in which it sat, and according to Wade Blanchard, there was a law enforcement member who had made it his job to catch Wade breaking one of the ridiculous laws.

"There have to be seven kinds of snacks on offer," Wade explained. "So he'll actually come in and count the kinds of tiny crackers that make up the bar mix we serve."

"That's insane," Annalee laughed.

"But true," Veronica confirmed. "You'll all have to come visit sometime."

I wanted to. I hoped that someday I could go wherever I wanted, see the country and the world, without worrying about being Chrissy.

Aubrey was smiling widely through the banter, leaning into Wiley's side. "I can't believe I haven't been out there yet."

"You were out there as a kid," Archie pointed out.

"I wasn't exactly dropping through bars back then," she laughed.

It turned out Aubrey and Wiley had known each other years before, when Aubrey and Archie's family had briefly lived in Southern Maryland, where Wiley and Wade grew up. Aubrey and Wiley had met again when he'd come out to help Archie get the resort bar set up—kind of a second chance romance, I guessed.

When the meal ended, Aubrey organized us all in front of the big fireplace for a photo. I stood at Harrison's side, trying not to feel like I was in one of the cast photos they had taken every year for the show and instead imagining what it would be like to do a family portrait each Christmas. With him. And our family. But the thought made me sad. It could happen—his leaving didn't mean we were over—but it would be hard.

Next, Aubrey sat us down for a game where we could open gifts or steal them from each other. There was plenty of laughter and insanity, but Harrison stayed withdrawn, and I was beginning to worry that I'd said something wrong, or that maybe his dad had shared some bad news when they spoke, though he hadn't mentioned it.

"Everything okay?" I asked for the third or fourth time as we finished up the game.

"Just tired," he said, not meeting my eyes. I wondered if he'd figured something out, and I couldn't shake the feeling he was hiding something.

"Hey," I said, trying to capture his attention. "I have a gift for you."

"I have one for you too." His steely gaze flicked to mine, his jaw flexing for a second, as if he was grinding his teeth. The intensity in the look had me ready to strip off my dress right there in front of the fire.

"Upstairs?" I leaned in, letting the whispered question become a breath against his ear.

His answer was an arm banded around my waist as we turned toward the door.

"Goodnight guys! Merry Christmas!" Aubrey called after us. I turned and flashed her a quick smile over my shoulder, but Harrison maintained his singular focus on departing quickly, as if a band of Christmas elves was hot on our tail.

In the elevator, Harrison turned to me, caging me between his body and the paneled wall and dipping his head to crush his lips to mine. The kiss was demanding and possessive, and within seconds I was melting beneath him, my thighs slick beneath my green dress. Did this mean he wasn't upset with me?

As we stepped into the hallway, I tried to catch my breath. "Your gift is in my room."

"I'll wait." His voice was a growl, lower than I'd ever heard it, and he stood sentinel at my door while I retrieved the wrapped package from my bedroom.

Soon, we were stepping through his door, and his intensity —if it was even possible—had increased. He kept a hand on me, guiding me at my low back toward the center of the room, where

I sat on an ottoman in front of an armchair, my eyes never leaving his.

"Sit, and you can open this," I said. Then I realized that without looking, I'd managed to plop down on something hard that had been forgotten beneath the throw blanket on the ottoman. "Oof, what's this?"

As Harrison sat in front of me, his gift in his hands, I pulled a book out from beneath me. His brow wrinkled as I lifted it to read the title.

"*Empathy for Assholes*?" I laughed. "Are you reading this?"

Harrison didn't crack a smile. "I was reading it," he said. "It's pointless, though." He seemed upset, and I was back to worrying.

He took the book gently from me and dropped it to the floor next to the chair. "I had a gift for you, but it's not the right thing."

"It's not?" A little prick of disappointment went through me. He'd gotten me something, but he wasn't going to give it to me?

"No."

"Okay."

The intensity was still turned up to eleven and the air around us buzzed with something strange, an atmosphere that was making me both nervous and anticipatory. Harrison's constant glances as he opened his gift were predatory, full of dark promise, and my body was responding as if his hands were on me, every nerve ending firing to life.

"Maybe it's stupid," I said, second-guessing the gift even as he pulled the tissue from around it and lifted it to the light. I'd gone with the girls down to Denver and we'd made snow globes. I'd done my best to make the Kasper Ridge Resort, thinking that since Harrison was leaving, it might be nice to have something to remember the place by.

"It's not stupid," he said, his voice a whisper as those serious eyes took in all the details inside the little plastic globe. "It's beautiful." The eyes were on me now. "Did you make this?"

I nodded, pleasure at his response rolling through me, joining the heat he'd already sparked in my belly.

He set the globe aside and moved to the floor, kneeling in front of me, my knees in his chest. His dark expression didn't fade as his hands landed on my legs, sliding gently up my thighs until the met the hem of my dress.

A light sound pulled from my throat, need and desire mixed up in the strange mood that had surrounded Harrison all night. I wasn't sure what to expect from him and there was something wildly exciting about that.

"Can I?" He asked, his voice a deep scuff in the quiet room. His fingers were dipping beneath the hem of my dress, urging it up my thighs. I nodded and his palms slid along the sides of my thighs until they wrapped around behind me. My dress was at my waist, and Harrison's fingers were pulling the thin fabric of my thong, slipping it off as I lifted my hips to help.

I watched him, feeling almost like he was a stranger—this uber serious version of the man I'd come to know, or though I did.

"Is everything really—oh!" Harrison's strong hands tugged my body forward on the soft ottoman, scooting me toward him and pressing my legs to either side of his chest.

I was suddenly completely exposed to him, and seeing his eyes go glassy and dark as he gazed down at my apex gave me an intoxicating sense of power. His eyes flicked up to mine for a brief moment, seeking consent, maybe? Whatever he found in my face must have said yes, because in the next moment I was laid back, my weight on my elbows, as Harrison's mouth explored the hot wetness between my legs.

His tongue and lips were tentative at first, sweeping through my folds, glancing over my clit in a way that made me want to grab his head and hold it where I needed it.

"Please," I heard myself whisper.

Harrison answered with his tongue, finding a steady unrelenting rhythm right where I needed it as his hands moved over my body.

I reached for him, finding my hands buried in his soft hair as his tongue continued its constant undulating pressure and my thighs began to shake as my stomach dropped inside me.

"God, yes," I moaned as the most tenuous tension coiled within me and I had fleeting thoughts of need and desire and wonder all at once. When I moaned again, Harrison increased the rhythm and added a thick finger to the assault, slipping into me and expertly pressing into the tender spot that he worked expertly. I unspooled, his mouth on me, his hands doing things I'd only imagined, and I heard myself coming undone, my voice desperate in the quiet air of the cool room.

I'd barely finished, when I heard Harrison release his belt, my eyes dropping to where he was unzipping his fly, ripping his shirt over his head, that same steely but dazed determination in his beautiful eyes.

"So serious," I whispered, but Harrison didn't answer. He'd taken himself in his hand and without dropping my gaze gave his length a couple hard strokes before rolling on a condom.

And then he was on me, climbing up my body, pushing my dress over my head as his warm heat surrounded me, the velvet head of him plowing the hot wetness of my entrance.

All I knew was heat and pressure, and his mouth taking mine again, his tongue sweeping my lips apart even as his thick steely length invaded my body—a welcome intruder. He thrust into me, his mouth still holding mine captive, and my hands scrabbled for purchase as a whole different kind of pleasure built inside me.

Harrison was claiming me, taking me in every sense of the word, and I was completely here for it. No one had ever commanded my body quite like this, and I loved being on the receiving end, giving everything up for him even as he wrung pleasure from my body that I didn't even know it was capable of producing.

He was moving more slowly suddenly, lengthening every thrust until my body was screaming for him with every absence, celebrating and clutching at him with every renewed invasion. "God, Penny," he murmured, releasing my lips only long enough to stare into my eyes for a moment.

His face held an expression I didn't recognize. Sorrow? Regret? I didn't have time to think about it, because his mouth was on my throat in the next second, and my body was clenching around him as if trying to keep him there forever.

"Oh my god, Harrison," I moaned, as hot pulsing pleasure rolled through me, exploding in my center and radiating out in waves that felt never ending.

"Penny," he gasped a second later, dropping his head to my chest as his body shuddered through his pulsing orgasm. I could feel every movement of him inside me, every throbbing, forceful release.

We lay there for a second, and then Harrison stood abruptly, tucking himself back into his pants after removing the condom, and turning away from me. I felt suddenly embarrassed. Exposed. I sat up, picking up my dress and holding it in front of me as he busied himself picking up the discarded paper from his gift.

"Hey," I said, my voice a whisper, like I was afraid of spooking him. "Are you really okay?"

He turned to face me, one hand holding a fistful of green tissue, and the other rising to grip the back of his neck. His face was a mask of pain. "Yeah."

"Wait," I stood, dropping my dress, forgetting my nakedness for a moment and pressing myself against him. "What's going on?"

He stared into my eyes for a long beat, then his arms slid around me and he kissed me again. "Nothing," he said. "Just . . . I'm going to miss you."

The words felt raw and wounded, and I wondered at the strange shift in him, even as I let him kiss me, lead me to the bathroom and run a steamy shower for us both. He'd brought up us leaving soon, and I'd thought it was his way of reminding me that we shouldn't get too attached, shouldn't forget that this was only for now. But maybe I'd been wrong?

I wasn't sure, but with my track record and knowing what I was hiding, it seemed like making big promises was probably not the right thing to do. It had been a long night, and we were both sleepy and worn out. I'd bring it up in the morning, when we were both fresh.

Harrison didn't say anything else either, our bodies speaking for us as we went to bed, making love again, but this time doing it carefully, lovingly.

And as I nestled against the rigid planes of his chest in the darkness, I realized something I'd been trying to avoid.

"Truth?" I whispered into the darkness. The only response was Harrison's steady soft breathing. "I'm so in love with you it scares me," I told the darkness. I was going to miss him too.

* * *

The next morning I jolted awake abruptly at a banging on the door of Harrison's suite. My heart leapt into my throat and panic surged through me before I realized where I was, that I was okay.

"Brainiac! Penny!" It was Archie's voice. Something was wrong.

"I'll get it," Harrison said, rubbing a hand through his messy hair and stumbling to put on some boxer briefs before heading out to the living room. I heard him pull the door open.

"What the hell?" he asked.

"Put on some pants man, and tell Penny to get dressed. Her mom is here."

The words filtered through the quiet morning sunlight in the room, and at first I didn't register the meaning. But then I was completely alert, out of bed, shock and something that felt like terror racing through my body. Why was my mother here?

Chapter 24
A Holiday Surprise

PENNY

Archie walked me down to the lobby, Harrison following just behind us, though I'd told him he didn't need to come. Realistically, I had hoped he wouldn't come.

Mom was unpredictable at the best of times. But if she'd driven herself to Colorado on Christmas, through snow and heaven only knew what else? This was probably not the best of times. We hadn't spoken in weeks. I'd sent her an email to wish her a happy Thanksgiving.

"There you are! Darling, Merry Christmas!" Mom was

some version of herself I hadn't seen since I was a child. This was the Mom who dressed and behaved the way she thought wealthy women in show business circles should, and it was painful to witness. She was decked out in slim black cigarette pants and high open-toed heels, despite the three feet of snow piled up outside. She wore a red sweater with sequins smattered across the shoulders, and something akin to red peacock feathers adorning the sleeves. It was loud and pretentious, and all just so. Very. Mom.

"Mom, hi," I said, stepping close enough for her to pull me into her arms and trap me there, her heavy perfume filling my nose and mouth and making me cough. "What are you doing here?"

She stepped back, holding me at arm's length, her taloned nails digging into my shoulders beneath the flannel shirt I'd pulled on in Harrison's room. I was also wearing a pair of athletic shorts that belonged to him, and my feet were covered in thick socks he'd handed me. It wasn't what I'd intended to wear downstairs on Christmas morning, but I also hadn't expected Mom to appear like the Ghost of Christmas Drama.

"I wasn't going to miss seeing my only child on Christmas," she said, glancing around at Archie and Harrison, smiling and batting her eyelashes as she produced a false laugh.

This was my least favorite version of Mom. My stomach churned as I released myself from her grip and stepped back.

"Mom, this is Archie, he and his sister Aubrey own the resort," I told her, waving a hand to Archie.

He stepped forward with a huge smile and an extended hand, which Mom ignored as she pulled him into a hug instead. Archie's surprised voice said, "So nice to meet you."

"And this is Harrison," I said. "Who you don't need to . . . hug."

But Harrison had already stepped forward, arms

outstretched, and pulled my mother into an embrace that looked as awkward as I felt.

"Well no wonder Penny doesn't want to come home," Mom said, looking between the tall handsome men. "I'd probably stick around too, if there are more men that look like you fellows up here."

I felt sick. I didn't want my mother here, and the thought of her staying for any length of time sent my mind swirling down a road strewn with worst-case scenarios.

"Well Ma'am," Archie said, looking around the lobby. "Do you have luggage? Shall we get you set up in a room?"

"I do have a bag out in the car," she said, pulling her keys from the sequined purse hanging from her shoulder and handing them to Archie. "If you wouldn't mind parking it for me too, darling. I wasn't sure where to put it with all this snow!" She sounded like the snow was some kind of unexpected surprise, not a completely predictable occurrence at ten thousand feet in Colorado in December.

"I figured I'd stay with you," Mom said, turning to me as Archie went outside obediently.

I cringed, trying to keep my smile in place. "You'd be more comfortable with your own room, don't you think?"

Mom's face fell, and I could see her considering which form of drama would make the most sense here.

"The rooms are huge, and if you want, you can probably stay in one of the rooms just down the hall from me. That way you'll have your own bathroom and your own bed."

She tilted her head to one side and gave a little wave of one hand. "Well, I suppose," she said. "That sounds nice."

Archie returned with Mom's bag and set her up with a room, and then we headed upstairs, leaving Archie down in the lobby looking a little gob smacked.

"I'll get this for you," Harrison said, shouldering Mom's knock-off Louis Vuitton bag.

"Thank you," she responded, her hand wrapping Harrison's bicep as we stepped into the elevator. I cringed again. Cringing was becoming my normal state of being this morning.

"So," she drawled, tilting her head up to gaze at him. "What do you do here, Harrison?"

"When the resort is running, I manage the ski operations," he said. "We closed down for the week between Christmas and New Year's though, so right now, I guess I'm just on vacation." The smile he gave her was glorious, and I felt a misplaced pang of envy. He hadn't smiled like that at me in at least twenty-four hours. I watched him surreptitiously, trying to figure out what had happened the day before to twist things up between us.

"I see," Mom said lightly. "And you and Penny are a couple?" Despite all her put-on affectations, Mom didn't miss a thing, and she had no compunction about poking her nose into something even our good friends were considerate enough not to ask outright.

"Ah, well," Harrison's gaze flicked to mine. "I admire her very much, ma'am, and yes, we have been seeing each other for a little while."

A tiny "humph" came from my mother, whose gaze swung immediately to the opening doors of the elevator, and I felt the cold judgement swirling around us as we stepped out into the hallway. I was going to hear about how I never shared anything with her, about how I was keeping her out of my life. She wasn't wrong, but I had good reasons.

"It'll be down here," I said, leading Mom to a room a few doors away from mine. "Most of this wing is empty—it's the staff wing for now, hasn't been redone like the guest wing."

"Oh," Mom said, and I could hear the note of disappointment in her voice.

"That wing is completely empty right now since there are no guests," I said. "It would be pretty creepy to be by yourself there."

"Right, of course," she said, stepping into the room I'd unlocked and looking around her approvingly. Whatever might be outdated or dusty here was still miles ahead of her ratty Englewood apartment, I was sure.

"Well, thank you, Harrison. I suppose we'll see you later." Mom gave Harrison a quick nod and dismissed him, sending irritation ratcheting through me.

He turned to me, his eyes searching my face. I wondered what he was seeing there—did he understand how complicated my relationship with my mother was? How very much I wished she weren't here?

"See you later," he said, leaning in to kiss my cheek.

"Okay," I said, wishing we could have stayed in bed and let Christmas morning dawn around us quietly, lazily instead.

When the door shut behind Harrison, Mom turned to me with a bright smile and flopped into a chair. "That drive was horrendous."

"Then why did you do it?" I asked, crossing my arms. If Mom was going to act like a brat, I would treat her like one. I didn't have any patience left for her, and the fear that she was going bombshell in here and explode everything I'd managed to find for myself was making me feel panicky.

"You weren't going to invite me. I had to invite myself. And what better time for a visit than the holidays?"

"Some notice would have been nice."

"You don't answer my calls," she pointed out.

"Email works." I already felt completely exhausted, and sank into a chair facing my mother.

"Well, I'm here now. Might as well catch up." She glanced around. "Don't supposed that cute redheaded bellboy could get us some champagne and orange juice? Doesn't feel like Christmas without a mimosa."

"The cute redheaded bellboy is Archie Kasper. He owns the resort, which I told you. I'm not going to ask him for anything else. Giving you a room free of charge seems like enough."

Mom sniffed, letting a bit of her pretense slip and settling into her chair. "Tell me what's been going on. Have you talked to Paul?"

"I have spoken to my agent," I said. "And Paul knows that I'm not planning a return to show business."

"But the reunion?" Ever hopeful that her cash cow might once again begin to produce.

"I'll do the event, announce my retirement, and then come back here. I have a job. A real job."

"And a handsome boyfriend. Is it him? Is he distracting you from your career?" She sat forward pointing a long red nail in the direction Harrison had gone.

"No. He's leaving, actually." I did not want to talk to my mother about this. I didn't even know exactly how I felt about things, and now she was here, muddying the waters.

"Then why stay here?" Of course Mom would see the absence of an interested man as a reason to leave.

"Because I have a job that I like. I keep the books for the whole resort, and I'm good at it."

She wrinkled her nose in disgust at the mention of real work. "This is such a waste of your talent."

I sighed and sank back into the chair. "Mom," I said slowly, testing my words. "I'm trying to build a real life for myself. Something I can be proud of. Something that's my own. I'm sorry I can't support you anymore, but maybe it's time for you to do the same thing? Grow up a little. Take care of yourself?"

Her face registered shock for a split second, then the devastated mask slid into place. "Since your father died, things have been so hard, Penny."

"Which is why you decided to convince Aiden to film he and I together and sell the footage? What was your cut?" The man I'd dated briefly had emailed me with an apology. Evidently he didn't believe my own mother would go through with the plan to release the video to the tabloids and he'd gotten cold feet and demanded it back when he understood that she was serious. He said he didn't keep what was supposed to be his half of the payout and gave it all to her. I didn't know if I believed him. He had no real reason to lie now. None of it mattered.

"I would never—" Mom had the grace to look offended, bringing a hand to her heart and letting her mouth drop open.

"I already know it's true," I told her.

She pouted for a moment, undoubtedly searching for a new angle.

"Listen, Mom." I stood up. "I'm going to go take a shower and get dressed. You can stay here, but if you do, you will be polite and quiet. No stories about the past, no talk of television, nothing about my previous life. You will be gracious and demure, and keep your mouth shut."

She shook her head, her eyes wide. "Of course, but . . ." A strange expression slid across her face, her brows lowering. "That Harrison fellow. Is he after your money? Is that why you don't want any reminders of your career?"

"My career is over, and I get to be a real person here. And the fact that you think there's money... it just shows how totally out of touch you really are. And no. Harrison doesn't even know about Chrissy."

She laughed loudly at that. "Of course he does."

"He actually doesn't. He didn't watch television growing up and doesn't follow pop culture at all."

"Surely someone else has told him how famous you are."

I shook my head. "Anyone who knows is keeping it quiet. We don't want paparazzi here or to have anything else overshadow the opening of the resort. So far, everyone's behaved. Will you?"

"He's lying to you, darling."

I sighed, exhausted by my mother's constant requirement for drama. "He's not."

"Honey, you're so naive. Of course he is. He knows who you are, certainly, and he's waiting to see what you can do for him."

I had a flashing thought about what I had done for him in the shower the night before, but pushed it away quickly. "You will keep your mouth shut," I told her. "Don't leave this room until I get back." I hoped she'd listen, but wasn't feeling overly confident.

"Fine," she said lightly, waving a hand at me. "If that's how you want to play this."

Because to my mother, everything in life was just another role to play.

Chapter 25
Secrets Don't Stay Secret Forever

HARRISON

I'd hoped to spend Christmas with Penny. Despite my knowledge that getting even closer would only serve to devastate me further when it was time to walk away, what else could I do? My heart was driving at this point, and it seemed oblivious to the danger my mind could see clearly ahead.

Penny's mother, however, had other plans. I didn't even see Penny until the afternoon, and her mother, who told us all to please call her Deirdre, was inserting herself constantly between us. I couldn't get close enough to touch her, talk to her, anything.

At one point, we took Deirdre outside to show her the fire pit and the yurts out back. As we stood on the patio, warming our hands over the fire, she turned to me and gave me what felt like a very judgmental up and down look before saying, "Penny tells me you're not a big television fan, Harrison?"

Penny was on the other side of the fire pit, having been dragged away with Aubrey to talk about something that had come up with payroll and needed a quick fix, and I had a burning desire to leap across the flames, both to be closer to her and to be away from her mother, who clearly didn't like me.

"Uh, no," I answered. "Not really."

"Sure," she said, as if I'd just told her I was the president of the United States. That's how clearly she believed me.

"My dad was a diplomat, so I didn't grow up in the US," I went on, simultaneously asking myself why I was justifying my lack of a television addiction and still desperate to do it. "I missed a lot of pop culture from my childhood."

"Oh, I see," she said, again making it clear she did not see at all. She stepped closer, leaning her head toward me, her eyes on her beautiful daughter across the fire. "Listen to me. Penny is bright and brilliant and talented, and she'll figure out soon enough exactly what you're after. You can play games all you want, but you're not fooling me."

I turned to stare at her. What the fuck had this lady been smoking? "Ma'am, I'm not sure I know what you're talking about."

"The money," she hissed. "Just forget it. Your plan isn't going to work."

"Is this about the treasure hunt?" I asked, my head spinning.

She frowned at me, something calculating in her eyes. "What treasure?"

I shook my head. "No, never mind. I must have misunderstood." I did not like Penny's mother. I had tried. But either my empathy had failed me completely, or she was just not a likable person. I wanted to try for Penny's sake, but I had to disengage. "I'm going to head inside. Can you let Penny know, please?"

Deirdre didn't answer, just turned back to the fire with a sniff as I essentially fled.

Inside, I bumped into Monroe coming through the front doors. "Hey, you," she said, stepping close to hug me. "Merry Christmas!"

"Yeah," I said, hugging her back, but then wondering if Penny's mom might be around, waiting to see me hug someone so she could accuse me of cheating on Penny or something. I froze and stepped back. "Uh, Merry Christmas."

"Yeah, you sound super jolly," Monroe said, laughing. Her cheeks were rosy and her eyes sparkled. My friend looked happy and I was glad. One of us should be.

"Where have you been?" I asked.

"Mateo's. We spent the night there so Lily would be at home on Christmas morning. She wasn't sure Santa would be able to find her if they stayed here."

I nodded, but my mind was still outside, piecing through the words Deirdre had said.

"You look a little lost, Brainiac."

"I am." I didn't like admitting it, but Monroe was the closest friend I had here. And I needed a friend.

"Come on," she said, taking my arm and turning me towards the bar. "Let's have a Christmas libation and you can tell me all about it."

"Um." Monroe left me little choice, and I let her lead me into the bar, where we soon had matching glasses of whiskey before us as we sat together at the end of the long space. No one else was in the bar just then, off celebrating the holiday in their own ways. We had plans for a big dinner that night, everyone together, but for now, the bar was quiet and I was glad.

"Penny's mom is here."

Monroe's eyebrows crept up. "Oh. Well that's nice. The holiday and all."

"I don't think it is."

Monroe frowned.

"I'm sensing a lot of weird vibes between Penny and her mom, and she definitely didn't ask her to come. She just showed up this morning."

"Oh. Weird," Monroe said.

"Yeah. And I'm getting the distinct impression she hates me, but I can't figure out why. She asked me a bunch of weird questions and suggested I was after Penny's money. But as far as I know, Penny doesn't have a ton of money. It doesn't make sense." I wanted to talk to Penny about all this, but hadn't gotten a chance with her mom constantly between us.

Monroe's face shifted into something thoughtful and a little bit wary. "What kind of weird questions?"

"About whether I watch television."

Suddenly, something in the bottom of Monroe's glass appeared to capture her full attention. She stared down into it, swirled the glass, and finally sipped slowly. My stomach dropped.

"What?"

She knew something she didn't want to tell me. She might have been named for an actress back in the fleet, but she was terrible at trying to play anything off.

"What do you know?" I asked her.

She glanced up at me, a question in her eyes. "Do you really not know who Penny is? Or who she was before?"

"What? What does that even mean?" Even as my brain whirled, I felt some puzzle piece sliding slowly into place.

Penny didn't talk about her past, her childhood. Not at all. Was there a reason for that?

"Penny's famous," Monroe said finally, after a deep breath. "She was on this show back in the day. *Our Girl Chrissy*. She was Chrissy."

Something vague pinged in the back of my mind. I'd heard of it. Maybe.

Monroe pulled out her phone, tapped the screen a few times, and then dropped it in front of me. There, on the little screen, was Penny as a child. She was impossible not to recognize. And the unmistakable titling of a sitcom splashed across below her. *Our Girl Chrissy*.

"Why would she keep this a secret? That was a long time ago." I couldn't take my eyes off this different version of the woman I loved. I didn't understand.

"The show was a big deal," Monroe said. "It was super popular. *She* was super popular."

"But it's over, right? That was a million years ago. She's clearly moved on."

"I think she's trying. I think that's why she didn't tell you."

"The rest of you knew?" Frustration began to overtake confusion inside me. Why would she keep this from me?

Monroe lifted a shoulder and dropped my gaze.

"I don't understand."

"I should have told you. I'm sorry. But there's more," she said, taking her phone back and pulling up another screen. This image featured the Penny I knew in a photo, with a headline across the bottom of the screen. *Our Girl Chrissy is a Naughty Girl!*

"What the fuck is this?" I asked, anger on Penny's behalf roiling up in me suddenly.

"There've been a couple scandals. Sex tapes."

My chest clenched. Was that why Penny hadn't told me any

of this? Was she up here running from something? Was that why she didn't want to consider anything beyond this fling, this single season together?

"There's one more thing," Monroe said, scrolling through something on her phone. "I just found it, actually."

"Do I even want to know?" I downed my whiskey in one tilt of the glass, not sure what to do with any of this information. I felt sick, but nothing changed how I felt about Penny. I just wasn't sure any more how she felt about me.

"This article says she's planning to go back, to do a reunion season of the show. She's supposed to announce it at an event after the new year."

She had said something about taking care of something in LA after the new year. Was this what she meant?

I stared into empty space across the bar, trying to pull the ill-fitting pieces together in my mind. "I don't get it," I said, wishing I could disguise the confusion ripping my chest apart.

Was I so bad at reading people that I couldn't even see when someone close to me was lying to my face? Or did Penny just not trust me enough to share her whole self with me? Did she understand how broken I truly was, and realize that I couldn't handle it?

"I have to go," I said, sliding my glass toward the inside of the bar for someone to pick up later. I rose from the stool and turned to leave the space.

"Brainiac," Monroe said, meeting my eyes. I didn't want to see the look she held as she stared at me. Sorrow. Pity. "I'm sorry."

I didn't answer her, going straight to my room instead, where I immediately stuffed *Empathy for Assholes* into the garbage can and turned to the low banquet against the wall, picking up a bottle of whiskey and a glass. It hadn't helped me understand things better when I'd been let go from Archer, but it had made me care a little less. Maybe it would work again.

* * *

Hours later, the light had faded in my room as the sun dimmed outside and evening rolled in with thick-looking grey clouds and a noticeable drop in temperature. Even in my room, I could sense the snow coming.

A knock came at my door, pulling me out of my half-drunk stupor. I'd been sitting still, drinking, trying to process all of what I'd learned and make it fit with everything else I thought I knew.

So much for truth.

"Harrison?" Penny's voice came through the door.

My first instinct was to bolt to answer and pull her into my arms, let our bodies reassure me that this was all some kind of misunderstanding. But my first instincts weren't trustworthy.

I rose slowly and went to the door, fighting the emotions warring within me.

"Hey," she said softly looking up at me. She was dressed for dinner, wearing a black wrap dress with long sleeves, and bright red lipstick that made me wish to see her wrap those lips around me later. But that wasn't going to happen.

I stepped back, making room for her to enter, but I couldn't find words. Not yet.

"Is everything okay?" she asked. "I know my mom can be a lot. I'm sorry about the change to our plans. This is definitely not what I wanted to be doing for Christmas." She laughed lightly and turned to face me again as I closed the door.

"Worried she'll expose your secret?" I asked, crossing my arms over my chest.

"My what?" She laughed, but then her eyes found my face, and the laugh died in her throat. "My . . . oh. Harrison."

"So it's all true." She'd just confirmed it all and my heart plummeted to the floor.

"Yes, but that was my past. It's irrelevant now." There was a plea in her voice.

"Except the part where you think I'm after your money and the part where you're planning to leave to do a reunion show and didn't think to mention it to me."

She shook her head, her eyes widening. "What?" Penny took a step closer, her arm stretched out to touch me, but I moved away. If she touched me, I would be weak. I'd decide it didn't matter.

But it did.

"Harrison?"

"You didn't tell me the truth, Penny." It was as simple as that.

Her beautiful face fell, and she dropped my gaze. "I didn't. I had reasons for keeping it from you, though."

"I don't think they matter. You lied to me. You didn't trust me." I blew out a breath, my lungs feeling scorched and seared along with my heart. "I understand now why you aren't asking me to stay, even when I offered, why we can't talk about the future."

"What?" Her chin jerked up. "You're the one who's leaving."

"It doesn't matter now. We always talk about truth, and that's the one thing you didn't give me. I think you should go." I walked to the door and pulled it open, my heart screaming at me to reconsider, but my pride wouldn't let me.

"Can we talk about this? Can I explain?" Pain was laced through Penny's voice and it almost broke me.

"There's no point," I told her. What could she possibly say?

"I know everything now so there's nothing left to tell me. I know about the sex tapes and the reunion show. It's all laid out on the internet for anyone who cares to look."

"Harrison," she said, her voice cracking. She moved toward the door, but paused with one hand on my arm. "I'm so sorry. I just didn't want you to think of me that way. I wanted you to see me as Penny. As the real me. Not some version of me that never existed in the first place."

"Truth?" It almost killed me to say the word, the word that had meant so much to us. "I don't know the real you. I wonder if you do."

A tiny sob escaped her then, and it ripped whatever was left of my heart into pieces I knew I'd never put back together. I'd loved her. And it wasn't enough.

Penny left with tears streaming down her face, and I shut the door behind her. I moved to the bathroom, stripping clothes as I went, and then stood under the shower for as long as I could take the heat on my skin. And then I slid into bed, part of me hoping never to wake up again.

Chapter 26
Merry Merry Mom

PENNY

I stumbled away from Harrison's door in a state of shock. It had happened again—my past had crept near on stealthy paws and waited for the perfect moment to spring, destroying everything that came after it. For a long moment I leaned against the wall outside the elevator, unable to imagine sitting through a holiday celebration, faking a smile as everything inside me convulsed and shuddered. I felt sick, nauseous and shaky. I didn't want to go downstairs, I didn't want to go back to my room, and I didn't want to see my mother. Everything I wanted was in that other room, the one I'd just been sent away from.

Why wouldn't he let me explain? Why was he so determined to end things?

And when he said he'd offered to stay . . . why hadn't I made it clear that was all I really wanted? I'd been afraid, too worried that this exact situation would eventually arise, too certain that if I allowed myself to believe it was more than temporary, then it would be that much more devastating when it ended.

I was wrong. How could it be worse than this?

Mom was already downstairs at dinner, telling god only knew what to everyone about my life, about me. She'd been here less than twenty-four hours and had managed to explode every wonderful thing I'd finally built for myself. I needed to go do damage control if I possibly could. And then, I needed to explain to my mother exactly what was going to happen between us from now on.

I sat across from her, thankful we were at one end of the long table because it allowed me to keep my mood hidden, at least from most of the group.

There was laughter and conversation, lots of wine and holiday music playing in the background. Aubrey and Monroe had catered the food in but sent the servers home, so they'd set everything up on the table, family style. It smelled delicious, but I couldn't eat.

"Prime rib, honey," Mom drawled. "Haven't eaten like this in a while, huh?"

I couldn't look at her. I nursed my wine, which tasted like vinegar to me tonight, and waited until a reasonable time so I could excuse myself.

Sasquatch and Antonio were seated directly next to Mom and me, and while Sass explained how well Roscoe was doing with his training—and it seemed to be true, since the dog was curled up against the wall behind Sasquatch's chair, sleeping—Antonio gazed at me thoughtfully. I tried to avoid his eyes, but when I glanced up he tilted his head sideways and mouthed, "you okay?"

I forced a smile and nodded. But everything felt wrong.

"Actually," I said, turning to my mother. "I feel a little sick. Too much wine, maybe. I think I'm going to turn in early."

Mom's raspberry lips pulled into a frown. "I came all this way, and you're going to abandon me at Christmas dinner?"

I glanced down the table, full of people I'd come to love, representative of a life I'd thought I could have. It felt so wrong to abandon this, these people, to my mother. But wasn't that what my whole life had been about? My mother, telling people all about me, explaining who I was before I ever got a chance?

"Yes," I said, finding a small amount of steel in my backbone and standing straighter. "I am. And tomorrow, I think you should go home."

Her false smile stretched wider and she laughed lightly. "You're so funny. I'll see you in the morning, darling." She glanced around to see who might have heard this exchange, but Sasquatch was already deep in loud conversation with Lucy, Will, and Ernie on his other side. Antonio gave me a quick little salute, and I smiled at him. Then I turned and headed upstairs, my mind a dark black abyss.

Back in my room I pulled on my favorite sweats, swathing myself in a comfort I couldn't feel, and just when I thought I might lie down and try to go to sleep, my mouth filled with saliva and my stomach lurched.

I made it to the bathroom, barely, and as I slipped to sit against the wall on the cold tile floor after vomiting up what little food I'd had that day, it all felt just about right. This was what my life had always been. Doing what my mother wanted, supporting her desires and needs. And throwing up on

Christmas after being told to go away by the only man I'd ever loved? It just seemed like it fit.

Why had I thought I could escape my past? Why had I believed I could do anything different?

I'd been raised to be Chrissy. I might as well quit trying to do anything else.

* * *

I put Mom back in her car the following day.

"Drive carefully," I said, leaning into the passenger side window in front of the resort. "I'll see you in a couple days."

My flight was in two days. I'd already called Paul and let him know I was all in for the show, and now I just had to leave clear enough notes for someone else to pick up my duties at Kasper Ridge. Harrison wasn't going to be here, he didn't trust me anymore, and even though I wanted to keep this life, I saw now that it was pointless. It was like every step I moved away, I just boomeranged right back. Why not embrace it?

I hadn't seen Harrison at all since the night before, and part of me thought it was easier that way. If he didn't even want to let me explain, maybe we just made a clean break here. My heart was not on board with that plan, but what choice did I have?

"I'm so glad you've decided to embrace your talent, honey." Mom smiled and blew a kiss at me before driving away. She didn't care what I did, I knew. As long as I was able to support her. And since I'd given up my apartment, it looked like I'd be living with her for the time being, paying her rent and buying her food. She was ecstatic, and part of me hated her for not understanding what it all meant for me.

It had snowed lightly overnight, but the roads had been plowed and the sun was beating down this morning. It was a good day to travel.

* * *

I spent the next two days in my office, leaving notes and details about various processes and systems I'd barely gotten time to put into place myself, and training Annalee to hold down the fort until they were able to hire someone in full time to replace me.

"I can't believe you're leaving." She said this (for the fifth time) just as we finished up one evening. My flight was early the next morning. "I can't believe he's letting you."

I glanced up at her, aware that she was hoping to draw me into conversation about Harrison, who'd been practically invisible for days. They were good friends, I knew, and if he was going to talk to anyone, it would probably be her.

"Has he said anything to you, Annalee?"

She sighed and leaned one hip on my desk. "No, but he isn't much of a talker, you know."

"I just figured if he was going to talk to anyone, it would be you."

"It should be you."

"He's angry."

She nodded.

"I should have just told him the truth right out of the gate." I repeated the words I'd been telling myself for the past few days as the cold realization of Harrison's absence settled in. I hadn't been warm since my mother showed up.

"Why didn't you?"

I thought about that for a minute. "It wasn't that I ever decided not to tell him. It was just so nice having someone know me as Penny. Like me for Penny. My whole life I've been forced to be an illusion for everyone I met. They all know I'm an actual person, not the TV person I played, but no one is very good at separating the two. With Harrison . . . it was the first time I'd really felt like Penny. Just one hundred percent myself."

"Yeah. I get that. You think Harrison doesn't?"

"I haven't even talked to him since he found out. He told me to go. So I'm going." Pain lanced through me as I thought about driving away, leaving it all behind.

"You think he really meant that you should leave Kasper Ridge?" Annalee looked surprised.

I lifted a shoulder and gathered my few belongings into a tote bag I'd brought down with me. "He's leaving soon anyway. We were always temporary. We both knew it."

She blew out a sigh and stood, crossing her arms. "You guys deserve each other, I guess." She was frowning, and I wasn't sure what to make of her clear frustration, but it made me nervous She seemed almost angry. "He's such a child," she said. "You know he blames himself for this, right?"

I shrugged again, "I don't know. It was pretty obvious he blamed me for not telling him."

She laughed, and her face softened. My own anxiety calmed a bit when she relaxed. "He does this, takes on the blame for everyone else. He thinks he's bad with people, that he's not empathetic enough. Some instructor in the fleet told him that years ago, and then when he didn't get tenure, they said something similar. Now he's internalized that. So I'm sure this whole thing just played into his belief that he's bad at people."

Hadn't he said something like that to me? Had my lie somehow confirmed this stupid idea for him?

"It doesn't really matter, though," I said, my heart aching inside my chest. "I have to go, and so does he. We just got here a little earlier than expected."

"And that's okay with you?" Annalee wasn't the kind of woman who let the world push her around, and I suddenly envied her enormously.

"No, but—"

"Don't leave." She said it flatly, like it was the most obvious thing in the world.

If it had been Harrison asking me, would I have stayed?

"I have to. At this point, I've signed a contract and they're expecting me. Harrison was clear enough, and eventually we'll both get over whatever this was." I didn't believe a word, but the contract part was true enough. If I didn't show up now, the network could sue me. "Thanks for the help here." I couldn't keep talking about this. I'd made my decision—Harrison had helped make up my mind. It was for the best. A clean break. A return to the path my life kept trying to keep me on.

I didn't see him again. And the next day, I was on a plane back to Los Angeles. Where I belonged.

But my heart hadn't made the trip, and there was an aching void inside me where it had once been.

Chapter 27
Whiskey and Movies

HARRISON

She left. She really left.

I watched through the lobby door as she slid into the black town car and pulled the door shut, everything inside me fighting a violent war as I tried to decide if I should run outside and stop her or if I deserved the pain of watching her leave.

It was my own fault in the first place. I hadn't been the kind of person she felt comfortable confiding in, so how would we have ever managed a real relationship? Those, from my understanding, were based on honesty and trust. Penny had neither of those for me, and while I wanted to blame her for keeping her secrets, I knew it was my fault. I wasn't the kind of partner she needed, the kind she would have been comfortable leaning on, being vulnerable with.

"You beating yourself up some more?" Monroe's voice came from behind me, and I turned, trying to pretend I hadn't been staring out the doors after Penny's car, which was now gone.

I cleared my throat, shoved a hand through my hair. "No."

"Right."

I sighed, dropping the act. "Need something?"

"Let's ski."

The resort was going to be quiet for a few more days. It was a good time to take advantage of the lack of crowds.

"We'd need the guys on the lifts."

"Sass and Antonio are running the bottom and Ghost and Fake Tom said they'd run the top for a little while. We're all going."

Maybe skiing would help clear my head. Drowning it in whiskey hadn't helped. "Okay."

"Meet you out back in ten."

I turned and headed for my room, dressing and grabbing my helmet and goggles. I tried to forget the time I'd spent teaching Penny to ski, but it was as pointless as trying to forget her in general. Everything about Kasper Ridge reminded me of being with Penny. And that was why, when we all sat around the blazing fire pit out back that afternoon after taking turns running the lifts and flying down runs, I told Ghost I had to leave too.

"You're kidding," he said, sounding disappointed. "This is about Penny leaving?"

I sipped my beer, wishing everyone here didn't see my pain so clearly. "No. It's the job I took in Cali. They need me to start as soon as possible. I've been holding them off." It wasn't a lie, Gator had called a couple times, asking again about dates.

"But not like, immediately, right?"

I wanted to leave now, to run away like Penny had, to pretend none of this had happened and hope that distance and a change of scenery combined with challenging mental work would erase the pain inside me. Or at least let it fade to a dull ache.

"Pretty immediately, yeah." We'd originally planned for May, but I couldn't imagine staying here five more months without Penny.

Ghost bobbed his head. I hated letting him down, and even though I'd seen no signs of it, I still worried sometimes that he might crack. We all did. We'd seen it once before, and it had been one of the worst times of all our lives. We protected Ghost, looked out for him. And me leaving early? It was just one more way I was letting people who cared about me down. But it felt like I might die if I stayed here. It was too hard. Too painful.

"Yeah man, if that's what you need. We'll get someone else running the program."

I hated the disappointment in his voice, and I knew I was letting him down. "How about this – I'll come back for weekends? Fly out on Mondays, come back Thursday night? I've got the plane." What good was the plane and my license if I never used them?

Ghost's eyes held mine, like he was looking to see if this was a serious offer. "Yeah. That'd be good. For a while at least."

"And I can hire someone," I said. I hated interviewing but it felt right that I should have to endure that as penance for leaving early.

"Or maybe Antonio?" Ghost asked.

We both glanced across the fire at the soccer player. He was a solid guy, responsible and reliable. And a gifted athlete. His talent seemed to extend beyond the soccer pitch to the slopes. He was a good fit.

"Yeah," I said. "If you can spare him, he'd be good. He's very empathetic. He'll be a good manager."

Ghost gave me a look that told me he understood the comparison I was making and didn't necessarily agree with it. "Whatever you need, man," he repeated.

* * *

In my room that night, I emailed Gator to let him know the plan, and then I paced. The walls, which once had echoed Penny's soft moans now seemed cold and hard, and they felt a bit like they were closing in on me.

I couldn't settle. I couldn't spend all my time drinking, though part of me longed for the oblivion of not thinking about what had happened, not believing I could have stopped it somehow. I couldn't run, not with all the snow outside, and I couldn't wander the resort without bumping into people who would cast pitying gazes on me.

Instead, I pulled up the list of movies from the last page of Ghost's album and started streaming them over the next nights and weeks—sometimes in my quiet room, sometimes in my even quieter room in a hotel in Sacramento. I watched them all, one by one, immersing myself in the past in ways that were only slightly less painful than picking apart the disastrous way the happiest time in my life had exploded.

I also watched every episode of an old sitcom called *Our Girl Chrissy*. And even though she was young here, even though the plots were trite and the canned laughter grated my nerves, I realized I was desperately in love with Chrissy.

As I watched Penny as a kid, her smile still slicing through my heart, her voice achingly familiar in the quiet of my room, I realized I loved her still. Even this version of her. Did it matter who she was in the past? I was in love with Chrissy and Penny and whoever she wanted to be in the future.

We were both in California now, most of the time at least. But it was too damned late.

Chapter 28
Plans We Hate

PENNY

Paul and Mom were both ecstatic that I had agreed to stay on for the reunion series. Of course they were, they were both like vultures, circling overhead as I went through the motions of living, waiting to take whatever was left.

"Aren't you glad to be home where you belong?" Mom was asking for the thousandth time after we'd returned home from Paul's office where I'd reviewed the contract I had signed digitally from Kasper Ridge. My stomach hurt and I felt sick.

I looked around Mom's dark one-bedroom apartment. The

walls were stained, the couch against the far wall sagged, and the lingering smell of cigarette smoke gave the whole place a discarded feeling. I felt discarded here too, forgotten. Which was strange, considering all I'd really wanted lately was for everyone to forget who I was. Or who I'd used to be, at least.

"Penny, I know you're feeling down, honey," Mom said when I didn't answer her with joy about my current situation. "But things are about to change for us! All that money in your new contract, and we can get a nicer place, do a little shopping." The glee in her voice turned my stomach. "You'll see. It'll be like old times."

I stared at her, the gaping emptiness inside me making it impossible to feel anything except slightly sick and completely exhausted. "I don't want old times, Mom. That was the whole point of going to Kasper Ridge. I'd finally found something else, the kind of life normal people have."

She wrinkled her nose. "Why on earth would you ever want to be normal?" She sank into the faded floral armchair across from where I sat in on the brown couch. "I've been normal, Penny. My whole life was normal, and it wasn't pretty. Scraping money together, worrying all the time. Did you know that my mother cleaned other peoples' houses?" She spat this as if she'd just admitted something disgusting.

I nodded. Grandma had died when I was little, but I remembered her soft voice, the way she smelled. She was kind, and hardworking.

Mom had worked too, as a cashier at the grocery store, which was where she met my dad. He'd been a financier, but not the smart, responsible kind. More like the kind with the fancy car and the promises of ridiculous returns that he could never deliver. And when the market turned, Dad lost it all. By then I was about four, and I became plan B.

We passed the days this way, in a state of mild disagreement. Mom dragged me to high-end stores, and restaurants, spending the advance I'd been given on the contract while I tried not to examine the feeling that I'd sold myself out somehow.

I considered texting Harrison—several times a day. But I had nothing to tell him, not really. He wasn't wrong. I'd lied to him. And how did you come back from that?

But my heart didn't really understand the logic. It ached and longed for him, for the way he'd looked at me, the way he'd traced his fingers gently across my cheek, pushed them into my hair as he'd kissed me like he wanted to own me. My body missed him too, bringing up sudden memories of the security and pleasure I'd found in his arms, in his room. At Kasper Ridge.

I missed the life I'd created in so short a time, and when Bennie called, it was hard not to let on. I'd texted her that I was leaving, and I missed her terribly. But I didn't want her to worry.

"I wish you'd come back," she said.

"I can't. I signed a contract."

"I guess I just don't understand why. You wanted to get away from all that." She sounded far away and I closed my eyes, imagining the soaring trees surrounding her little home, the cool crisp mountain air, and the expansive silence of night in Kasper Ridge.

I lay on the air mattress we'd set up in the dining room, shielded by folding screens. Mom had tried to convince me to sign a new lease in Brentwood, but I'd told her we should wait. She was doing a good job spending wildly on her own, I wasn't sure we'd be able to cover an expensive lease.

"I did. I do."

"Then why, Penny?"

"I fucked everything up. I couldn't stay. I lied to Harrison, and when he found out the truth, he was so angry." It hurt to admit my mistake, but I knew Bennie would understand.

"Why didn't you just tell him?" she asked.

I'd asked myself that question so many times I'd run out of potential answers. "I don't know. I wanted to keep Chrissy as far away from that new life I was building as I possibly could, I guess."

"Would it have brought her into it if you'd told him?"

"He'd see me differently. Everything would have changed."

"You don't know that for sure."

I shrugged, though she couldn't see me.

"I miss you up here," she said. "And I bet he does too."

"I haven't heard a word from him."

"Phones work both ways."

When we hung up, I stared at the water stain on the grey ceiling overhead for what felt like hours. How had everything wonderful turned so sour in such a short amount of time. I wanted to blame my mother, but the only person who really deserved the weight of the responsibility was me, and the knowledge made me feel physically sick.

I turned over to my side, hugging my knees up to my chest, wishing to rewind time. The best I could do was to replay the movies from my time in Colorado against the inaccurate screen in my mind.

Chapter 29
Here, Hold My Beer

PENNY

"You won't regret this, doll. They love you," Paul told me as we rode to the reunion event in the back of a stretch limousine he'd brought to pick us up. His steely hair was slicked back from his red face, and his shiny tie fell to one side of his voluminous gut beneath the expensive suit jacket he wore. It would have been funny if I didn't feel so sick inside, the shiny big car pulling up to the equivalent of a roadside motel as Mom's neighbors peered out of windows and open doors, scratching their heads. Planes rumbled loudly overhead, making it feel like the very air was being ripped apart as I stepped out of the shabby building in the red sheath dress and stilettos, followed by Mom wearing more sequins that I would have thought you could fit on a size two dress.

I didn't answer. It seemed unnecessary when Mom was there to speak for me. "She knows, Paul, and can we just say how grateful we are that you've kept us in mind through everything?"

We. Us.

There was no me. There was only Chrissy and what she could do for the "us" that Mom depended on.

"Our girl here is a star, that's just a fact," Paul said. My stomach turned. I didn't want to be his girl.

We pulled up behind a row of long black and white limousines, the other cast members arriving for the red carpet moments ahead of the reunion kickoff event. I actually felt a little bloom of warmth at the idea of seeing them again. We'd been close once.

As we drew up in the line, I could see the red carpet, the photographers packed against the velvet ropes next to it. I watched, feeling a bit like I was in someone else's body, someone else's life, as Edward Page exited the limo ahead of us, his wife on his arm, and paused to pose for photographers. Edward had played my father on the show, and his genuine kindness shined through even his show-business smile. I was happy to see him. One bright spot to all this, I supposed.

"Ready, doll?" Paul and my mother were both buzzing with excitement.

I'd tried to summon some enthusiasm, but the best I could manage was a strange bubbling unease deep in my gut and the same worrying nausea I'd felt since everything had fallen apart with Harrison.

"Here we go!" Mom sang as the valets pulled open the back door and Paul stepped out, turning to offer his hand first to

Mom, then to me. As my feet contacted the pavement and I slid forward far enough to lean out of the car, the noise of the gathered crowd notched up noticeably. When I stood, in full view, there were screams and cheers, and enough applause to make it feel like the noise was coming from inside me. My stomach turned.

We stepped forward and I tried to call on some ancient muscle memory to force a smile, to bring my hand up to wave happily at the photographers. Mom stuck close by my side until we were in the center of the red carpet, when she kissed my cheek and waved to the crowd, stepping away so they could get photos of me by myself.

I posed, looking out at the gathered swarm of people. They were calling out questions.

"Chrissy! Are you happy to be back?"

"Penny, do you think doing the show will help the public forget the scandals?"

"Penny, we heard you left show business, what made you change your mind?"

We were always instructed not to respond on the carpet, to look happy and agreeable but not to engage. I forced the wide smile to stay on my face as I posed and swiveled, eventually receiving the nod from the event organizer at the end of the carpet, signaling that I should continue walking to my seat.

We entered the antique theater, taking our seats at the front of the space where our names had been hung on the red velvet with little printed signs. I sat in the first row, right in the center, with my cast-mates all around me. Mom and Paul sat a few rows behind, and I felt relieved to be separated from them and their pressing expectations.

"So good to see you," Sasha Lane told me, leaning close from the next seat. She played my little sister on the show, and we'd never been close but I liked her well enough. "You doing okay? With everything?"

"Yeah, thanks," I said. Sasha had had her share of scandals too, but I suspected she cultivated them herself, sharing my mother's belief that as long as your name was in the press, it didn't matter why.

"Welcome, ladies and gentlemen!" The emcee of the event stepped onto the stage and the auditorium hushed, the lights dimming slightly. "We could not be more excited to have you here today, to witness the official announcement of an event years in the making!" The announcer turned to look behind him, his arm swooping to indicate a huge screen dropping from the ceiling onstage. When it was down, the theme song to the show started up loudly, and the opening montage from *Our Girl Chrissy* began to play, followed by a series of photographs that had appeared in the press over the years as the show had gained popularity.

The music was too loud, and my head—already throbbing— threatened to explode as my stomach continued its constant churning. My skin felt slightly clammy, and I forced myself to take several deep breaths. I would have to step onto that stage and speak soon enough. I needed to gather myself.

As the music faded and applause roared around me, the emcee welcomed several members of the cast to the stage, including Sasha, who grabbed my hand and squeezed it before running up to meet my television parents and other actors in front of the audience. They took seats up on the stage after being introduced, and finally, the announcer looked around at the gathered press and fans.

"And finally, the part we know you came for. It took some convincing, because she's very busy these days, as you can imagine. But we finally managed to secure a commitment from Our Girl Chrissy herself, Penny Davis! She kept us hanging, playing out the anticipation as only an excellent performer knows exactly how to do.

"Ladies and gentlemen, please welcome her to the stage to say a few words about this exciting new run of our favorite show . . . Penny Davis, Our Girl Chrissy!"

The theater exploded in noise around me, and my stomach dropped as I stood up, suddenly unsteady on my feet. Nerves had never been a big problem for me, but I was better in the studio than I ever had been live. Still, the way my blood raced in my ears and my vision seemed to be spotting didn't feel right. It all combined to make me believe I was making a terrible choice. I should never have agreed to this.

I made my way to the stairs at the side of the stage, thankful for the usher's steady arm as I climbed the steps. Sweat had gathered on my upper lip and brow, and I tried to wipe it away surreptitiously before stepping up to the stand under the bright lights.

My heart was hammering in my chest, and though I forced a smile, I wondered if it looked as sick as I felt.

The announcer took my arm, walking me to the podium, and then kissed my cheek, stepping back to give me the floor. I peered out into the sea of faces, the flashes of cameras doing nothing to help the dancing spots before my eyes.

"Hello," I managed to say, my voice somewhat shaky in my own ears. "Welcome back, everyone. It's amazing to see the support and enthusiasm that a fifteen year old show can still generate among its true fans, and I—" I paused as my stomach clenched. I clamped my lips shut. I was not going to vomit on stage. The press had enough to work with if their goal was humiliate me. I didn't need to add that to their arsenal.

I swallowed. Hard.

"Sorry," I said, laughing at my own nervousness. "I guess it's been a while since I've been in front of an audience."

The crowd tittered obediently at my bad joke.

I clutched the edges of the podium, my legs shaking beneath me.

"I just . . ." my vision darkened as my heart hammered in my chest and that dogged nausea flooded me again. "I, uh," I heard myself say. Then everything went dark.

Chapter 30
Chrissy Gets a Surprise

PENNY

As I lay in a hospital bed in the emergency room, Mom at my side in her over-the-top sequins, I couldn't help feeling relief. Being there, in front of all those people, all those cameras—it wasn't the right thing for me. I was sure of it now. It didn't matter about the money, or my mother. I couldn't do it.

Mom told me I'd slumped dramatically to the floor on stage, necessitating an ambulance as I slowly regained consciousness, there on the stage in front of everyone.

It wasn't the show they'd planned, but the drama I'd

brought had been over and above what anyone had hoped for, especially me.

"Mom, I'm sorry, I—"

"Honey, no need to apologize. You were nervous! That's normal. It's been so long. And honestly, you probably built more anticipation for the show than the silly event ever could have managed without the—"

"No." My voice came out much stronger than I felt. "You aren't listening. You never do. I'm not going to do the show. It's not right for me. Not now."

"You signed the contract," Mom reminded me, her eyes narrowing on my face.

"I'll talk to Paul." He'd want the advance back. He'd try to convince me to stay. I didn't care. About any of it.

She shook her head. "You're just not feeling well. We'll talk about this later at home, when you're better."

"Mom, no. I think this is why I'm not feeling well. I don't want to do it. This part of my life is over."

Mom opened her mouth to respond, but just then, the doctor pushed through the curtain into the space, a tablet in her hands. "Penny, hello."

"Hi," I managed.

"How are you feeling? That IV should be helping with the dehydration." She glanced at the tube attached to my arm.

"Yes, better," I said. I did feel better. Had I just been dehydrated?

"Well, we drew some blood when you first arrived, and I just wanted to review the findings with you." She glanced at Mom. "Do you, um, would you like privacy for this?"

"You can tell us both," Mom said.

The doctor looked at me for confirmation, and I said, "It's fine." If I asked Mom to leave, she'd just cause more drama, and since there was nothing to hide, I didn't see the point. Mom took my hand as if preparing for bad news. I sighed, letting her. This could not be over soon enough.

"Well, your bloodwork shows that you're about twelve weeks pregnant, Penny." She raised an eyebrow, as if uncertain whether this would be good news or bad.

"I'm . . ." I swallowed hard as Mom's hand tightened on mine. "I'm pregnant." It wasn't a question. It was the answer. No wonder I'd been feeling the way I had. It explained the nausea, the vomiting. Maybe it explained the brain fog and the confusion. I knew it couldn't explain the heartache . . . but in some way it made me feel a tiny bit closer to Harrison.

Harrison.

I squeezed my eyes shut, trying to imagine what would happen next.

I needed to tell Harrison.

The doctor had begun speaking again. "So we'll let that bag run, get you out of here today, and then you'll need to see an obstetrician regularly for prenatal care. And if you need, I can send a counselor in to review your options with you."

"That won't be necessary," Mom said abruptly, releasing my hand.

The doctor's gaze swung back to me. "It's fine," I said. "I'm fine."

"All right. Someone will be in to discharge you soon."

Four hours later I sat on the couch in Mom's dark apartment, my laptop on my knees as I bought a ticket back to Colorado.

Chapter 31
No Spare Barns Around

HARRISON

It was possible I'd actually begun to hallucinate.

By my count, Penny had been gone a full month, and I'd spent a good portion of that time flying back and forth from Kasper Ridge to Sacramento. I was exhausted and unhappy, and when I wasn't flying or working, I spent my time drinking whiskey and watching old movies in a futile effort to learn something that would help me become a better, more relatable human being.

So far, the whiskey had led me to feel like shit most mornings, and the movies had taught me that if you had a real problem, one surefire solution was to gather some friends and put on a show. This worked best if you had a spare barn, it seemed.

I knew I needed to quit both habits, but finding the motivation to do anything was a struggle. I missed her.

I missed the way her laugh would start low, almost like she was trying to hide it, and then escalate until it ricocheted through my heart. I missed the way her wide eyes would scan my face when she thought I might not be okay, and the way her full lips would pull into a smile when she saw me. I missed having her close in my bed during the cold winter nights, and knowing she was right there, on the other side of the patio window during the day when she was working in her office.

Which was why when I saw her standing in the lobby at the reception desk, talking to Aubrey at the end of another long day helping tourists learn to ski, I assumed I'd finally just lost my mind completely.

She looked beautiful, her dark hair cascading in waves over her shoulders. Her cheeks were glowing, and a sweet rosy shade colored her full lips. Her eyes danced as she laughed at something Aubrey said, and she leaned forward, putting both hands on the desk, as if to brace herself as she giggled.

I stood to one side of the lobby, having been on my way to the bar to see if I could talk Wiley out of another bottle of whiskey to go. But I'd stopped against the wall near the elevator, stunned to immobility by the apparition of the woman I loved.

When she turned toward me, sensing my heavy gaze, maybe, I jolted back to reality. It wasn't a hallucination. She was here. Penny was back.

Her face didn't light up when she spotted me, not exactly. She smiled at first, but the pull of her lips faded slowly into something wary. She lifted a hand to wave at me.

My heart lurched. What did this mean? She was back, but now we waved at each other?

I moved toward her, stopping a couple feet away, nervous for some reason, and unsure how to handle the massive emotions surging through me. I was angry at her for leaving, for never calling. I was hurt that things had ended so abruptly. But mostly, I was desperate to tell her how I felt, to tell her all the things I should have told her before she left.

"You're back." My twisting mind settled on sending the most obvious statement available shooting out of my mouth.

Aubrey had become involved with another guest farther down the reception desk, and Penny stepped toward me, her eyes narrowed on my face.

"I am," she said. She stopped a foot away from me, and I could feel the pull of her body to mine, even from there.

"For how long?" I asked.

"I'm not sure," she said, dropping my gaze and staring down at her hands. "Hopefully, for good."

Neither of us spoke for a second, the noise of the resort filling the silence between us. Then Penny looked up, meeting my eyes with a gaze that looked lost and hurt, and that made me want to step closer, to pull her into my arms. But it didn't feel like I had any right to do it, so I stood still. Cleared my throat.

"Harrison," she said softly, "we need to talk."

"Yes," I agreed. I needed to tell her what she meant to me. I needed to ask her forgiveness for being such a clueless asshole. I needed to see if we could try again. "Upstairs?"

She nodded. "Aubrey gave me my old room. Maybe you could give me a few minutes to get settled, and then come over in a bit?"

"Okay," I said.

Together, we stepped into the elevator, my mind flashing scenarios to my body like suggestions. Take her hand. Cage her against the wall of the elevator and kiss her. Drop to your knees and profess your love.

I stood still, following her from the elevator car and down the hall to my door, where I stopped, watching her proceed to her own room.

"See you in a few," she said, disappearing inside.

Penny was back.

And my head was a spiraling mess.

I dashed to my desk, pulling out a notecard and writing down the things I needed to say. I made a bulleted list so I wouldn't miss anything, and tucked it into my back pocket. There. My mind was organized. Now I could tell her all the things I should have said in the first place, before I let her leave.

Maybe there was still a chance.

When exactly fifteen minutes had passed, I took a deep breath and headed to Penny's room, knocking lightly on the door.

She opened it, stepping aside to let me enter.

"You're going to want to sit," she said, giving me a look I couldn't decipher as she turned to face me.

I did as she said, sitting in one of the two arm chairs facing one another. Penny took the other chair, her hands on her knees. Then she took a deep breath and spoke again. "Harrison. I'm pregnant."

"What? Wait . . ." I should never have let my mouth open. My mind had barely begun to process the fact she was here, physically here, not just a conjecture I'd managed in a drunken stupor. And now, she was saying things so outside the realm of what I'd expected we might talk about that my haywire mind couldn't respond appropriately.

"I'm pregnant. With a baby," she said, adding the explanatory phrase at the end for those of us having trouble with basic concepts. Her expression was wary, almost scared.

"And it's mine?" I asked.

Even as the words were streaming from my lips, I knew they

were wrong. I wished I could rewind and pull them back, rephrase my question or consider the wisdom of asking it at all. Why would she be telling me this if it weren't my baby? But I had watched a few of the dramatic entertainment news segments that had aired when the sex video of Penny and some man had been leaked. They'd insinuated that she was less than selective about partners.

But that was the point of sensationalist new shows, wasn't it? And I knew Penny better than they did.

Penny was already rising, moving to open the door of the suite.

"Wait, Penny."

"You should go," she said, and her voice shook.

"No, I just—"

"Please get out."

I had no choice. I stood and moved like the gob smacked zombie I'd become back out the door of her suite. When it shut in my face, my world seemed to click off at the same time. Nothing made sense.

What did I do now? How did I fix this?

Chapter 32
Of Course It's Yours

PENNY

Sending Harrison away hurt. I wanted to curl up on the couch and cry, but I knew doing that wouldn't help matters. Instead, I took a deep breath, pulled myself together, and called Bennie. Within an hour, she had arrived, her hands full of more bags and boxes than I would have thought one small woman was capable of carrying.

"Oh my gosh, come in," I said, taking her roller bag out of her hands. "You planning on staying a while?" I was joking, but I had invited her to stay overnight. The idea of being alone, knowing Harrison was right down the hall was too much. His reaction to the news . . . I still didn't really know what to think of it. It certainly wasn't good, though.

"I'm staying exactly as long as you need me to," Bennie said, dropping a bag onto the couch and then carrying the rest of her things to the table to one side of the room and putting everything else there. "So I brought my stuff for work."

I had poked my nose into one of the brown grocery bags on the couch. "I don't think this ice cream will keep until tomorrow. I've got a mini fridge, but no freezer, Ben."

"That's for us," she said, producing two spoons and another pint of ice cream. She grinned and brought it with her to the couch, where she sat, pulling her legs up beneath her and taking the lid off her ice cream.

"You got my favorite flavor," I said, picking up the pint of salted caramel and doing an internal wellness check. Could I eat ice cream right now? My stomach felt settled, despite the scene with Harrison not long ago. I got comfy on the couch, facing her. "Thanks for this."

"Of course. Now tell me everything, starting with the moment you left here."

In that moment, I felt a surge of love for my friend, for this place. She had already demonstrated more genuine concern for me than my mother showed in the time I was home. Bennie didn't care what I could do for her. She had done all this for me, dropped everything and rushed over here to take care of me.

With a lump in my throat and my heart a little bit lighter than it had been before, I told my friend everything.

"'Is it mine?' You can't be serious. What an asshole." Bennie dropped her spoon into her empty pint of ice cream on the low table next to the couch.

"I know, right?" I said, not quite able to bring myself to certainty that Harrison was actually an asshole. "I mean, I guess he was surprised."

"Um, yeah, but so were you."

"Right, but I've had a little time to get used to this. I kind of sprung it on him." I felt my initial anger at him dissipating a bit as I thought about it from his point of view.

"Maybe, but still, what a loaded question!" She pushed a corkscrew curl off her face and wound it back into the bun on top of her head.

"I know. I mean . . . I guess he's seen the videos by now, and all the news. They say really awful things about me. And if he went all the way back and watched the ones from right after the first scandal . . ."

"Then what?" Bennie asked, sounding angry. "Then he'll find out that you were ridiculously famous and that people tried to take advantage of you at every turn. Even your own parents!" Her little chin lifted, and her eyes glittered.

My heart warmed inside my chest. This was friendship. A friend who liked you enough to feel anger on your behalf. Bennie looked like she was ready to kick someone's ass.

So when a knock sounded at the door and Harrison's voice followed soon after, I was a little worried for him. Bennie bolted to answer it.

"You've got a lot of nerve."

I couldn't see Harrison—Bennie had barely opened the door a crack.

"Can I see her, please? I owe her an apology." He did sound sorry, and my heart lurched.

"Hell yes, you do. You owe her more than that."

"I—Bennie, please."

"She's not up to dealing with this right now. Give her the night to get settled. Maybe that'll give you time to get your head out of your ass."

"I . . ." I heard Harrison drop a heavy sigh, as if he was

carrying the same overwhelming burden inside him that I'd been hauling around since I'd left. "Yeah, okay."

Bennie shut the door, and I felt a little flame extinguish inside me. "Maybe I should talk to him," I said, my voice weak.

"You will," she said. "But let's give him enough time to really get his head around what happens next."

"What does happen next?" I asked, trying to laugh. I'd thought about things a lot, and I was pretty sure I knew what I wanted, I just didn't know what he wanted. I was keeping the baby, and I'd give it the childhood and life I'd never had a chance to have. With or without Harrison.

"That's one hundred percent your choice. And I'm behind you no matter what you choose." Bennie sat down closer to me now, wrapping an arm around my shoulders. I let my head fall to rest on the soft blue sweater she wore, pulling reassurance from my friend's fierce protection of me.

"I'm going to keep the baby," I said softly. "No matter what Harrison does."

Bennie's hand tightened on my shoulder, and I let her hug me for a while, feeling some of her strength penetrate the fierce hug, feeling my heart lift just a bit. We wouldn't be alone, I realized. Even if Harrison wanted nothing to do with us.

"I'll talk to a lawyer," I said softly. "Just in case, so I'm ready. If he's not interested in being in the baby's life, that's fine. I just want him to sign something saying he's not going to change his mind."

"You want him to sign away his paternity rights?"

I nodded, even though hearing the idea out loud was crushing. "Only if he doesn't want us."

"Okay," Bennie said. "CeeCee's cousin is a family practice lawyer in Denver." She patted my shoulder and rose, pulling a thick book out of one of her many bags. "Now, let's learn about this little peanut inside you. What week are you on?"

"Thirteen," I said, sitting up a little straighter. I'd been so mired in emotion, I hadn't really done any research about what was happening inside me. But suddenly, I was filled with curiosity.

Bennie flipped the pages of the book and then stopped, spreading it open on her lap. Then she began to read, telling me that my baby—barely more than a concept before this minute—should be as big as a lemon already. She said that the eyes would remain shut for a while, but that vocal cords were forming and the head was roughly half of the baby's total size. I almost made a joke about Harrison's call sign, Brainiac, and how the baby's brain would probably be huge, but that felt like something that was probably off limits, considering I didn't know yet what he wanted.

I sighed heavily, and Bennie looked at me a long moment. "It's pretty fucking real, isn't it?"

"Too real. Scary real," I said, nodding.

She closed the book, setting it on the table. "I have one more thing for you. And then bed." She rose and dug around in another of her bags, and then pulled out a tiny, crocheted sweater. It was cream colored and delicate, and so small it seemed made for a doll, not a human.

"Oh my god, where did you get this?" I asked.

"I made it," she said, her lips in an uncertain smile. "I started it as soon as you called me."

"But that was less than a week ago!"

She lifted a shoulder. "I've been crocheting since I was small. My grandmother taught me. I'm quick now, and it gives me something to do while I watch TV. This sweater is courtesy of a binge of *Upload*."

"I don't think I've heard of that one."

"You're missing out. Robbie Amell. Deep sigh."

"I'll add it to my list. I think I'm going to have a lot of quiet nights on the couch while I work on growing this human being." I held the tiny sweater to my stomach, feeling that same surge of love rush through me that I'd felt earlier. What a strange mix of emotions—my heart was in pieces over Harrison, and especially his reaction to the news of the baby. But at the same time, I felt surrounded by love here, and certain I'd come to the right place, no matter what Harrison decided. I was surrounded by love here in a way I'd never been before, and there was a security in that. In this place, and these genuine people I'd come to love right back.

"Thanks for everything, Bennie," I said, rising to go get ready for bed. "I love you."

"I love you too, girl." She hugged me tight, and then held me by the shoulders. "Tomorrow we'll get your first appointment set up, and then we'll start talking about the shower." I imagined what that would be like—everyone celebrating with me. Friends who really cared about me. I'd never had any of it before. I felt so lucky.

It was all a lot to process, but I smiled at my friend. "That sounds good."

She kissed my cheek and let me go.

"That turns into a bed," I said, pointing at the couch.

She nodded and turned, pulling sheets and a comforter from another bag. "I know! I've got it handled."

"Do you teach tomorrow?" I asked her, realizing it was Sunday night.

"I have a sub tomorrow. It's baby day, like I said. But I'm prepared for work Tuesday, even if I'm still here with you."

"You didn't have to do that."

"I did, actually. That's what you do for friends." She said this in a way that didn't invite further discussion, and I went back to my bedroom, piecing through the strange cloud of feelings inside me. I'd been alone my whole life, even when my parents had been with me, even while Paul looked after my professional life. No one had ever really been in my corner. But now, with this baby coming and my friends at my side, I had the sense I'd never really be alone again.

As I closed my eyes to sleep, I forced my mind away from the one tender spot inside me, the place where Harrison's love was supposed to be. God, I missed him. This would all be perfect if only I didn't love him so much.

Chapter 33
When Men Stop Being Morons

HARRISON

"You said what?" Monroe's beer splashed over her hand as she set it down fiercely on the bar in the Toothy Moose, where we'd gone for a meal when she'd found me moping around the lobby, scaring the guests.

I'd called Gator, let him know I might be a couple days late back to work in California this week. We were between deliverables, so it wasn't a big deal, and he even suggested I could work remotely for the week if I was tired of flying back and forth.

I was, but I had bigger issues.

"Tell me again. Exactly what you said," Monroe said, her

eyes narrow as she looked at me. She looked settled, confident, and I envied her ease in the world. She and Mateo were building a house in the neighborhood connected to the resort where Lucy and Will had begun construction of their home too. Until the snow cleared, though, everyone spent most of their time in the staff wing at the resort, though Mateo and Lily maintained their home too, and sometimes Monroe stayed with them. I envied the confident happiness I saw in my friend. She'd figured her life out. I wanted the same.

"I asked if it was mine."

"I'm surprised she didn't light you on fire, you moron." Monroe shook her head, laughing at my evident stupidity.

"Maybe she should have. Put me out of my misery."

"Oh for fuck's sake. Are you still doing this moping thing where you whine about how you aren't soft and fuzzy enough?"

"I lost a job because I wasn't empathetic enough, Monroe. It's a real problem."

My friend stared at me over the rim of her beer as she swallowed several long, slow gulps. I got the distinct impression she was trying to make me uncomfortable, but I was already so miserable it didn't make a dent.

"It's a real thing," I said again, sipping my own beer as she put hers down.

"You sure have made it one. It's a good excuse too, I guess."

A little bolt of anger flared in me, causing me to lean in a bit. "What?"

"You're sitting here telling me that there's something wrong with your personality and that you can't 'people' well enough, while the woman you love, who I'm pretty sure loves you back, and oh, by the way, who is carrying your baby"—Monroe's eyes flared wide as she said this—"is back at the resort believing you think she's some kind of slut who sleeps around mountain towns getting knocked up."

"I don't—"

"I know you don't actually think that. I know you didn't even doubt it was yours in the first place." Monroe was on a roll, her cheeks flushing pink as the words rushed from her. "Did you?"

"No."

"Brainiac. Your issue isn't that you don't have enough empathy."

"It's not?"

"Let me ask you this. Did you basically abandon everything else going on in your life to come up here when Ghost called you and said he needed help?"

"Well, yes, but—"

"Why would you do that? You needed to find a real job, to be all professorial and shit. Why would you agree to come up here and wander around an ancient resort with a bunch of former pilots you used to know?"

"Ghost needed help, and I worry about that dude."

She nodded. "Because . . .?"

"Because we're friends?"

"And?"

I shook my head. "This." I jammed my finger into the bar top, and the bartender jumped, rushing to bring us two more beers. I nodded my thanks and lowered my voice, keeping my hands in my lap. "This is the shit I'm no good at. I don't know what you want me to say."

Monroe smiled as if I'd just made her point for her.

Fuck. I'd never figure people out. I drank half the new beer in one long swallow.

"You still don't get it?" she asked, leaning in close.

"No."

"You worry about Ghost because you know what he's been through. And you felt for him when that was all going on. You worry about him because you care about him. And you do the same for me all the time."

"You're my friends," I pointed out, a tiny light threatening to illuminate all the dark stupidity in my mind suddenly.

"And that, sir, is empathy. I'm sorry to tell you that you have it."

"But—"

"Hey, being empathetic doesn't mean you can't also be an asshole sometimes."

"Well that's a relief. Didn't want to have to give that up."

"Course not."

I chuckled and sat quietly with my friend for a minute. And then I realized I still had no idea what to do.

Monroe must have read my mind. "So what do you do now?"

I shrugged. "Go back to Penny. Say more stupid shit and hope some of it comes out okay?"

"What do you want, Brainiac?" Her voice was soft, understanding.

I hesitated. I knew what I wanted, but it seemed so impossible now. "I want to be with her. I want her to be with me."

My friend nodded. "And the baby?"

The word, the very thought of it sent a confusion whoosh of emotion twisting through me. Excitement, hope, fear, and a strange sense of enormity. Like knowing there was a baby coming connected me somehow to the global community or to some greater humanity than I'd felt part of before. It was humbling and terrifying.

"I want to be with Penny. And raise our baby."

"So tell her that." She smiled in a self-satisfied way, like she'd just mastered the issue of climate change.

"Think it's really that easy?"

"Maybe."

* * *

The next day I went looking for Penny in her office, but she wasn't there. Aubrey sat at her desk and grinned when I opened the door after knocking.

"Hey, Harrison. What's up? Thought you'd be off to California by now."

"Working remote this week. Penny around?"

Aubrey shook her head. "First doctor's appointment," she said. "Bennie's cousin got her in when someone else cancelled I guess, so she kinda rushed out."

My heart fell like a hard apple inside my chest. I hadn't even thought about that. Of course there'd be doctor's appointments. I should be there with her. But would she even want me there?

"Do you know when she'll be back?" I asked.

"Should be soon," Aubrey said. "She's been gone a couple hours."

I nodded, feeling directionless. I wanted to see Penny. Needed to see her.

"I'll let her know you're looking for her," she said as I turned.

"Thanks."

"Hey Harrison," Aubrey called when the door was almost shut. I poked my head back in. "You're going to fix things now that she's back, right?"

I sighed, accepting that literally everyone knew every bit of my business up here. "I'm gonna try."

I didn't get the chance until later that night. It took all my nerve to walk down the hall to Penny's room and knock, and then I stood there hoping Bennie wasn't going to come to the door. She was small, but she was fierce, and I didn't know if I could manage convincing her and then having to talk to Penny too. The little package I held in my hands felt inadequate, stupid.

The door opened slowly inward, and Penny stood before me in black leggings and a big Kasper Ridge sweatshirt, her feet bare and her hair down around her shoulders. She looked young and so beautiful it made my skin ache.

"Hi," she said softly.

"Hi," I returned. "Could we talk for a minute?"

She nodded, stepping backwards and then going to sit on the couch. I closed the door to the suite and followed her, sitting a little way away.

"I need to talk to you anyway," she said. "I spoke to an attorney today, and there are just a few things I'd like you to sign."

"Sign? What?"

She looked hesitant, but then took a deep breath and went on, talking so fast I had to squint to keep up. "I don't know what you want, but I definitely don't want you thinking you don't have choices. I didn't come back here for you, to rope you into anything. I came back because I feel like this is where I belong. And you don't have to be a part of that.

"So I got these papers drawn up for you if you want them. To relinquish your paternal rights. We can do this officially and then you won't ever have to worry about me coming to you for anything, or about having to do anything for the baby." Her voice was strong and clear, and she tilted her pretty chin up as she spoke.

I shook my head. "I don't want to do that," I told her.

"But you can. I'm letting you walk away. I don't want you to be with me because of a baby."

"Penny," I said, my voice cracking. "I don't want to walk away. I want to do the complete opposite of that. I want to stay, to be with you. And to raise our baby with you."

The words sounded foreign coming from my lips, but they also felt more right than any I'd spoken before. *Our baby.*

Penny didn't speak. Her lips parted and then closed again, and she shook her head. "I knew you would do this, that you would try to do the right thing. That's why I want you to sign the papers, so you don't have to feel obligated—"

I putting the little gold-wrapped package aside and took her hands in mine, dropping to the floor in front of her. "Penny, stop. I don't feel obligated. I feel a lot of things, but that isn't one of them. Mostly I feel . . ." I swallowed hard. "I feel like I should have told you a long time ago that I don't care about your past. I only want your future. And I want to be in it."

Penny's eyes held mine, and I watched as hers bean to shine with unshed tears. "Harrison, don't—"

"I should have said it before you left. I love you. And I already love this baby. And I can't think of anything better than being with you, raising a baby with you, building a life."

"I love you too," she whispered, the tears finally rolling down her pink cheeks.

I reached a thumb out to press one away, and Penny caught my hand, kissing my fingers and then dropping her cheek into my palm, holding me there. "I missed you," she said quietly, her eyes shut.

"I missed you too," I said, whispering for fear of breaking the moment, waking up from this blissful dream.

"I have something for you. Your present."

"From Christmas?" Her smile widened, even through the tears.

I nodded and handed her the little box, the gold wrapping glinting in the soft light of her room.

She accepted it and untied the red ribbon slowly, glancing up at me. "I thought you decided it wasn't right or something."

"Maybe it wasn't at the time. Now I think it is." I hoped she would understand, that she would like it.

Penny opened the tiny box to reveal the necklace inside, a simple gold chain with the word "Truth" in the center in script. It had been meant to be an inside joke, and had felt silly and trite on Christmas eve, but now, after everything, it felt meaningful.

"I love it," she said. "It's us. Our word."

I nodded.

"Will you help me put it on?"

I clasped the gold around her neck as she turned away, loving the look of the gold against her skin.

"Kiss me?" she said turning back around, her eyes glittering dreamily.

"I can do better than that," I said, moving to the couch and pulling her into my lap. I took her beautiful face in my hand and let myself look for a long moment at the woman I loved, the mother of my child. And then I kissed her, long and hard, pushing every ounce of longing and passion I felt for her into the press of my lips, the pulse of my tongue. And Penny responded in kind, winding her arms around my neck and pressing herself against me.

A second later, she stiffened and pulled away, and fear gripped my heart. Had she changed her mind? Decided this wasn't right after all?

"I have to get something," she said, sliding off my lap.

"Right now?" Relief wound around the stress inside me, relaxing it only a little. "Can it wait?"

She shook her head and disappeared to the side table near the door, digging through a bag that was lying there. A moment later she returned, holding something in her hands, a piece of paper, which she held out to me.

It was fuzzy, a black and white print out, but I knew exactly what it was. Who it was. "This is our baby?"

She nodded, her eyes shining.

"Did they show you what was what? Can you help me?" I squinted at the fuzzy shapes, wanting to see my baby, to see my future. My chest felt tight as Penny slid back onto my lap and took the paper, turning it so we could both see.

"This," she said, her finger tracing a round shape in the center, "is the baby's head."

The tightness in my chest grew stronger and I swallowed hard.

"And this is the body, the spinal cord."

"And it all looks good? Everything is okay?"

Penny set the paper on the table in front of us. "Everything is perfect." She wrapped her arms around me and for a long moment, we held each other as thoughts of the future—of my baby, our baby—made me feel like I might cry. Being close to Penny helped, and the overwhelming feelings ratcheting through me slowly became easier to bear.

"Can I take this off?" I asked, pulling up the hem of her sweatshirt and letting my palm glide along the silky curve of her ribs.

She nodded, helping me push it off over her head.

For a moment, I just stared at the beauty of her exposed skin, soft and smooth and pale. And then I bent my head to kiss her, trailing kissed from her clavicle between her breasts, flipping her so she was on her back on the couch and I was crouched above her, continuing my trail farther south.

I took my time with her, lavishing every inch of exposed skin with kisses, tiny nips of my teeth, and letting my hands slide along the sides of her body as my mouth dropped lower, to kiss along the waistband of her leggings.

Soon, the leggings were off, and Penny lay on the couch

before me, every centimeter exposed to me, every centimeter perfect. I sat up, letting myself take her in for a long moment, my eyes trailing down her body, committing it to memory once again.

"You're making me nervous," she laughed, pulling at my shirt, coaxing me to take it off. I whipped it over my head.

"Nothing to be nervous about. I'm just admiring you," I said. "How the hell did I ever let you go?"

"You didn't let me. I left."

I shook my head, preferring not to think about that now.

I took her mouth with mine again, bracing myself over her so I didn't crush her beneath me, but Penny's hands were pulling at my back and her body was arching up into me.

"I want to feel you on me," she breathed into my mouth.

"I don't want to crush you. Or the baby."

"You won't."

I gave in, sinking my weight onto Penny's softness, still careful to brace myself a bit. Feeling our skin pressed together, the warmth we created, had my head spinning and my breath coming faster. My jeans were becoming uncomfortable, and I reached to unfasten them, push them from my body.

For a moment, we lay like that, our bodies pressed together, the heat and comfort working together to make my brain short-circuit so I could think of nothing but Penny. But then, I had a thought.

"Let's go to the bedroom." I raised myself up to move.

Penny pulled me down. "It's so far," she said, her voice a whine.

"It'll be worth it." I stepped back, taking a moment to regain my balance and then scooped the woman I loved off the couch and carried her to the bedroom, where I deposited her gently onto the bed and then climbed on beside her. I lay on my side, letting my hand explore Penny's body as I watched her face.

When my fingers traced downward, over the smooth flat stomach where somehow, miraculously, our child lived, Penny sucked in a sharp breath. I petted her folds, gently, taking her mouth in mine, and then used her wetness to coax her open, to find her clit and tease it.

Penny moaned into my mouth, and I used two firm fingers to begin a steady rhythm, circling and coaxing her along as her breath came faster.

"Please," she moaned softly, and at that moment I knew I'd give her anything she wanted.

She reached for me, her cool fingers wrapping my thickened cock and guiding it toward her.

"I didn't bring a condom," I said, my fingers never leaving the work of making her writhe and gasp.

"Doesn't matter now," she said, sliding herself toward me, demanding with her body what her words weren't saying.

I put a leg over her, keeping our bodies pressed together, enjoying every point of contact with her skin and unwilling to let it go. And like that—with every part of me dying to be as close to her as possible—I slid home, nearly passing out from the joy and pleasure of it.

"Oh god," Penny moaned. "God, I missed this."

I was beyond words, but the kiss I gave her answered her, and when her teeth nipped at my bottom lip, I almost lost it.

I moved in and out of her, each thrust celebrating the welcoming heat of her body, each movement away, a tiny loss that nearly broke me. I felt like all that I needed in the world was to stay here, to stay inside Penny, to be with her in every way possible.

But when I stopped thrusting, Penny moaned and took over, moving her body beneath me in a way that gripped and pulled at every inch of me. She moved, setting a pace of her own, and it was the most exquisite ecstasy I'd ever experienced.

"Holy shit," I breathed, as Penny began making a rhythmic cry that told me she was close. I was teetering on the brink, in the midst of more pleasure than I'd thought my body was capable of.

It was all I could do to brace myself, let her take me on this ride, and not take over by force, thrusting madly into my release. Penny was in charge, and I was going to let her see it through, even though it might kill me.

After a moment of the most delicious torture I'd ever known, Penny cried out and stilled, but I could feel the fluttering pulses inside her as she came. "Oh god," she cried, her arms tightening around me, her body arching into mine. "Oh my god."

That was it, her desperation and release pushed me over the edge, and I didn't even have to move as a shiver of lightning started low in my spine and then slashed its way up, sending stars shooting in my vision. I felt myself thrusting, milking the last of my release, as we cried out together, and when it was over and I'd come back to myself slightly, I rolled to one side, keeping Penny in my arms, our bodies connected.

"Truth?" I said softly.

"Always."

"I love you so much," I told her.

"I love you too."

As Penny drifted to sleep in my arms, my brain spun. I had to do this right. Decisions needed to be made, things needed to be aligned. A baby was coming, and I was going to do everything in my power to make sure its life, and Penny's, were as good as they could possibly be.

Chapter 34
Tiny Clothes and Enormous Wraps

PENNY

When I woke up the next morning, grey light was filtering through clouds outside, casting my bedroom in a gray pall. I was in Harrison's arms, and for a long while, I forced my eyes to stay shut, kept my mind from working too hard.

But there were so many questions to be answered still.

I turned to face the man I loved and blinked my eyes open to find him staring at me, his stern face dreamy in the soft morning light, but those steel eyes sharp.

"Hi," I said, snuggling in closer as his arms tightened around me.

"Good morning," he whispered, tucking his chin to the top of my head.

I breathed him in, the comfort and reassurance of his mountain man smell settling me somewhat. But not completely. Something was still not right.

"Truth," I whispered. It was a question this time, and Harrison understood.

He sighed. "I don't know if we can stay here, Penny."

I didn't move, but my blood, which had been flowing warm till now, turned chill. "What?"

"A ski bum can't raise a family. Not the right way. And I've got a good job in California."

Now I moved back slightly to look into Harrison's face. His brow creased and I understood the steel in his eyes was worry. "I don't want to move," I said. "I love it here. These people are my family now." I thought about Bennie and CeeCee, about the resort staff. "And I like my job. I'm good at it." They hadn't hired anyone to replace me yet, so it was still mine, according to Aubrey.

The worry line deepened between Harrison's brows. "I know." He sounded so miserable. I lifted a hand to smooth the brow, to trace a line down his stubbled jaw.

"We can stay here," I said, hoping to convince him. "I have some money. And our baby doesn't need a lot. As long as we love them, we'll be fine."

Harrison's eyes dropped shut for a long beat, and when he opened them, I saw a resolve there that broke my heart. "I don't want to scrape by, to worry about money and security. It was fine when it was just me, my risks were my own. But for you, and for our baby . . . I want more."

"We only need you."

"And you have me. But the job in California pays well, Penny. Security, benefits. All the things a family needs."

"I don't want to go." I hated the plea in my voice, the way I suddenly felt perched on the edge of a canyon, about to plunge back into uncertainty and darkness. Would I survive again?

His eyes dropped shut and when he opened them again, I saw clarity there. Determination. "Okay. If that's what you want. I'll keep doing what I've been doing then. Working there during the week, coming back on weekends," he said. "We need the benefits. The security. I can't leave the job."

I frowned. It wasn't what I wanted, but it wasn't awful, either. "I wish you could just stay here," I tried again. "With us."

He sighed. "I know. Me too."

I'd been working on a benefits package for the full-time staff at the resort, but we weren't ready to roll it out yet. "I guess so," I said, but my heart wasn't agreeing with the plan. "I just hate the thought of being here without you."

"You won't be alone," Harrison said softly. His hand drifted to my stomach and rested there, and I wondered if he meant the baby or our friends here in Kasper Ridge. He was right. I wouldn't be alone, not really. In fact, now that a child was on the way, I felt a little bit like I'd never be quite alone again. Not in the same way.

* * *

Harrison stayed a week more, and then left for California on a Monday morning. And we went on like that for months.

I missed him desperately, but work was busy now that the resort was at full capacity, and my evenings were full, when I wanted them to be. Bennie, CeeCee, Lucy, and even Annalee had become the baby's unofficial extended family, calling themselves the "Cool Aunt Posse." It was touching, actually—they took it completely on themselves to outfit the baby and make sure it had every accessory known to man.

"This is some kind of fancy wearable baby thing," Annalee was telling me, holding up a piece of fabric that was long and frankly very intimidating.

"The baby wears that? It looks huge," I said, a hand on my stomach.

"No," CeeCee laughed. "It's for you."

"I've seen moms wearing these when they drop their older kiddos off at school," Bennie said, taking the wrap from Annalee's hands and holding it up, her face wrinkling into a frown of concentration. "You must put your arms in here, then wrap one of these things around this way, and . . . Annalee, did you keep the directions?"

Annalee shrugged and knelt to dig through the packaging materials she'd crumpled and discarded when she took the wrap out. "I can't find them," she said. "Oh, but I almost missed this!" She held up a book. "It's for Brainiac."

"*Fatherhood for Assholes?*" Lucy laughed.

Annalee grinned. "Perfect for him, don't you think?"

"He's not an asshole," Bennie said. "He just takes a while to grow on you."

"Didn't take long to grow on me," I said. "He's definitely not an asshole." My voice might have gotten just a bit wistful.

"How's that all going?" CeeCee asked. "The flying back and forth thing?"

Brainiac had been commuting to California for the new job for three months now, and it was wearing on us both. He'd come back early for one doctor's appointment, but it felt like he was missing everything else.

"It's hard," I admitted. "We talk on the phone a lot, which is weird, but it's all we have."

"He looked exhausted last time he was here," Lucy said. "I

can't imagine that's easy, working all week then hauling yourself halfway across the country to work more for the weekend."

"I think it *is* exhausting," I said, thinking about the few weekends he'd missed because he'd gotten stuck at work and then been too tired to fly. He beat himself up for letting me down, for asking Antonio to work the weekends too. I hated the uncertainty of not knowing if he'd make it back to Colorado. I felt like I was always on edge, always vulnerable to his schedule, his job.

"Is he coming next week?" Bennie asked. "For the shower?"

The girls had planned a baby shower for the following Saturday, and I was looking forward to it, but couldn't help wondering if Harrison would make it. "I hope so."

"He'd better," Annalee growled. I loved the way her friendship with Harrison had turned into complete loyalty to me and this baby. "Or I'll have to give him a stern talking to."

"Glad it isn't me," CeeCee said, laughing. Annalee was intimidating without trying, but when she was angry, she was downright frightening. Something about the former fighter pilot vibe, I supposed. I certainly didn't want to end up on her bad side.

"Okay, we'll let you get some rest," Lucy said, picking up the wrap and frowning at it. "And if you'll let me take this, I'll look up the directions online and next time you see me, I'll be a crazy wrap garment thing expert."

"Okay," I laughed. "Thanks."

The girls left, and after cleaning up the packaging, I stared at the growing collection of baby items in the corner of my suite. I didn't have a crib yet, but there was a car seat, a swing, piles of onesies and burp cloths, diapers in boxes, a terrifying-looking pump contraption for breast milk, and other things I hadn't even really begun to figure out. Everyone here was excited about the baby.

I was too. But I was also terrified and surprisingly lonely. The growing bump had begun to feel more real to me. My pants were no longer fitting, and Bennie had given me these little extenders I could fit between the buttons on jeans to wear them a bit longer. But most of the time I wore leggings and big sweaters, and I was starting to wear some of the maternity things I'd ordered online.

Mom had sent a package too, though we hadn't actually spoken since I left. Mom had been angry and hurt, and Paul had been too. But Paul had been surprisingly understanding, and the network had let me out of the contract due to the baby. Chrissy couldn't be pregnant, they said. It wasn't part of their vision for the character.

There was no card in the package sent from Mom's address, but the box had a tiny white gown inside it with teeny satin shoes and a little bonnet. There was a picture, too, of my parents holding me as a baby. I was wearing the gown. My christening, I supposed, staring at the photo. My parents were both beaming down at me in it, and in that moment, we looked like a regular family. Like a couple with a new baby they were going to love and cherish.

But that isn't what we'd been.

Still, the gesture from Mom felt meaningful, like maybe the beginning of a bridge that could mend the gap between us. I didn't like the idea of her alone, and thought that someday I might be able to reach back to her, even invite her to join me here. But that was in the future.

Right now, I had other things to worry about.

Chapter 35
A Different Kind of Shower

HARRISON

I had a problem.

I loved my new job. I was back in the lab, working with software and mechanical engineers and consulting on avionics for the product Gator was developing. I didn't feel awkward or ill at ease. On the contrary, compared to many of the guys I worked with, I felt like the socially adept cool guy most of the time. It was a lot like being in the squadron, surrounded by other engineers and computer science majors. People seemed to have the impression that fighter pilots were mostly jocks, but the truth was, a lot of us were pretty geeky.

Those were my people and I loved feeling like I belonged somewhere again.

But I also loved Penny and Kasper Ridge.

There was a strange part of me that found I actually missed the day-to-day variety that running the ski program had brought. I was so busy believing I hated interacting with the public that I hadn't noticed it had started to grow on me.

But what I really missed was her.

It wasn't even the obvious stuff, the kissing . . . the sex. I definitely missed that.

But it was more about the little day-to-day glimpses I'd enjoyed when we'd worked in the same location. I'd loved catching sight of her grabbing a coffee from the stand outside when I was picking up a new ski student from the patio meeting area. I'd loved seeing her across the lobby in the middle of the day, heading in to get her lunch, and those stolen moments when we actually had a little time together during the busy days. It felt a lot like Penny was my partner. My person. Seeing her, even if we didn't have time to speak or touch, bolstered me in some small way, made me feel a little less alone in the world. She was there. And she loved me.

But I was here.

And when I wasn't in California, working long days and crashing at night only to do it all again, I was flying back to Colorado and trying to pack as much into every weekend as possible. It was exhausting, but I didn't feel right letting Penny see how tired I was. Instead, she caught me falling asleep in movies or drifting off on the couch when the crew got together up in Ghost's room.

That was why I took a whole week in April for the baby shower. The shower itself was only one Saturday afternoon, but this gave me the opportunity to attend a doctor's appointment with her and relax a little bit.

"And you're definitely coming?" Penny had asked, sounding nervous as I finished my pre-check in the plane.

"I'm literally in the plane. I'm coming."

"Okay." She still sounded uncertain.

"I'll see you in a couple hours."

"See you soon."

Penny's hesitation stoked a little coal that had been burning inside me the last couple months. The physical distance between us felt like it was starting to affect us in other ways.

And that terrified me.

When I arrived at the resort, I was exhausted as usual, but determined not to show it.

"You're here!" Penny greeted me at the door and threw her arms around my neck. The little bump that had begun to emerge from her flat tummy had grown bigger, and I could feel our baby pressed between us. My heart hurt as I thought about how much I had missed.

I hugged Penny tightly, breathing her sweet scent and letting it wash through me. I was home.

"Are you tired?" she asked, stepping back with one hand on her belly, almost like she was protecting our baby.

"Nope," I lied. "Just need to put my stuff away and then we're headed to the shower."

"Okay," she said, checking her watch. "We have a little time still."

I wiggled my eyebrows at her. "How much time? Time for a real shower?"

She laughed. "No, I already did my hair and makeup. We can do that later."

"Promise?"

She rose onto her toes and planted a kiss on my lips. "Let's put your stuff away."

The baby shower was happening out back in one of the

yurts, which Aubrey still hadn't had much success renting. Glamping didn't seem to be much of an attraction when there was a fully outfitted resort just around the corner, but the yurts made good event spaces, so she'd begun renting them out for parties.

Inside the space, everyone was gathered, and there was a huge table strewn with gifts, and another with food. We hadn't found out the gender yet, so there was a mix of soft yellows and purples everywhere.

Lucy, Bennie, and CeeCee ran the party, insisting that we play a variety of insane games, one of which involved sniffing brown smears in diapers (which turned out to be chocolate bars).

"I draw the line!" Sasquatch bellowed when he was presented with a diaper to smell. "A man has to draw the line somewhere!"

"So you draw the line at poop sniffing," Ghost said, grinning, "but you're perfectly willing to shit can someone you don't like."

"I apologized for that." Sasquatch lifted his chin and looked indignant.

"For what?" Lucy asked, her attention pulled to the story we were clearly all about to hear.

"Do we really want to know?" Bennie asked.

"Probably not," Ghost said. "But now I feel like we have to share."

"It's contextually relevant," Fake Tom pointed out.

"But disgusting," Monroe added.

I knew the story, and did not particularly want to share this side of squadron antics at our shower, but it seemed everyone was about to hear it anyway.

"Okay, tell us," Penny said, grinning and looking around the room. Her eyes fell on me. "Do you know it?" She took my hand and squeezed.

"Yes, but I wasn't there. Tom was."

Fake Tom glanced around and then grinned. "So Sasquatch had a little issue with this guy Alphabet—"

"Alphabet?" Lucy asked. She'd clearly caught on that the reasoning behind a lot of call signs was more interesting than the names themselves.

"Long name, lots of letters, totally unpronounceable," Sasquatch supplied.

"Which was part of the issue," Fake Tom went on. "Sass started calling the guy Alphabet because he couldn't be bothered to learn how to pronounce his name properly."

"He didn't already have a call sign?" Bennie asked.

"He arrived with something ridiculous like Turbo," I explained. "Couldn't let it stand."

"Course not," Sass said.

"But he didn't like Sass's new one. Said it was disrespectful." Fake Tom said this in a way that made it clear he agreed with Alphabet. "Anyway, Alphabet reported Sass for shooting personal video from the cockpit over San Diego on a training flight, and Sass thought he needed payback for getting him in trouble, so he delivered a little present to the guy's office when he wasn't around."

"Took him two weeks to find it," Sass chuckled.

"A present?" CeeCee asked.

"The story started with the term 'shitcan,'" I reminded them.

"Oh my god," Penny breathed.

"That's foul," Lucy said.

"The smell sure was," Sasquatch laughed.

"I kinda side with Alphabet on this one," Penny said softly.

"We all did," Fake Tom assured her.

"What was his real name, anyway?" Penny asked.

"Sergei Rozhdestvenskij," I said.

"Did you ever master it?" she asked Sasquatch.

"I would have," he said, looking slightly abashed. "But the guy never spoke to me again so I didn't get the chance."

"This isn't really what I saw us all chatting about at Penny's baby shower," Aubrey said, sipping her champagne.

"Let's do presents!" Lucy cried.

Bennie picked one up, but Lucy took it back from her, shaking her head. "This one is last."

Penny opened all the packages, handing a few to me to open. We amassed a collection of adorable little outfits, more boxes of diapers than I could imagine we would actually use, and some bottles and plastic bags and pacifiers and bibs. Babies, I realized, took a lot of stuff.

The package Lucy had taken back was nowhere to be seen as people started to rise and clean up before saying goodbye. When it was just me, Penny, Aubrey, Wiley, Lucy and Fake Tom, Lucy pulled the box back out.

"You can open this one now," she said, handing it to Penny with a tentative smile.

Penny opened the package, revealing two matching yellow PJ sets with feet and little blue elephants stitched onto them. "These are adorable," Penny breathed, grinning at Lucy and Fake Tom.

"There are two," Lucy said, something edgy in her voice I didn't understand.

"I see that. Thank you so much," Penny said.

"For two babies," Lucy added.

I frowned, wondering if she'd had too much champagne. "We're just having the one as far as we know, but this will give us a backup."

"One is not for you," Lucy said, still grinning a little maniacally.

"She okay, man?" I asked Fake Tom.

He was barely suppressing a laugh as he looked at Lucy. "Honey, I don't think they're getting it."

"Are you trying to tell them that they're having twins?" Wiley asked, looking as confused as I felt.

"That doesn't make sense. A doctor would have mentioned that. Not Lucy," I muttered.

"She's trying to tell you that there will be two babies," Fake Tom said. "But only one of them will be yours."

"This is getting super weird," I said.

"Wait a second," Aubrey said, leaping to her feet. "Are you guys having a baby too?" She practically screamed this last part, and the rest of the group let out a series of "oohs," as understanding dawned.

Lucy nodded eagerly with an enormous smile on her face, and everyone cheered.

"Oh my god," Penny cried, jumping to her feet. "When are you due?" She rushed to Lucy and took her hands.

"About two months after you," Lucy said, suddenly looking shy.

"I can't believe you haven't said anything," Penny said.

"We didn't want to steal your thunder."

"My thunder? Oh my gosh, I'm so excited to have someone to share this with! I've felt so totally alone!"

As Penny and Lucy hugged, the worry I'd been feeling eating away at me gnawed a supersized hole in my gut. This wasn't right. Nothing was right. Penny shouldn't be feeling alone. Not now, not ever.

I shook Fake Tom's hand and congratulated him, doing my best to stay chipper as everyone headed out carrying gifts back to the resort for us. When the shower officially ended, Penny was exhausted, so I sent her back to her room, promising to clean up and come find her later.

Besides, I knew I had to do something, and I was going to need help.

Lucy, and Aubrey were still in the yurt, gathering the gifts together as Fake Tom and Wiley cleaned up plates and glasses. CeeCee and Bennie had come back to help clean up too.

"Ladies," I said, feeling nervous suddenly when four pairs of female eyes landed on me. "I'm going to need your help with something."

Chapter 36
Sleigh Ride

PENNY

I went back up to my room and laid down on the big bed, letting my eyes slide shut as I pulled the comforter up around me. It was peaceful and cozy in here, and the room had begun to feel like home. And that made me sad.

I didn't want to be at home in a hotel. There was a permanent state of impermanence about that, wasn't there? And I didn't want to feel so at home all by myself.

But I did.

Harrison was rarely here, and nothing I said could convince him that his physical and emotional presence was more important to me than his money, his college funding, his health benefits. We could figure all that out, but this time—when we were supposed to be nesting and preparing—we'd never get it back.

So I was alone. And even though it was early in the evening, I drifted off to sleep, emotionally and physically exhausted. At least he was staying a week this time.

At some point during the night, Harrison slipped in beside me, and though I didn't wake to full consciousness, my dreams became sweeter, my mind calmer once he was there.

I expected to wake to find him at my side in the morning, but when I rolled over and stretched, opening my eyes slowly, there was a rumpled spot where he'd been. And a note.

PENNY:

i HAVE A FEW THINGS TO TAKE CARE OF TODAY. PLEASE SLEEP IN. EAT WELL, AND BE IN THE LOBBY AT 3PM SHARP TO MEET LUCY.

HARRISON

I rolled over, holding the note with Harrison's sharp and masculine writing in front of my face, feeling a whirl of disappointment. Why couldn't I make him see that all I cared about was his actual, physical presence?

Whatever he was off taking care of—if it wasn't work, at least—was probably something he thought he needed to do. For me, for the baby. But all we really needed was him.

The one thing I couldn't seem to have.

A sinking depression pressed me down into the mattress. This wasn't working. Maybe this wasn't going to work. I'd thought everything was good when he came back, when he told me he loved me.

But now?

I wasn't sure we could keep this up.

* * *

At three, I was dressed and in the lobby, feeling only slightly better about things. At least I was going to see him, I figured. We needed to talk. I couldn't go on like this.

"Ready?" Lucy asked, grinning at me as she rose from where she sat in the corner of the lobby on a long bench. Now that I knew about her pregnancy, I could see just the slightest hint of a bump beneath her sweater.

"I guess so," I said. "I have no idea what I'm doing, so . . ."

"I'm glad you brought a jacket," she said, nodding at the long parka in my arms. "We're going to be outside for a bit."

She gave me a reassuring smile and took my arm, and together, we went through the massive front glass doors of the resort. Lucy's grandfather, Ernie, was waiting there at the curb, sitting atop an actual horse-drawn carriage just like the ones I'd seen in Central Park when I'd been in New York for an awards show as a kid.

"What is this?"

"Your chariot," Ernie said, taking a moment to hop down and offer me a hand after pulling out a small stool to make a step up into the carriage.

I looked over at Lucy. "You and I are taking a romantic carriage ride? This is Harrison's plan?" He was going to be absent, even from the romantic part of his own plans.

She winked at me. "This is just the beginning. Have a bit of faith, okay?"

I was running out of that particular thing, but I shrugged and let Ernie help me into the carriage, where there was a fuzzy blanket to tuck around our knees. Lucy joined me after kissing her grandfather on the cheek.

"Ready, ladies?" Ernie asked us, turning with a grin to make sure we were comfortable.

A few guests had gathered on the sidewalk to watch us take off, and I heard them asking whether this was something the resort offered. I knew Aubrey was going to be inundated with requests for carriage rides.

"Where did the horses come from?" I asked Ernie.

He chuckled and said, "Well, darlin', When a mommy and a daddy horse love each other very much—"

"Funny, Papa," Lucy cut him off. "They belong to a friend of Papa's who has a ranch a little east of here."

I laughed. Despite the dark feelings I'd been having, it was impossible not to enjoy the feel of the horses pulling the sled around the curves in the two-lane highway just outside the resort entrance. I was a little worried about blocking traffic, but Ernie guided the horses back off the road a few minutes later, through a second Kasper Ridge Resort gate that was just a little farther down the road from the resort. I'd never really noticed it before.

"This is the entrance to Kasper Ridge Estates," Ernie said,

sounding like a proper tour guide. "Marvin added this property to the resort when he reopened it. His dream was to build a neighborhood for full-time staff and other folks who wanted a proper community up here in the mountains."

That rang a bell. I looked at Lucy. "This is where you and Will are building your house?"

"Right," she said. "We had to stop for the winter, but we're hoping to get it finished about the time this bun is done in the oven." She patted her stomach and I felt a warm smile of understanding cross my mouth. They were nesting. Getting ready for their baby. Together.

As we rounded a wooded curve in the road, I could see the neighborhood they'd spoken about. There were several partially constructed houses in various states of completion, a few with what looked like foundations poured, and several more empty lots.

Harrison, however, did not seem to be here. What was going on? Disappointment threatened to ruin what was meant to be a lovely outing.

"Ladies," Ernie said, pulling into the snowy driveway of one of the more complete homes. "We have arrived."

We scrambled carefully from the sled, and Lucy turned to me with a bright smile. "Ready?"

I shook my head. I wasn't. I had no idea what we were doing here. "I guess?"

She took my hand and led me to the front door of the house, knocking resoundingly on the front door before opening it.

Harrison and Will were waiting in the entryway, both of them grinning widely.

"There you are," I said, my heart filling at the sight of Harrison. He reached out and pulled me into a hug.

"Sorry I disappeared. I had some work to do."

The warm happiness inside me dimmed. Work. Of course. "Sure," I muttered.

"Come see this house," he said, taking my hand and pulling me along. "Lucy and FT agreed to let us have a look at it today."

I raised an eyebrow and glanced back at Lucy and Will, who were both smiling a little too widely.

We walked through the big house, getting a constant narration of which rooms would be which from Will, who guided us upstairs and spent a little extra time talking about the nursery. I could picture it all, though the rooms were just framed in wood so far and the plumbing consisted of the ends of pipes jutting up through the floor in various spots.

"This will be so nice for you guys," I said, trying not to feel envy creep through my body. Why were we here, looking at someone else's happy future?

"This house has an extra wing," Lucy was saying. "Like an apartment, kind of. For Papa. But the others aren't planned that way. Of course, plans can always be adapted."

"Sure," I agreed, feeling like I was in some alternate dimension. This was all interesting, but . . .

"You're probably wondering why we brought you here," Harrison said.

"Well, yeah." I turned to him, trying to perceive an answer in those steely eyes, the firm serious set of his mouth.

"Bear with me just a little longer," he said, his gravel voice stirring desire inside me even as I considered the fact I was losing him.

"Okay," I said, my voice soft. I didn't know what to think, how to feel. So I held Harrison's hand and let him lead me to the back deck of Lucy and Will's dream house.

"Do you see that?" he asked, pointing just past the edge of where their fence was marked out.

There was a playground set up. Brightly colored plastic and

composite slides and a jungle gym and a little arch with hand-holds on it for climbing. There was something that looked like a little treehouse, and from one side of a it, a swing set. It was adorable.

"This house shares the green space behind it with the one that will be built just there," Harrison said, pointing to where another house would clearly back up to the park. The basement had been set, the foundation poured, and it looked like some framing had begun.

"Oh," I managed.

Harrison pulled me down the steps of the deck and through the snowy yard to the playground, where he sat me on a swing. The bright blue sky spread over us and the towering trees seemed to lean in to hear when he began to speak.

"Penny," he said. "You know I love you."

I dropped my eyes to my knees, letting the slight motion of the swing calm me. I was sure his next words would begin with a 'but.' I wasn't mistaken.

"But we can't go on like this."

I nodded, miserable. "I know. I realized it too."

"It's too much. The constant travel, the feeling like no matter where I am, I'm missing something important. It's not fair."

It wasn't fair. Not to him, not to me. Not to this baby.

"I've been wracking my brain for a way to fix things," he said.

"But you can't," I told him, deciding to be strong. I looked up into those beautiful blue-gray eyes and dug deep for the strength to let him go. "You can't, and I can't fix it either. It's okay."

Harrison's face was hard to read at the best of times. At that moment, it was impossible. "I can fix it," he said, sounding almost offended.

But I didn't have a lot of time to think about his tone, because in the next moment he was dropping to his knee in front of me.

"I'd like to try at least," he said.

"Penny, I can't imagine a life without you."

I drew a shuddering breath, my heart pounding fiercely in my chest, but Harrison kept speaking.

"I can't imagine a life where I'm not here, one hundred percent of the time, with you and with our child. And we already know that kind of life doesn't work—the kind where I'm flying back and forth, trying to be everything to everyone.

"It's not making me happy, but more importantly, I can see that it's making you miserable. And I'm missing everything. And god, I miss you. So much. I can't do it anymore."

Little pricks of shock mixed with the confusion I felt, sending my heart racing. Was he proposing?

"Penny, I'm trying to tell you that I want to stay here. Both of us. All the time. And that this house?" He pointed to the one behind Lucy and Will's. "It's ours if you want it."

I felt my mouth drop open. "What?"

"I talked to Gator, and we agreed that there are parts of the job I can do remotely. I've proved that a few times since I started. Not the whole thing, but enough to keep the benefits and a portion of the salary. And I can stay on to run the ski school at Kasper Ridge seasonally. And we can be together, Penny. And raise this baby."

I shook my head, unable to find words.

Harrison's smile dropped. "You're saying no?"

"No!" I struggled to make my mouth say actual coherent words as surprise and excitement and love all battled for prominence inside me. "No."

Harrison grinned, letting out a laugh. "You just said no again."

"Wait, no!" I cried, standing. "I'm saying yes to all of that," I told him, tugging him to his feet. "If that's what you really want."

He stepped close, pulling me into his arms. "It's all I want. *You* are all I want."

I gazed up into the fierce eyes of the man I loved, feeling the broken pieces inside me align, beginning to mend. "Then yes," I said, locking my arms around him, reveling in the solidity of him against me. "Yes, let's get married."

He kissed me then, and the world seemed to soften and remake itself. Instead of a place where I was fighting, always struggling to find a path for myself, I felt a road clear ahead of me. One I'd walk with this man, with these friends, in this place where I was finally a complete person. I wasn't Our Girl Chrissy anymore, though she would always be part of my identity. Now, with Harrison beside me, I felt like I could finally be Penny—complete in myself.

"I love you so much," I said, tucking my head into his chest and staring at the foundation of our future home. Our lives.

"Truth?" He said softly.

"Always," I told him.

"I love you both," he said, dropping a hand to my stomach. "I can't wait to be a family."

Epilogue

HARRISON

Three months later...

"This really looks okay?" Penny stood in front of the floor length mirror in the suite we were now sharing, turning from one side to the other in a form-fitting burgundy dress that hit her just below the knee, hugged her perfect body, and made me want to rip off the tie I'd just put on and take her back to bed.

"It looks incredible," I told her, coming up behind her to put my arms around her. I rested my hands on her gorgeous round belly and stared at us in the mirror. "You look incredible. And if we had more time, I'd already be proving it to you."

She smiled, meeting my eyes in the mirror and leaning her head back into my shoulder. "You look good too."

"Thank you." I kissed her neck and inhaled her scent, feeling a warm happiness spread through my chest.

"I guess we should go down," she said, turning to kiss my cheek and then moving to pick up a sweater and a little purse.

"Probably," I agreed, and after adjusting my tie once more, we headed downstairs to Lucy and Fake Tom's wedding.

Part of the back patio had been sectioned off, set up with chairs and a pine and floral arch to one side. Guests still sat on the other parts of the patio, maybe more than usual since the crowd dressed up for the wedding was attracting a bit of curiosity.

The rows were filling up with familiar faces, along with a few I didn't know. Penny and I parted ways to go find the bride and groom.

Soon, the music was starting and the small crowd gathered in the folding chairs became quiet as Will walked toward the arch at the end of the aisle. He was followed by Archie and Bennie, Wiley and Aubrey, Sasquatch and CeeCee, Mateo and Annalee, and finally by Penny and me.

There was something right about walking among all these people with Penny on my arm, and while we had no plans to get married right away, it felt a bit like practice. I couldn't wait to marry Penny, but it was strictly a formality. She was my family, my wife, my life already. I kissed her on the cheek as I moved to stand for Fake Tom and she stepped to take her place in line with the other bridesmaids.

The music shifted and the crowd turned to watch Lucy walk down the aisle on Ernie's arm.

I'd heard it said that pregnant women glowed, and in Lucy's case it was absolutely true. She looked beautiful, her cheeks flushed and her eyes bright as she moved toward her fiancé. I actually got a tiny bit choked up, thinking about how happy she and Fake Tom were, how right this all felt.

The ceremony was short and sweet, concluding with a kiss and a lot of applause before we all moved inside for the reception. Once Lucy and Fake Tom had picked a date, we'd raced to ready one of the event halls on the second floor of the guest wing of the resort. They were huge open spaces that could be configured for conferences or parties, and with the new chandeliers, fresh carpet and modern touches, this room was perfect for wedding receptions.

I sat with Penny, and tried to enjoy myself. The entire afternoon had been somewhat colored by my nerves—I had to give a speech for Fake Tom at dinner, and I'd been struggling for weeks with what to say. It didn't help that his father was present, and Mr. Cruz had been a high-ranking officer in the fleet, always stern and usually not in a very good mood. He was intimidating, to say the least.

"Pretend he's naked," Penny suggested when I mentioned that his presence was ramping up my nerves.

"That definitely doesn't help," I said, wishing then that I could erase the sudden image of Fake Tom's fierce father with all his dangly bits out.

"You've got this." Penny squeezed my hand as I stood to speak, turning to face the little table where Lucy and Fake Tom sat up front.

I stumbled a bit at first, but soon was able to get going with the words I'd prepared.

"I've known you for years, Will, though it's still hard for me to call you Will instead of FT. But now that you're married, expecting a baby, maybe it's time I figure that out."

I turned to look around at the crowd. "Will was an incredible, intuitive pilot," I told them. "He was one of the guys you definitely wanted up there with you when things were dicey. We flew together in Afghanistan a while back and Will's quick thinking and calm attitude saved one of our buddies when his plane had some mechanical problems on a mission.

"The guy hadn't flown a lot—he was one of the most junior pilots in the squadron, and he was on Will's wing when his plane threw up a bunch of alarms. Not to get too technical or specific, but those planes were pretty old, and even when they were technically mission ready, that was sometimes only after our maintenance guys had worked some magic getting parts from downed planes or sticking things back together with gum and glue."

I glanced at Will's dad as I said this, hoping he wasn't going to take offense. He knew about the readiness issues with our jets just as well as I did, but it wasn't something we talked about a lot. He gave me a curt little nod.

"This guy's cockpit air flow was failing, so he was starting to lose oxygen, and it was getting a little warm inside the plane. In Afghanistan, as you can probably imagine, it's already pretty hot, so that's not really ideal.

"Anyway, the guy was getting panicky, and talking about ditching, and I just remember hearing this calm, cool voice over the radio, seeing Will on the guy's wing, and listening as Will talked him back to base. He was cool and steady, didn't give off even a hint of worry, and I think he saved the kid's life that day just by being completely calm in the face of a terrifying situation."

I turned to look at Will and Lucy. "That's how I know he's going to make a great husband, and an amazing father." I raised a glass to them, and the gathered crowd joined me. "I watched a bunch of old movies recently, so I can't take credit for this line, but it seems to fit here. 'Life isn't about getting good cards and winning all the time. It's about how you play the cards you're dealt, how you bluff and bet, and how you keep your cool when you lose.'"

I made eye contact with Lucy then. "You're in good hands," I told her. "Will's the guy you want next to you when you've got crap cards. But I hope that you will both enjoy good cards from here on out, and that your life will be full of laughter and joy."

"Here here!" Sasquatch called loudly from a nearby table where he sat with CeeCee, Antonio, Bennie and Archie. Roscoe barked once from where he lounged by the wall. The dog had become Sass's shadow, and when Roscoe was silent, I hardly noticed him at all anymore.

Everyone drank and ate, and the room filled with the sounds of a party as I enjoyed the fact my speech was over and Penny was at my side. When dinner had concluded and the dance floor was filling up, Ghost appeared at my side with Aubrey next to him.

"That thing you said," he said, his cheeks flushed and his eyes bright. "Where'd you get that?"

"The thing about the cards," Aubrey supplied.

"One of those old movies I watched off that list in the back of the album. The one where you got those." I pointed at a green necklace sparkling on Aubrey's neck. They'd had all the jewels appraised and found that they were mostly costume jewelry, though there'd been a few very valuable stones in the lot and they'd sold those. It seemed Aubrey had kept the rest.

"Uncle Marvin used to say that all the time, and he said it was one of the best lines he ever wrote," Aubrey explained.

I pulled out my phone and brought up the entry I'd made in my notes for all the movies I'd watched. "It was this one, "Love in Las Vegas.""

Aubrey took my phone and scanned the movie information.

"But Uncle Marvin isn't listed as a writer on that one. It just says 'Written by MTP Studios.'"

"MTP? Like Mountaintop?" Archie asked. "Wasn't that the studio Rudy Fusterburg was part of?"

I shrugged. They'd fallen back into sibling speak and I was a bit lost. We'd been so busy with weddings and babies and resort guests that there hadn't been much talk of the complex red herring-laden trail of the treasure hunt.

"But why would Uncle Marvin say he wrote that line if he didn't?" Aubrey asked.

Ghost shook his head, but then his mouth lifted into a half smile. "Maybe he did."

"What?"

"Maybe that's what he's trying to tell us."

"What, that he wrote movies he didn't get credit for?" Aubrey said, sounding like this was far-fetched.

"Exactly. Remember the words from the poem? Copyright? Writer? Greed?"

Aubrey and I nodded in tandem as I realized Ghost was probably right. Was Marvin trying to tell us that he didn't get credit for movies he'd written?

"We need to do some more digging," Ghost said, turning as if he was going to leave the reception to do it right this minute.

"Maybe after the wedding?" I suggested.

Ghost's smile dimmed a bit, but he nodded. "This is it, guys. This is what we needed. Brainiac, you figured it out!"

I shrugged. I didn't feel sure I'd figured anything out, but if the heartbreak I'd felt when I thought I had lost Penny was going to pay off, I was glad for it.

"See?" Penny said at my side. "All this because you decided to immerse yourself in pop culture."

"I'm not sure old movies count as popular culture."

She smiled and pressed herself into my arms. "Maybe not, but I bet you're right about this. I can't wait to find out."

I held my fiancée against me, our friends all around us in the low lights, dancing and smiling and happy. "I can't wait for lots of things," I told her, thinking about our own marriage, our baby, our lives together—all of it stretching out ahead of us.

"Oh really?" She asked, smiling up at me with dancing eyes.

"I love you, Penny. You've made every day something I'm excited to live."

"You do the same for me," she said, her arms wrapping around me. "And I can't wait either."

"Dance with me?" I suggested.

Penny's face shifted then, and she looked worried. "Oh," she said, her face clearing. "Harrison."

I felt the frown pull my eyebrows down. "What's wrong? Are you okay? I knew a wedding this close to your due date was a bad idea."

She shook her head. "It's just all the good things happening at once."

What?

"Maybe on the same night."

"What?"

"My water just broke," she said, and I looked down to see that she was right as panic surged inside me.

The next hours were chaos, at least in my mind. I sat Penny down and CeeCee stayed with her while I went upstairs to get all the things we'd need. Then, I pulled the car up and CeeCee helped me get her into the car.

Inside, I was a storm of emotions, but my training served me well. On the outside, I did my best to portray a veneer of calm. Turns out flying jets does have a practical application to real life.

Penny was mostly relaxed, a tiny flicker of worry on her face as she gritted her teeth through the contractions that were just beginning. We'd left as quietly as possible, hoping to keep from causing a huge distraction at Lucy and Will's wedding.

"How are you doing?" I asked Penny as we drove toward the Kasper Ridge Hospital.

She was sitting still, her hands on her stomach and her head turned toward me. "I'm good, I think," she said. "Maybe a little scared."

"You don't seem scared," I told her.

"And you seem like you're driving us out to get some frozen yogurt, not about to meet our son or daughter."

I took a deep breath. "Truth?"

"You know the answer."

"This is me freaking out. This is literally the most exciting moment of my life."

"Wow. You should consider pro poker as your next gig."

We pulled up to the front curb of the hospital, and I rushed around the car to help Penny out. After taking her inside and ensuring that she would be taken care of, I drove the car around to the parking lot. I found a spot, turned off the engine and sat, only for a moment.

"Deep breaths," I told myself, staring out the front window at the three-story hospital building sitting across the dark parking lot ahead of me. Inside that building was the woman I loved and my child, who I was about to meet. And suddenly, I didn't want to waste another second.

I jumped out of the car, took Penny's bag, and raced back to the check-in area.

"Oh good," Penny said when she saw me, and then her eyes squeezed shut and her face reddened as she sat in the wheelchair someone had found for her.

"Ready to go?" A nurse approached and pushed Penny down toward a set of double doors.

I wasn't sure if I was supposed to go, but as they approached the doors, the nurse turned back and looked at me. "Dad? You coming?"

The next four hours flew by. Penny was braver than I was, but everything went as planned. The entire thing felt like a dream, like someone else's life. And the very best part was when the doctor turned to me, placed a squirming bundle into my arms, and congratulated me.

"Meet your daughter," she said, turning back to Penny to finish attending to her.

I stared down at the red, wrinkly bundle in my arms, and my heart stopped beating for a few moments. She was beautiful, and as I looked down into the tiny face, her eyes opened and stared up into mine for what felt like eternity. And in that time, my world shifted, spinning around me and reorganizing into something unidentifiable. Something wonderful and new, something full of possibility and promise.

"Let me see her." Penny's voice broke through the fragile wonder I'd found, and I looked up at her to see tears running down her face. Moving to her side, and offering our beautiful daughter to her, I realized that nothing would ever be the same. From this point forward, my heart would live outside my body. I was vulnerable in a way I'd never been before, in a way I'd always feared.

And it was wonderful.

Penny took our daughter from me, gazed down into her little face as one tiny hand rose up toward us, reaching. I met the little fingers with my own, and looked up at Penny.

"You're crying," she whispered.

I was. And I couldn't remember the last time I'd done so.

"I'm happy," I answered. "Happier than I've ever been."

"Everything is going to change," she said.

"Everything is going to be perfect," I told her.

"Just you, me, and Magnolia," she said.

And that was the beginning of the rest of our lives.

"I love you." I leaned down and kissed my girls, Penny and Magnolia, and felt the air around me slow down and the very atmosphere in the room focus on us, there in the middle of the hospital. I was excited for everything to come, but the world was sending me a message to slow down, and right then I decided to savor this moment. There would be plenty more moments, I hoped—but I was going to work hard to enjoy every single one of them.

Also by Delancey Stewart

Want more? Get early releases, sneak peeks and freebies! Join my mailing list here or scan the QR code and get a free story!

The Kasper Ridge Series:

Only a Summer

Only a Fling

Only a Crush

The Singletree Series:

Happily Ever His

Happily Ever Hers

Shaking the Sleigh

Second Chance Spring

Falling Into Forever

Singletree Box Set 1

Singletree Box Set 2

The Digital Dating Series (with Marika Ray):

Texting with the Enemy

While You Were Texting

Save the Last Text

How to Lose a Girl in 10 Texts

The Text Before Christmas

The MR. MATCH Series:

Prequel: Scoring a Soulmate

Book One: Scoring the Keeper's Sister

Book Two: Scoring a Fake Fiancée

Book Three: Scoring a Prince

Book Four: Scoring with the Boss

Book Five: Scoring a Holiday Match

Mr. Match: The Boxed Set

The KINGS GROVE Series:

When We Let Go

Open Your Eyes

When We Fall

Open Your Heart

Christmas in Kings Grove

The STARR RANCH WINERY Series:

www.ingramcontent.com/pod-product-compliance
Lightning Source LLC
Chambersburg PA
CBHW071211210726
48293CB00002B/380